RULE-BREAKER

What was she—Gillian Ames, bastard and lowly housemaid—doing wearing emeralds? She should be thrilled at finally starting on the path to her dreams. She had wealth, support, and most of all, the opportunity for a fine marriage that would establish herself and her mother for the rest of their lives. She should be dancing on the rafters in excitement. Instead, all she could think was that she was a thief and a liar living someone else's life. Her breath caught on a sob, and she felt Stephen's hands tighten on her shoulders in surprise, turning her around so he could look directly into her eyes.

"Amanda? What is wrong?"

"I-I do not belong here," she gasped, then felt her eyes widen in shock. "I mean—"

"Shhh, it's all right. You are Amanda Faith Wyndham."

"No—"

"Yes. Amanda, listen to me. You are an earl's ward and a beautiful woman who has already become an Original even before your come-out."

She blushed. "Do not be absurd," she whispered, not comprehending the husky timbre to his voice or the almost desperate sound to his words. The mesmerizing golden flecks in his eyes filled her thoughts, and she felt her heart beat faster as he drew a ragged breath.

He leaned down, his dark hair brushing against her forehead as his breath mingled with hers. And then without even realizing that she was the one who moved, she found herself in his arms, straining upward as his lips descended to hers.

Katherine Greyle

Rules For A Lady

LEISURE BOOKS NEW YORK CITY

A LEISURE BOOK®

January 2001

Published by

Dorchester Publishing Co., Inc.
276 Fifth Avenue
New York, NY 10001

Cover Art by John Ennis
www.ennisart.com

ISBN 0-8439-4818-3

Printed in the United States of America.

Visit us on the web at www.dorchesterpub.com.

To the woman who taught me to be a lady,
my mother Jane;

and to my children
Amanda and Sherilyn,
who have their own lists of rules.

Prologue

A lady always wears her hat in public.

"Do you repent now?"

Gillian Ames paused in the clearing behind her cottage, fighting a chill that had nothing to do with the late-winter snow falling silently into her hair. Then Reverend Hallowsby's voice came again, echoing in the frigid air even though the man was inside the small building.

"Mary Ames, I ask you again, do you repent? Your daughter is dead. Your sins exposed. Do you repent?"

Gillian hurried to the back of the cottage, crouching beside the wall as she strained to hear what was happening inside. She closed her eyes, imagining the scene. Her mother would be huddled by the fire, coughing that hacking cough that had sent Gillian out searching for herbs.

Reverend Hallowsby would be towering over her, his narrow face and clutching hands no doubt florid with holy fervor.

But then Gillian heard other sounds. A murmured agreement, a whisper of encouragement. At least five "amens."

The biddies were with him. Reverend Hallowsby's two holy women were always there, acting as his chorus as he went out to terrify people to heaven.

"Repent, Mary Ames! Repent, I say!"

Gillian pressed her fist against her mouth, stifling the rage that burned within her. She wanted to dash inside. She wanted to rush to her mother's defense with a broad stick and use it to beat the sanctimonious reverend about the head until he bled.

She had done it before.

But she could not. Not this time. She was supposed to be dead. So she stood in the snow, quivering with anger, powerless to stop the holy harangue.

"It is too late for Gillian, Mary Ames. She now twists in the eternal fires of torment. God takes His vengeance!"

Then her mother responded. "Aw, go on w' ye. Git out already. 'Tis time I took a piss."

Gillian froze at her mother's deliberately coarse tone, knowing that if she allowed herself one breath she would burst into laughter. She should know better than to imagine that the arrogant vicar could intimidate her mother. Mary Ames was made of sterner stuff than that.

Gillian pressed her ear to the back wall, trying to hear more. The deafening silence from within told her that her mother's visitors were shocked speechless. Imagine anyone having the audacity to mention bodily functions before the holy reverend!

"Very well," continued her mother. Then she paused as a coughing fit consumed her. Gillian waited, afraid that this might be the time her mother failed to catch her breath. Was this the fit that would . . . The coughs ended; then Mary Ames spoke again, her voice strong in the still air. "Ye can watch me if ye like. We ain't got no curtain, and I'm too old to be going outside." Gillian heard the telltale sound of the chamber pot being dragged across the floor.

"Good God, Mary, have you no shame?" That was Mrs. Smithee, her voice shaking with horror, her prune face likely squeezed into a knot of disdain.

"Wot I got is a touchy bladder an' a need t' piss."

There was another long moment of silence as the holy man apparently stood there, calling her mother's bluff. It would be a waste of time. After over fifty years on this earth, Mary Ames had no modesty left. She would do her business right in front of the good cleric and not think twice about it.

Gillian was not surprised when, moments later, she heard the sound of hurried feet as the

Reverend Hallowsby and his two harridans rushed out of the Ames cottage. Wishing to see their backs despite the risks, Gillian eased around the cottage wall. Her hand was still pressed tightly against her mouth to keep her giggles from escaping.

Typically, her mother had no such restraint. Mary Ames was cackling like a proud hen as she used her cane to thump on the front door.

"Go back t' yer parish, Reverend," her mother called. "On this moor, we like t' sin in peace!"

Gillian watched from the shadows as the reverend snapped the reins of his fine carriage and rode away in a huff. Though he did not deign to look back at the cottage, his two holy shrews did, managing to glare with both hate and pious disgust at the same time.

Gillian instinctively drew backward, hiding deeper in the shadows, too used to shrinking away from hostile stares to even wonder if they could see her.

Then they were gone.

Soon afterward, she heard her mother slam the door, thumping around inside the cottage as she released her anger. But Gillian did not enter. She stood where she was for twenty more minutes, shivering from the cold before finally daring to sneak inside.

"There ye be," her mother said with a cackle from her seat by the fire. "Ye missed that twit Hallowsby."

"I saw him," Gillian answered smoothly, pulling off her cloak and hanging it carefully on a peg. Then she stepped to the fire, touching the older woman as she passed, feeling warmth and vitality still in her mother's frail body. "I'm sorry you—"

"Don't apologize for 'im, girl," her mother interrupted, her accent smoothing out now that the minister was gone. "You 'ave yer own answering to do without adding 'is sins to yours."

Gillian straightened, turning to the fire, where she quickly set water on to heat. "Would you like some tea?" she asked.

Without waiting for an answer, Gillian pulled her mother's misshapen tin mug down from the warped plank that served as a shelf. Choosing carefully, she pulled a single leaf out of her pocket, crushing it before dropping it into the tin.

"This snow will kill off the new growth," she commented as casually as she could manage. "But the water will be welcome once it warms."

There was no answer. Truthfully she had not expected one, but she had hoped. So in the end she turned, facing her mother's steady regard with as much strength as she could manage.

"Mama?"

"It gives me chills, it does, seeing your name on her gravestone."

Gillian busied herself with pouring hot water into the cup and carefully offering it to her mother. "You should not be walking by the graveyard anyway. It is too far."

"I'll decide what is too far and not too far, my girl!"

11

Gillian nodded as she stood beside her mother, still offering the tea. In the end, it took another coughing fit before her mother grabbed the brew and began sipping. Moments later she put it down, her breathing noticeably easier.

"I leave early tomorrow morning, Mama. I need to explain some things before I go."

Her mother snorted, glaring across her tea at Gillian. "You'll put me in my grave with your foolishness, girl. There is nothing wrong with being a maid. I am proud to be a maid. My mama before me, too, and her mama before her. We 'ave served the Wyndhams for generations."

"And now we will be the Wyndhams," Gillian quipped as she turned away.

"Mind your tongue, girl. That's sacrilege, it is." Her words were sharp, but Gillian was relieved to see a flash of humor sparkle in her mother's eyes. "Besides, you are nothing like that namby-pamby Amanda Wyndham. See through you in a second, they will."

"No one has seen Amanda for nearly two years. I have run her estate, corresponded with the solicitor, and done all she would."

"You cannot go! It is evil thinking."

Gillian did not respond, knowing the words were nothing more than bravado. Her mother feared their coming separation, and in truth, Gillian shared some of her worries. But they had to do something quickly.

It had been a rough winter, and the harshness of it was etched in her mother's sallow features and the hacking cough that still shook her frail body. If the early thaw had not warmed the air, the woman might not have survived at all. Amanda had certainly succumbed, despite Gillian's nursing.

Now with Amanda dead, all Gillian's worries were for her mother. She and Mary had to find better circumstances before another Yorkshire winter. That meant Gillian had to marry well. But the only way to marry well was to become legitimate.

"I leave before dawn tomorrow, Mama. Mrs. Hobbs will bring you food and wood every Tuesday. She even promised apples later this summer."

"I despise her pasty-face ways."

Gillian sighed. Her mother had fought this plan from the start. She would rather die in honorable poverty than take matters into her own hands to achieve a better life. But Gillian was different. She would happily damn her soul to hell if it meant giving her mother a warmer home and some decent food.

She reached forward, clasping her mother's bony hands between her own. "You could come with me. As a lady's maid."

Her mother stomped her foot on the floor. "I told you. This is foolishness."

"But Mama, all her life Amanda wanted to be healthy and strong like me."

"And all you ever wanted was to be 'er."

Gillian grinned. "Now we shall both get our wish."

13

"You are a by-blow, Gillian. The old baron liked my smile and nine months later you were born. You will never be 'appy unless you accept that without wishin' to be something you ain't."

"Mama, I am ruler of the Wyndham estate. I have been for years. There is nothing his legitimate daughter could do that I cannot. There is nothing she could be that I cannot become."

"You are Gillian Ames and nothing will change that."

"Starting tomorrow, I am Amanda Faith Wyndham. And when I return from London, I will be a rich, married lady." Gillian leaned forward and dropped a kiss on her mother's wan cheek. "Then I will take you away from this hovel and set you up in style."

Gillian stood, meaning to tidy the cottage, but her mother grabbed her wrist, holding her still with amazing strength. "Take the cap."

Gillian's eyes went to her hated maid's cap, tossed in the corner the day Amanda had died. She'd sworn that night she would never put it on again. Gently disentangling herself from her mother's fingers, Gillian shook her head. "I have no need of it."

"There is no going forward, Gillian Ames, till you start in the right place. And you start there. With a mobcap."

"Not anymore."

She spoke the words, and she meant them. But in the morning, as she crept out of the tiny cottage, the maid's cap was buried deep in her valise.

Chapter One

A lady does not sit on top of coaches.

London was cold and wet and dirty. But for Gillian Ames, it held all the wonder of the royal palace. Every filthy street, every pathetic urchin fascinated her. All those people crammed together. It made her head spin, both literally and figuratively. As the mail coach worked its ponderous way through the smelly streets, Gillian found herself swiveling and twisting to see more sights, more buildings and shops, more and more people.

Why, there were so many people, a person could get entirely lost with no one knowing one's name or business!

It was marvelous!

She could not wait for the coach to stop.

15

Thank heavens economy had forced her to sit on the coach's upper perch. The view here was incredible, and she literally hopped up and down trying to see more.

They finally pulled into the courtyard of the Bull and Mouth coaching inn, and Gillian could not help but gasp. So many coaches and people. It seemed as if all of London had gathered on this drizzly day just to greet her. She knew, of course, it was not true, but it seemed such a delightful reception she did not care.

She waited for the inside passengers to disembark, and for once she thanked the delay. It gave her a moment to regain her bearings, as much as one could in this shifting mass of humanity.

The yard held four other mud-splattered, heavy-seated mail coaches, each in a different stage of unloading. The coachmen and regulators called cheerfully to one another while a line of postboys waited for the next conveyance to pull in. She spotted a pie man with a berry-stained apron; at least two cripples, one clearly a veteran; a hawker selling little toys; and a number of children and dogs dashing this way or that. She even saw a peep-show man with bells sewn onto his colorful jacket as he tried to lure people to his box of surprises.

"Look lively, miss!"

Gillian started out of her reverie to see the guard urging her to descend. With a small "Oh!" of surprise, Gillian dropped quickly to the ground next to her slight, battered valise.

"Thank you, sir," she called up to the heavy

16

coachman, grinning at his delighted wink. She knew his behavior was probably scandalous, not to mention her own, but it felt so marvelous to finally be in London, she did not want to bother about propriety.

She turned slowly around, trying to take in all the sights from ground level, but she never got the chance. She was quickly surrounded by vendors. The pie man pushed his meat pasties beneath her nose while the toy vendor offered her a miniature toy sheep.

" 'Ave a pie, miss? Just wot one needs after a long ride."

"Uh, no thank—"

"Young lambs to sell! 'Ow 'bout a toy for a little 'un, miss?"

"No, really—"

"Come see me surprises, miss. Pretty entertainment for a pretty miss." The peep-show man motioned her over, showing off his gaily colored boxes.

Gillian hesitated, sorely tempted. She ought to head straight for Grosvenor Square and the earl's residence, but it had been a long journey. Surely she deserved a treat.

But as she stepped forward, something—or, more properly, someone—bumped against her leg. She looked down, surprised by the dirty face of an impish little boy.

She reached out to touch the child's thin face, but with a quick grin, he twisted away and disappeared. She would have gone after him, but the show man pressed closer.

17

"Come see me box, miss. Mysteries to delight your lovely eyes."

"Uh, perhaps in a moment—"

"I believe, miss, this is yours." A deep voice cut through the clamor, effectively silencing everyone around her, even the jingling peepshow man. It was amazing, Gillian thought as she slowly turned around, that a single voice could hold such authority. It seemed to get inside her and force her to listen.

Who could have spoken?

At first all she could see were the polished buttons of a dark blue greatcoat. Looking up, Gillian took in broad shoulders, a firm chin, and dark hair topped by a tall beaver hat.

She bit back a gasp of surprise. If ever a voice matched a man, this was the time. It was not so much his height and size, which were remarkable. No, it was more the dark, stern lines of his angular face. Although he appeared perfectly congenial, Gillian saw no softness in his blue eyes, no laughter in the precise curve of his lips. She saw only an exciting hunger in his expression, a brooding intensity as he raked her figure with a long, appreciative stare.

He desired her, and he made no effort to hide the fact.

"I . . . I beg your pardon, sir?"

He did not answer her flustered question. Instead he held up the unmistakable worn blue fabric of her reticule, taking pains to direct her attention to the cut ends of the string that had once held it to her wrist. Then she noticed the wiggling, twisting child effortlessly restrained by the gentleman's other hand.

"That is the sweet boy who bumped into me!" she exclaimed, only now realizing what had happened.

"This is the sweet boy who *robbed* you."

She felt herself color, seeing what a country fool she must appear to this man. "Well, yes, I suppose you are right." She took her bag back and carefully tucked it into the pocket of her gown.

"Shall I have my coachman call a constable?"

Glancing at his face, she knew he cared little about her response, so long as they dispensed with the boy quickly. His thoughts were clearly centered elsewhere, and she pulled her coat more tightly about her throat to cover the neckline of her dress.

"I ain't 'urt no one!" squeaked the boy, diverting her attention away from his captor. "Don't give me over to the constable, miss! Please!"

"Oh, dear." Gillian bit her lip as the gentleman handed the distraught child to a large man in burgundy livery. The boy was a tiny scrap of a thing, dwarfed by the two men who held him. As if sensing her gaze on him, the boy lifted meltingly beautiful brown eyes up to her, silently imploring.

He was a pathetic sight. With the filth and the drizzle, the boy looked nothing short of a half-drowned puppy dog squirming in the coachman's hand. She shuddered to think what would happen to the child in a London prison. "No," she said softly. "No, I cannot think a constable will be necessary."

"Very well." The gentleman nodded to the coachman. "You may release him."

"No!"

Both men turned to her with identical expressions of shock. The gentleman went so far as to lift his quizzing glass. "I beg your pardon?" he drawled.

His tone finally stirred her outrage. She understood she appeared a countrified miss with more hair than wit. It was incredibly stupid to gawk at her surroundings without heed to her silly reticule. Still, he need not stare at her as though she were an escaped Bedlamite.

She pulled herself up to her full height, which though impressive for a woman, could not approach that of the dark gentleman.

"I suggest we talk to the child," she said firmly. Ignoring the coachman's undignified snort, she crouched down to look eye-to-eye with the boy. "What is your name, young man?"

He would not answer at first, but after a shake and a growl from the coachman, the boy spoke with a tiny explosion of anger.

"Tom!"

"Well, Tom, we seem to be in a bit of a muddle. You stole something of mine, and though I am reluctant to hand you over to the authorities, I find I cannot simply let you go free." She waited, trying to gauge the child's measure, and was startled to see the same calculating look in his eyes. "What do you suggest we do with you?" she asked.

It began as a slight glimmer in his soft brown eyes, but it quickly grew to a watershed of pathos. He spoke haltingly, sniffing into his sleeve and biting his lip. "Aw, miss," he stammered between sobs. "It be me poor mum. She died last year of a 'orrible sickness." He coughed once for effect, peeking at her face between his fingers.

"I see," she said dryly. "And your father?"

"Oh, 'e's a cruel 'un, miss. Drinks mean and knocks me about just for me earnings."

"But he is alive, and we can find him?"

"Oh, no!" the child quickly retracted. " 'E left us weeks ago. Years."

Despite the child's exaggerated display, Gillian felt her sympathies rise. Most of his story was probably true. "So you wander the streets cutting purses to survive?"

"Oh, no, miss. I am a good boy, I am. But I am terrible 'ungry." He clutched his stomach. "I just wanted a bite of black bread."

"Good boys do not cut purses, Tom." She tried to be stern, but it was hard when looking into such soulful eyes.

"I am a crossing sweep, miss." Then he dropped his chin and squeezed a fat tear from his left eye. "Leastways I was until someone stole me broom. It is 'orrible 'ard to sweep without a broom." Then he descended into loud wails of despair.

She was not fooled, of course. The child was simply playacting. And from his looks, the gentleman knew it, too. Still, it was excruciating to stand idle before an entire courtyard while a tiny child wailed at their feet. All three adults fidgeted as they encountered the icy stares of more than one casual observer.

The gentleman broke first. "This is outside of enough!"

"I quite agree," added Gillian, but Tom was so caught up in his performance he would not stop. "Very well, sir. I suppose we must call a constable."

She expected her comment to stop the child's wailing, but the sobs only intensified. He became positively hysterical. Glancing up, she saw the gentleman's face darken. The man was clearly at the end of his patience. He bent down, careful to keep his clothing out of the muck, and spoke fiercely and quietly to the child. She could not understand what he said, but she could hear the low throb of authority infusing his tone.

Tom stopped crying midwail.

Gillian breathed a sigh of relief. Whoever the dark gentleman was, he certainly possessed a talent for cutting through juvenile hysterics. But then she noticed the gentleman's clenched jaw muscles and decided to get man and boy separated as soon as possible. Patience clearly was not one of his virtues.

She smiled as winningly as possible. "Thank you for your help, sir. I believe Tom and I can handle things now."

He straightened, looking for all the world like

a large black panther slowly uncurling before his prey. "Truly?" he drawled. "I am absolutely breathless with curiosity. How do you intend to control the brat?"

Gillian winced at the cruel term and became more determined than ever to escape this domineering man. "I am sure Tom will control his own behavior. Am I correct, Tom?"

As expected, the boy nodded vigorously, probably intending to run the moment the coachman released him.

"Of course you will, Tom," she continued, "because you and I will find something to eat, and then we shall speak with my guardian. I am certain he can find a position for a good boy in his household."

"Indeed." There was a wealth of understatement in the man's one word, but Gillian was not one to be intimidated by his arrogance. "And just who is this paragon of virtue who will hire a cutpurse?"

Gillian grinned, anticipating her moment of triumph. "The Earl of Mavenford," she said loftily, "and a kinder, more understanding gentleman I have yet to find." Her expression indicated that the dark gentleman was nothing close.

But far from appearing stunned by the mention of her guardian, the man actually began to smile. It was a bitter smile, cold and mocking, and it sent a tremor of fear up her spine despite her confidence.

"I believe you are mistaken," he said softly.

"Nonsense. My guardian is Stephen Conley, fifth Earl of Mavenford."

"And you are Miss Amanda Faith Wyndham?"

She lifted her chin, determined to lie with a straight face. "Yes, I am."

"Well, Miss Wyndham, I am quite intimately acquainted with his lordship, and I can assure you, he is neither kind nor understanding."

"Piffle," she said, reaching for Tom. She was gratified to see the coachman release him, and the boy sidled quickly into her protective embrace. "In any event, this is no longer your affair."

She made to leave, taking Tom with her, but the gentleman reached out and grabbed her, his large hand clamping like iron about her arm.

"You are going nowhere, you impertinent chit!" His hand tightened around her arm.

"Sir, you are offensive."

"I intend to get a good deal more offensive before the day is much older. Where is your companion? And why were you on top of the coach?"

"Just who are you, sir, to demand such questions of me?" She had practiced that tone before, imitating her half sister at her most condescending.

"I, Miss Wyndham, am the fifth Earl of Mavenford." He smiled grimly. "Your guardian."

Gillian felt her jaw go slack in shock. It could not be true. Why would the Earl of Mavenford pick up his nearly impoverished cousin from a coaching inn on a drizzly, gray day? At most he should have sent a servant, and she had scrupulously checked the courtyard for someone who appeared to be a footman or driver for the earl. No one had caught her attention, so she'd assumed the man simply had not bothered. After all, that was exactly what Amanda would have done if some nobody cousin came to visit her. It was inconceivable that this person could be the earl himself.

"I assure you," he said, clearly guessing her thoughts, "I am the Earl of Mavenford."

Despite his words, desperation compelled Gillian to glance at the coachman. He gave her a single, grave nod, and for the first time in years, Gillian wished she had died at birth.

"My . . . my lord—"

"Do not bother cutting up sweet, my dear. I assure you, you have already used up my store of patience."

"But—"

"I suggest you let the boy go on his misguided way and apply yourself to finding an explanation for your outrageous behavior."

Gillian stared at the dark gentleman, narrowing her eyes as she came to grips with situation. The man was condescending, tyrannical, and arrogant to the bone. He had to be the earl. Still, she had spent the better part of her life nursing the shrewish Amanda Wyndham. She knew how to handle autocrats.

"I am sorry, my lord, but I am afraid I cannot

comply. I have made a promise to this boy, and I intend to keep it."

"A promise! What promise?" A vein in his neck visibly pulsed, but the earl kept his voice level, his blue eyes narrow and intense. Somehow his very control made her fear him even more.

"I . . ." She faltered, but was still determined. "I promised to help him find employment."

He did not answer, but she could feel his anger mount exponentially with his every indrawn breath. It practically vibrated in the air between them, and she wondered why the passersby did not flee in terror.

Gillian swallowed and tried a different tack. "My lord, surely you can see this child must be helped."

"He is a common cutpurse!"

"No, my lord. He is a child who needs a little guidance."

"You are a naive fool," he retorted.

"No doubt. But at least I shall have tried."

The earl fell silent, surprising her by appearing to consider her comment. Determined to take advantage of any tempering within him, Gillian smiled as winningly as she knew how. "Please, my lord. True, the child's a liar and a thief, but he is also alone and hungry. We cannot just abandon him."

She expected some softening in his expression, but to her horror, his face grew harder, colder, more filled with disdain. "You will do better not to try your wiles on me, Miss Wyndham. You will find me particularly immune."

"Oh!" Gillian actually stomped her foot in frustration, something she had not done in fifteen years. She knew the child was not evil; why could he not see that as well? "You cannot abandon him, my lord. It would be . . ." She groped desperately for the appropriate word. "It would be unpatriotic!"

That, at least, gave him pause. "Unpatriotic?"

"Why, yes," she stammered as she tried to explain. "Suppose you were in some foreign country, and you saw a destitute English boy. You would help him then."

"I would?" His disbelief was obvious.

"Of course you would. Have I not said you are the kindest and most understanding man?"

He folded his arms across his chest. "You did indeed say that."

"Then it stands to reason you would help a poor English boy lost in a foreign land." She pushed Tom forward. "Only think, my lord, Tom is English and destitute. You cannot penalize the child merely because he is orphaned in England rather than in some foreign part?"

"To do so would be unpatriotic?"

"Exactly!" She beamed at him, pleased he understood her twisted logic.

He shook his head. "This is why women will never be allowed into Oxford."

"And that is why men will never be allowed in women's drawing rooms!" she shot back.

He blinked at her. "I beg your pardon?"

"Oh, never mind. I needed to say something,

and that tumbled out." She saw the gleam of humor spark in his eyes and judged it the best time to press her case. "Please, my lord, could we not keep him?"

"Keep him?" The earl's eyebrows climbed straight up beneath his hair. "Like a pet?"

"No." She tried to smile, but she felt off balance before the earl, unsure of exactly how to act. "I mean care for him like a child who has nowhere to go and no one else to turn to."

Then Gillian saw something she never expected: the man's face shifted, not easing in the way of a man giving in to a pretty woman, but twisting as a man remembering something cruel that was finally over. He sighed heavily. "You cannot go about saving every lost soul in London."

"No, my lord. Just this one today. I promise to leave the others for tomorrow."

He released a sudden bark of laughter, apparently surprising himself as much as her. "Very well, though damned if I know what I shall tell my mother."

Gillian grinned. "Just remind her it is her patriotic duty. I am sure she will understand."

The earl glanced down at the dirty boy still clutched in her arms, then closed his eyes with a pained expression. "Clearly you know as little about my mother as you did about me." Then he gestured her toward a waiting landau. It was a grand four-wheeled vehicle with the earl's golden crest emblazoned on both sides. Only a fool could have missed it, she realized with horror, but truly, she had not thought he would send anyone, much less come himself.

She was still ruminating on her stupidity when the earl shut the carriage door. Though the landau was quite spacious, Gillian suddenly felt short of breath. The earl seemed to dominate the interior of his carriage, looming large as he peered at her from the opposite seat. Unconsciously she pulled Tom closer, as though the boy could protect her. But the child was more interested in the novelty of riding in a richly appointed carriage than in comforting her. Currently he occupied himself by rubbing his hands across the burgundy velvet squabs, a look of ecstasy on his young face.

"Do not imagine for one moment I have forgotten." The earl's low voice filled the interior, sending a small shiver of awareness up her spine.

"Forgotten what, my lord?" She strove for an innocent expression and knew he was not fooled.

"I will demand an explanation for your outrageous behavior before this day is over." He spoke congenially, but Gillian knew he was as good as his word. She would receive a severe drubbing very soon. She sighed unhappily, knowing better than to rail at fate. After all, what was the worst that could happen? He could refuse to frank her Season, send her back to York, and thereby condemn her to a life of hardship and brutality, if not worse.

Gillian dropped her chin into her hand, her

spirits lowering with every clip-clop of the horse's hooves.

At the moment, York almost seemed preferable to a severe dressing-down by her formidable guardian.

Chapter Two

A lady is always demure.

"But Stephen, I will not have it!"

Stephen Conley, the fifth Earl of Mavenford, took a long, sustaining gulp of his brandy and wished he could be somewhere else. Anywhere else. Even Spain would be better than this civilized torture known as polite society. But he was not in Spain. He stood in the elegant blue salon of his London home, staring into the gray ashes of a dead fire. Dinner was long since over, and rather than his comfortable brandy and Aristophanes in the library, he prepared to confront his willful new ward while his mother, the Countess of Mavenford, droned on behind him like a loud mosquito.

"Stephen, are you listening? We cannot have

that . . . that . . . filthy child in our home."

"He is only a small child, Mother. True, he eats enough for three, but even you must admit he is a small boy."

"For goodness' sake, Stephen, you are an earl."

Stephen sighed and turned to face his small but imposing mother. "I am well aware of my rank."

She responded with an imperious sniff. Sitting on the couch in a voluminous gown of dark burgundy, his mother appeared no more than a puffed-up bird. At least until she opened her mouth and one heard her deep, aristocratic accents. She would have done excellently on the stage, he thought idly. Her voice and carriage befitted the most formidable of women, and it never failed to surprise him how dainty she could appear while ringing a peal over his head.

"Earls do not employ cutpurses," she said with haughty disdain.

"Neither do they have willful, disobedient wards, but I seem to have inherited one anyway."

His mother blinked. "Well, what is that to the point?"

"Amanda . . ." He paused to stare pensively into the amber depths of his brandy. "Miss Wyndham took a liking to the boy."

The countess waved her hand in a dismissive gesture. "Ridiculous. I have a liking for small monkeys, but that does not mean I keep them in the house."

Stephen looked up from his brandy in surprise. "Why, Mother, I never knew. Perhaps I shall buy you one for your birthday."

"Stephen!"

"Enough, Mother. The boy stays. At least for now. Later I will see what can be done. But at this moment my first duty is to Miss Wyndham."

"Well, as to that, she appears thin, old, and hopelessly countrified." His mother raised her chin, her pale blue eyes sparkling at the onset of a challenge. "Still, I believe there is a glimmer of beauty beneath the grime. It shall require monumental effort to unearth, I cannot doubt, but I expect I shall make a credible chit out of her eventually."

"Then you hope more than I do," he said grimly. "The girl is willful, cheeky, and has absolutely no understanding of how to go about. Do you know she rode from York on the top of the mail coach?"

"The top!" Lady Mavenford forgot herself so much as to let her teacup clatter into its saucer. "Good gracious, did anyone see her?"

"Half of London, I shouldn't wonder. Though I doubt any would recognize her once she is rigged out for the Season."

"But with that hair of hers, who would fail to remark it? Oh, we are undone before we even begin! Whatever shall we do?"

Stephen shrugged and looked away, his mind on the flashing mahogany tresses that first brought his disobedient ward to his attention.

He had been contemplating the dismal London weather when he chanced to look up. It seemed at first an angel of the autumn had flown in to roll back time to a glorious fall.

Though her hair no doubt began the day in a tight chignon, at least half of it had escaped to curl and dance in the setting sun. Even from across the courtyard, he could see the healthy glow on her cheeks and full mouth, both grown red from the wind. Her gown was drab, the color of an old tree trunk, but nothing could dim the life pulsing just beneath her dull covering.

Then he drew near and saw the warmth of her green eyes. In that moment he knew he had misjudged her. She was not an angel of the fall, but of the spring, of new life throwing off its heavy winter covering. Her eyes were lush and dark like a primordial forest. And when she became angry, they darkened like a spring storm flashing lightning bolts of fury at him.

In short, she was magnificent. Within seconds of seeing her, he had decided to bed her—until that horrible moment when he discovered she was his ward.

Life was indeed cruel.

"Stephen, you are not attending!"

"Of course I am," he responded evenly. "You spoke of how we are undone."

"Do not make light of this situation," his mother snapped. "It is touchy enough with us just out of mourning. But to sport an aging spinster who goes about on the top of mail coaches . . . well!" She placed a delicate hand on her breast. "I shall have to get my vinaigrette."

"Yes, ma'am," he responded automatically, handing her a glass of sherry instead. "Tell me what you know about the girl."

She took a long, fortifying drink from her glass, then cradled it protectively in her lap. "Well, as to that, you already know as much as I do."

"Humor me, Mother."

She glanced up, clearly trying to gauge his mood. He kept his expression bland and excruciatingly polite, and so eventually she had no choice but to continue. "Very well. Amanda is the daughter of my sister and her husband, that wastrel George Wyndham, Baron Thews. Marie died in childbed and George proceeded to carouse himself into an early grave. A common brawl, I think, finally did him in. Most vulgar."

She gave a delicate shudder while Stephen toyed with a tiny china shepherdess on the mantel. "How long ago was that?"

"Eight years."

"And the girl has lived alone in York all that time?"

"Well, your father hired a companion for her—"

"She did not come with Amanda."

"And, of course, there was that other girl."

From his mother's disdainful tone, Stephen knew she would give him a ripe tale. Twisting around, he gave the countess his full attention. "Other girl?"

She leaned forward, keeping her voice low while her eyes sparkled with a gossip's delight. "Well, it seems George got a brat on some maid, but rather than pay to have the woman removed from the household, he let both maid and child stay on. Apparently George was quite fond of the little girl. Amanda was not yet born, and so she was his first. Mr. Oltheten, your father's solicitor, told me she is quite bright. Studied plants or some such thing and became the local physic. That is how she came to tend Amanda."

Stephen nodded. This was familiar territory. "And did Amanda resent having her half sister tend her?"

His mother shrugged. "As to that, I cannot tell. According to Mr. Oltheten, they had little choice, as Amanda was quite ill and the closest doctor resides miles away." She furrowed her brow in concentration. "Consumption, I believe. It is quite remarkable, really, that she made such a recovery. I understand she was ill for many, many years."

"She certainly did not seem sick this afternoon," he commented dryly.

"Just as well. A few more years and there would be no hope for a respectable match. She is nearly cast away as it is."

Stephen nodded, his mind still on her strange childhood. "Whatever happened to the girl, the by-blow?"

His mother stared at him, her eyebrows

arched in surprise. "I have no idea. Whatever difference does it make?"

Stephen shrugged, then drained the last of his brandy. "None, I suppose. I was only curious."

His mother watched his movements with a careful eye. "Will you speak with her now?"

Stephen set his glass down with an audible click. "I shall speak *to* her, Mother. If she wishes to remain in my house enjoying our sponsorship, then she had best listen."

He did not miss his mother's self-satisfied smile. "Excellent. Between you and me, I have no doubt we shall make Miss Wyndham toe the line."

"Precisely my thought, Mother." Then, with a respectful bow, he made his way to the library, already rehearsing his words to the headstrong Miss Wyndham.

Thirty minutes later he completed his speech. His hands remained firmly at his sides, and he made sure to maintain his cold gaze on his ward's face. It was one of his better speeches—clear and to the point, with just the right touch of outrage, anger, and a healthy list of cut-and-dried rules.

Perfect. Except he had the distinct feeling he had made no headway at all.

He had watched her closely from the moment she entered the library. Since she had taken dinner in her rooms, pleading a headache, he had pictured her appearing for her scold with drooping shoulders, a sullen expression, and perhaps a faint sheen of illness coloring her skin.

Instead she'd arrived at the library neatly attired with her riotous curls pulled into a tight coil at the base of her neck. Her face remained as clean as her freshly pressed dress, although this, too, was as drab as her traveling outfit.

He told her rather curtly to sit down, and she obeyed with the demure courtesy required. She even kept her brilliant green eyes lowered, respectfully shielded by her thick lashes throughout his speech. Yet he had the distinct impression Miss Wyndham was anything but docile.

"Furthermore," he began again, "you shall follow my mother's fashion dictates to the letter, including wearing a hat at all times outdoors. You will never venture out without the company of a maid or a groom, you shall not dance or comport yourself with anyone of whom we do not approve, and you shall speak softly at all times. In short, I expect you to act with the decorum befitting the ward of an earl."

He stopped his speech, having said everything he planned and a few things besides. Now was her chance to speak, to assure him with soft phrases and sweet smiles that she would make him proud.

He waited. She looked up and blinked.

He raised his eyebrow.

Finally she found her voice. "Is that all?"

"What?" He was so startled by her odd response that he was momentarily stupefied.

"Is that all?" she continued. "No hair shirt, forty lashes, maybe a ritual sacrifice of my scandalous underclothes?"

Stephen felt his color rise at the images flashing into his mind. "You have scandalous underclothes?" he choked out.

"I have no idea," she responded with an airy wave. "Except, of course, to mention that they do not include whalebone and can on occasion be comfortable."

He frowned at her. "Miss Wyndham, it would seem my lecture has had no effect on you whatsoever."

"Of course it has." Her voice was high and bitter, and not at all the demure tones he anticipated. "It has impressed upon me, ad nauseam, exactly how horrible you intend to make my Season just because I cared for a small, destitute boy."

He slammed his hand down on his desk, the loud slap reverberating against the heavy wood. "This has absolutely nothing to do with Tom. You sat on top—*on top*—of the mail coach. And where, might I ask, is your companion?"

"What companion?"

He leaned forward for emphasis, using his superior height to intimidate the disobedient chit. "The young lady my father hired to stay with you."

"Oh, that peagoose. I sent her away."

He gaped at her. "Impossible! We have been paying her salary for the last eight years."

She tilted her head and regarded him with

her forthright stare. "As I am my own best companion, I saw no reason not to be paid for my excellent efforts on my own behalf."

He blinked, sorting through her words. "You took the companion's salary?"

"I paid myself for my work."

"This is outrageous!" He started pacing, marking off the carpet behind his desk in long strides. "Can you not see how important a true companion is? She could have taught you appropriate behavior. She would have kept you from sitting on top of the mail coach."

Amanda shrugged. "I liked it there, and it was cheaper."

"What has that to do with anything? It was not proper."

"Then I suppose I am not a very proper girl." She looked completely unrepentant, as if she had not just confessed a heinous sin.

Suddenly Stephen felt the weight of his responsibilities descend upon him with the force of a battle drum. She was his ward, and yet she displayed no understanding of how to get on. She would soon make her first bow to polite society, and yet she thought nothing of sitting on top of mail coaches and dismissing her companion.

He might have managed somehow if this were not his own first bow as the new earl. If she could not toe the line, then how would he ever manage a credible standing as an earl?

He bit down on his temper. He had not failed when knee-deep in a Spanish swamp, and he refused to be brought low now by a willful chit who ought to know better.

Stepping out from behind his desk, he approached Amanda just as he would a green recruit with more sauce than sense. He kept his tone level but firm, using every inch of his intimidating height to impress upon her his absolute authority.

"Let me explain something to you, Miss Wyndham. If you intend to spend time under my roof, sponsored by my mother, then it is time you learned how to become a proper miss. If not, you will find this a very, very short Season."

Her eyes were huge as she looked up at him, and he thought he detected a tremor of fear skating across her features. Squelching an urge to temper his tone, he pushed ahead, his voice as cold as before. "Do you realize the importance of a first Season? One wrong step, one wrong word, and you shall be tossed back like a smelly fish. And I shall have no compunction about throwing you back to rot in the wilds of York. Do I make myself clear?"

He watched her swallow nervously, her delicate neck muscles straining to remain relaxed despite the fear he tried to instill in her.

"Very well," she said slowly, as if she weighed every word. "I understand your point." She bit her lip, her small white teeth pressing into the delicate pink flesh. "I suppose I will become a proper miss."

He breathed a heavy sigh of relief. "Thank heaven!"

"But I shall not wear a hair shirt!" And with that, she stood and left the room. He gaped after her, amazed at her show of spirit. He knew grown men who could barely stand after one of his dressing-downs, and yet there she went, her head high, her lithe figure as arrogant as . . . as his mother's!

Stephen felt his knees grow weak, and he reached for his glass of brandy. Good heavens, he thought with a sudden surge of panic, he was surrounded. Between his mother on one side and his ward on the other, he was to be squeezed into the most uncomfortable debacle of this, his first Season as an earl.

He glanced at a calendar and counted out the days before the Season began in earnest. Perhaps there was still time to run to France and find an honorable death trying to kill Boney. Lord knew a war was nothing compared to the female fireworks he anticipated in the next weeks.

He sloshed another finger of brandy into his glass with a heavy sigh. There was one hope, a slim one at best, but manageable: if he could keep a tight rein on his headstrong ward, then his mother would continue to rule the household as she saw fit. That, of course, would leave him in peace as he dodged matchmaking mamas and sought solace in Aristophanes. Then, with luck, he would marry off Miss Wyndham to some naive fool and escape to Shropshire for blessed peace.

Yes, he decided. It was a good plan. Now all he need do was make sure Miss Wyndham became as docile as a newborn lamb.

Gillian stepped into her bedroom and released a sigh of delight. She had been in the earl's home for nearly five hours now, but she still could not believe she lived in such luxury. Why, her bedroom alone was grander than anything she had ever seen before.

To begin with, it was huge! Her entire cottage at home was this size. And the furniture here! The room contained an enormous wardrobe, large enough for her to lie down in. She knew because she had already tried it. Her bed had four posters and a thick, feather-tick mattress. There was a chair, a dressing table, even a little writing desk the housekeeper called an escritoire. She could hardly believe this was her very own room. In London. In an earl's house so grand she clenched her jaw shut just to keep it from hanging open like that of a dumbstruck cow!

Giving in to an impulsive giggle, Gillian spun around on her toes until she dropped with dizzy abandon onto the plump pillows of her bed. This will be so much fun, she nearly cried aloud. More fun than she had ever dreamed possible.

With a soft sigh, she rolled over, burying her face in the soft fabric of the coverlet. Even the earl's drubbing could not dim the joy bubbling up within her. Actually, it seemed almost funny, the way he had prosed on about proper behavior.

She should not fight him at every turn. He was a powerful man—powerful in terms of the gentry, but also in sheer physical presence. Every time she went near him, she felt her breath shorten and her chest squeeze into a tight knot of anticipation. But some demon in her made her challenge him at every step, measuring her will against his force. Perhaps her illegitimate side was coming out, but every time he put his hands on his hips and ordered her to do something, she lost all her good sense. She found herself looking for ways to bait him.

It took all her willpower just to agree to behave like a proper miss.

Her! A proper miss! The thought made her giggle into her coverlet. Of course, she had said the words. If she had refused, he would send her back to York on the next coach. But proper was the last thing she would ever be. Amanda had been all that was proper, and it had gotten her absolutely nothing. It certainly had never attracted any suitors.

Jumping up from her bed, Gillian danced over to her mirror. She could not wait to buy new clothes. She imagined herself dressed to the nines in costly silks, jewelry adorning her body while men fell at her feet and promised their devotion.

It would be glorious!

Her? A proper miss? Never. God had not made Gillian to sit with her hands folded waiting for life to come to her. She had plans and dreams for this Season and only a few months to see to them all. She would catch a rich husband, see the sights of London, and most of all, throw away a lifetime of demure habits.

Looking at herself in the mirror, she lifted her chin, picturing her admirers, seeing the silks.

But the image wouldn't form. Try as she might, she just couldn't see it, and somewhere in the back of her mind, she heard Amanda's voice laughing at her, calling her hateful names, and, worst of all, ordering her to perform all manner of drudgery or idiocy just to relieve the spiteful girl's boredom.

Looking down, she felt her spirits sink. How could she do this? What imp had convinced her that she could pretend to be Amanda?

She did not want to be Amanda! She did not want to be cruel or bitter! She wanted to dance!

Suddenly spinning away, she twirled about her room. No, she would not sit and wait to be admired like the real Amanda. She would not lounge like a stuffed bird on a couch while people spoke pleasantly to her face but cursed her behind her back.

No, Gillian would spend her days exploring London, and her nights dancing! Her feet would be lighter than air as she twirled in some handsome gentleman's arms.

Yes, she decided with a happy sigh as she

once again fell back onto her bed. Yes, she had definite plans for her Season, and none of them included acting the earl's idea of a proper miss.

Gillian woke to the chaotic sounds of a London morning. Although a bird trilled nearby, its song was nearly drowned out by the sounds of carriages, hawkers, and servants performing their daily activities. Still, even their noisy clamor could not compare to the song in her heart.

Today was her first day in London!

She jumped out of bed, dismayed to see the late hour. She usually rose with the sun, but last night she had been too excited to sleep. So when she finally drifted off to dream of elegant balls and ardent suitors, her body overcompensated and she rested far too long.

She chose her dress quickly. Truly, there was little to pick from her half sister's drab outfits. For the last year of Amanda's wretched life, the girl had barely left her bed, and then only to go to the privy. Everything she owned was years out of date and extremely heavy, to ward off her constant chill.

Shrugging on the shapeless fabric, Gillian promised herself new clothes soon. Not a maid's costume, not Amanda's shapeless drapes, but beautiful clothing of rich colors.

But not today. Today she had an entire list of places to visit. She practically danced down the stairs, bestowing her brightest smile on the footman waiting there. He seemed momentarily stunned, and she felt a deep thrill inside her. Would the earl ever look at her like that? With shock and awe in his eyes?

Yes! she cried silently to herself. When she dressed in silks and jewels, he would bow low before her and kiss her hand, whispering scandalous words of adoration. Oh, she just knew this would be a glorious day! She felt so young and carefree, as if the old Gillian had never existed and this was her true self springing alive for the first time.

Following the footman's directions, she made her way to the breakfast room, remembering at the last minute not to skip.

The first thing she saw as she opened the door was the countess excavating the last bit of a boiled egg with a slim spoon. She had met the woman only briefly the evening before, but by the time the interview concluded, the two had reached a state of mutual dislike.

As usual, Lady Mavenford appeared everything Gillian admired about the aristocracy. She was delicate and graceful, with a natural beauty that defied time. But Gillian already knew the illusion would shatter the moment the woman spoke. The countess was not shrewish. Far from it. She appeared polite and considerate, her voice low and extremely polished. But the words! The woman's questions were pointed and her eyes missed nothing, from the stray curls bobbing about Gillian's cheeks to the mud stains splattered across her skirt.

In her presence, Gillian felt nothing more

than a dirty mongrel who muddied the countess's pristine floor. She had never been so aware of her own lacks as when faced with this woman. And now she had to take breakfast opposite the imperious biddy? Gillian was sure the countess would find something to criticize.

With an inward sigh and an outward smile, Gillian resolved to make the best of it. She would not allow Lady Mavenford to ruin her pleasure on this glorious day.

"Good morning," she said sweetly as she moved into the sunny room. As she crossed the threshold, she saw the earl and her step faltered. Her earlier experiences with him had been in the gray light of a dismal afternoon. Later she saw him outlined by the softer glow of candlelight. Today she met him in the full brilliance of a beautiful morning.

Before, she had thought him large, powerful, and elegant in a dark way. Today she saw how truly handsome he was. He was dressed immaculately in a dark blue that matched his eyes to perfection. With the sun streaming in behind him, she saw the full width of his broad shoulders and the lighter blue highlights in his smooth black hair. She lowered her gaze and nearly gasped in surprise at the muscles clearly defined by his tight buff pantaloons. How could a town dandy be so well defined, so clearly masculine in every way?

Disconcerted by the odd tingling in her breast, Gillian turned away to the sideboard.

"Good morning, Amanda," the earl said, and

Gillian felt a shiver of delight at his rich tones.

Then his mother spoke. "Humph. I am pleased to see you rise early, my girl. I have always abhorred the town habit of sleeping in past noon. I find so much more can be accomplished when one rises early enough to read the post before breakfast."

Gillian kept silent. If this was what the countess meant by rising early, then Gillian could sleep in every day! Careful to dim her smile to a demure half curve, Gillian carried her full plate to the table. The countess, she noted, eyed the heaping mounds of food with dismay, but Gillian did not care. She was hungry and had no intention of viewing London's premier sights on an empty stomach.

"So have you plans for the day?" asked the earl.

Gillian brightened at once, unable to keep her excitement from animating her entire body. "Oh, yes. I hoped to take Tom to see the Norman Crypts below St. Mary-le-Bow Church. Boys always like crawling about in dark, dusty places."

"You cannot be serious," came the countess's shocked tones. "Stephen, tell me she is not serious."

"She seems serious enough, Mother." The earl looked up, his blue eyes warming as he gazed at Gillian. "I think she does not yet realize a lady never travels alone."

"But I will not be alone. I will have Tom with me—"

"The cutpurse!"

"Well"—Gillian bit her lip, trying to find the best way to phrase her thoughts—"who better to spot trouble than a former cutpurse? He will know all the tricks to avoid."

The earl made a peculiar choking sound, and he hastily reached for his tea. His mother, however, was not so polite. "If you think that . . . that jesting about a thieving boy is appropriate breakfast conversation, then you are sadly mistaken."

"But it was not a jes—"

"And as for going out, you shall not set one foot outside this house until I am sure you will do us honor as the ward of an earl."

"But—"

"Enough. We have an appointment at Madame Celeste's in an hour. That should take most of the day." She stood, looking down her dainty nose at the food piled high on Gillian's plate. "I do hope you will not overindulge in food. You are already too old. To add a heaviness in the jowls would be ruinous."

Gillian stared at the dainty woman with open resentment. Perhaps the countess's tiny figure did not require sustenance, but God had built Gillian on sturdier lines. She speared a large kipper with her fork, then looked up with an innocent smile. "Oh, I should not worry about jowls, my lady. I find I can eat almost anything without detriment to my figure. How unfortunate you must be wary of yours."

She expected an angry hauteur from the

countess, but was shocked to catch a gleam of appreciation in the woman's eyes. "Your tongue is most sharp," the countess said without heat. "It is a good thing your lessons begin tomorrow. If you work very hard, and I am very diligent, I might just allow you to be seen when the Season begins." Then she turned and sailed out of the room, leaving Gillian to stare openmouthed at the door as it slipped shut on all her plans.

"When the Season begins? But that is not for—"

"Three weeks," finished the earl.

Gillian set down her fork as her food turned into a heavy lump at the pit of her stomach. "Three weeks? But when will I see the crypts?"

"Poor Amanda," he said softly. "Did no one tell you of all the work in preparing for a Season?"

She shifted her attention to the earl, angered more by the tears of disappointment blurring her vision than by the thought of her ladyship's plans. "What lessons do I need?"

The earl shrugged, his tight waistcoat shifting in distracting patterns along his chest. "Deportment, dancing, music, that sort of thing. Never paid much attention to it myself, but Mother seems to think it important."

"And she would know best," Gillian added with a bitter twist of her lips.

He glanced up at her. "About how to go about in society? Yes, Mother knows best, and you would be wise to listen to her."

Gillian sighed, realizing he was probably

right no matter how much it galled her to think of it. "But when will I see the Tower and the menagerie or—"

"The crypts?"

"Yes. And what about Tom?"

He smiled gently at her. "I have already taken care of Tom."

"What? How?"

"And as for the crypts," he continued as if she had not spoken, "perhaps if you work very hard with Mother, I could take you to all those places. We have three weeks, you know. Surely we can manage to find you a free moment somewhere in that time."

She looked up gratefully at him, reassured she would eventually see the attractions touted in her London guidebook. And somehow the thought that he would accompany her made it easier to bear a delay.

"Oh, all right." She sighed. "I have waited to see London for five years now. What could another three weeks be?" She dropped her chin on her hand, her joyous mood now colder than her morning chocolate.

"Five years. As long as that?"

"And time goes very slowly in York," she intoned, remembering all too well the cold nights in her mother's cottage when she had nothing to do but recall bitter memories and empty dreams.

Suddenly she felt his hand on hers, covering it with a warmth that tingled up her arm. She glanced at him, unexpectedly lost in the deep sea of the earl's gaze.

"I will speak to Mother about Thursday next."

"We will go to the crypts?"

He nodded, though his expression looked pained. "I promise we will go there, if you wish it. In the meantime, try to get along with Mother. She absolutely delights in shopping, you know, so you should have an easy time of it."

Shopping. The word penetrated her disappointment like a ray of sunshine cutting through the fog. *Shopping!* "I shall be able to get rid of these awful clothes!" She lifted her chin off her hand. "What do you think, my lord? Shall I choose red or blue for my first ball gown? Or maybe a shimmering orange-red. I saw a fall leaf one day of that color and thought it the most stunning leaf in all the world. I dipped it in wax to preserve it and brought it along. I passed so many nights imagining dresses made in that very color."

She was so caught up in her dreams of her first ball, she did not at first notice his uncomfortable silence. But when she did, it brought her back to the present with an awkward thud. "My lord?"

"Perhaps you were unaware . . ."

Gillian felt her spirits sink with his every word. "What?"

"Well . . ."

"Oh, for pity's sake, do not drag it out. What horrible shock am I in for now?"

He sighed, and for a moment he seemed sorry for his words. "I think the orange-red would look wonderful on you, but all girls in their first come-out wear white."

"White!" She could scarcely believe her ears. "White? But I hate white, and I can never keep it clean. I am always smudging it somewhere or another. Surely you must be mistaken."

The earl shook his head sadly, denying the words even as he spoke them. "Maybe you are right. You must take it up with my mother. Now if you will excuse me, I have an appointment to attend to." He rose from the table and gave her a quick bow before disappearing out the door. Gillian watched him go, then slowly let her gaze drop to her cold plate.

White? She despised white. And as for speaking to Lady Mavenford, Gillian suspected the woman would take great pleasure in dressing her from tip to toe in that hateful color.

Oh, her Season was already cursed from beginning to end. And what had they done to Tom?

Chapter Three

A lady is grateful for a man's protection and assistance.

Stephen did not wait for his mother and ward to depart. He made his escape directly after breakfast, heading straight for Oltheten and Kersten, Solicitors at Law.

He did not suspect anything out of the ordinary, he told himself as he rode down Broad Street. It simply behooved him to learn as much as possible about his new ward. Any good soldier knew that seeking knowledge was always advisable. Unfortunately, his solicitor, Mr. Jeremy Oltheten, was distinctly unhelpful.

True, the offices of Oltheten and Kersten had assisted the earl's family for years. However, Mr. Jeremy Oltheten, a young lad of twenty-seven, had not helped Stephen's father with the terms of his guardianship of Miss Wyndham. That task had fallen to Mr. Oltheten's father, James Oltheten, who had retired last year due to serious illness.

So nearly three hours later, after one traffic upset, two wrong turns, and an interminable wait in a dimly lit drawing room, Stephen finally stepped into the sickroom of his father's former solicitor, squinting through the gloom to make out the details.

His first impression was of austere simplicity. From the rich furnishings of the house, Stephen expected the man's room to be similarly grandiose. It was in fact, quite plain, with only the absolutely necessary accoutrements, and it spoke well of the owner's practical inclinations.

As he entered, his gaze connected with a young woman, presumably a daughter. She wore a simple dress over a modest figure. Her hair was neatly plaited and her face remained calm, if a bit sad. She stood immediately upon his entrance, gliding silently forward as she dropped into a demure curtsy before him.

"He woke not more than five minutes ago and wished to see you directly," she said. "But please, my lord—he tires easily."

"I understand," Stephen responded. The woman nodded, then quietly withdrew, leaving Stephen to step closer to the large bed, which held a small, frail man. "Good afternoon, Mr. Oltheten. I appreciate your time."

"Not at all, not at all, my lord," the gentleman

said in a wheeze. "Always a pleasure to receive a visit, especially from your lordship. Tell me what has happened to your family."

Stephen settled into the nearby chair and embarked upon an edited recitation of his family's recent losses, much as he would for an elderly aunt. He spoke of his father's death and his brother's more unexpected one. He mentioned his hasty return from Spain and of how much the younger Oltheten was helping him adjust to the responsibilities of the earldom.

As he spoke, he carefully watched the man his father once depended on so heavily. The solicitor's hair was a dull gray where it wisped about his head. He was impossibly thin, his bony hands like long spindles where they rested on the coverlet. But what most concerned Stephen were the man's eyes. They were large and brown despite the wrinkles surrounding them, no doubt made from years of squinting at documents. But Stephen could not help but be dismayed at the vague cloudiness hovering there. Occasionally they would narrow, and Stephen would catch a glimpse of the man he must have been. But then the next moment Oltheten's glance would turn vague, and he knew the solicitor's attention wandered.

I had better get on with it before I lose the man entirely, Stephen thought grimly.

"Mr. Oltheten, sir, do you perhaps recall a Miss Amanda Wyndham in York some years back? Her father, my uncle, died, leaving a small estate that you supervised."

The man's eyes glazed over, and Stephen feared his trip wasted; then suddenly they cleared and the old solicitor let out a loud wheeze. "Oh, yes, Wyndham. One daughter. Bitter little thing. All encased in white." He glanced up, his face twisted in a short cackle. "Sort of like me in this damn shroud."

Stephen smiled, unable to deny the man his sickbed humor. "She is in London now as my ward. We are to sponsor her Season."

The old man pursed his face, frowning in confusion. "Miss Wyndham? For a Season? I never thought she would make it here."

"Sir?"

But the man was already lost in his own thoughts as he released another cackle. "Sort of gives me hope, if that girl could survive."

"She was very ill?"

"Death's door, I thought. You say she is here for her Season?"

"Yes, sir."

"Well," he said with another wheeze. "Maybe I ought to send for that by-blow girl myself."

Stephen blinked, wondering if the old man had faded into some imaginings of his own. "I spoke of Miss Wyndham, sir. Miss Amanda Wyndham."

The old gentleman twisted around to glare at Stephen. "I know who you meant. I am talking about her half sister, the one who knew herbs. She made me some tea, as I remember, on my last visit. Helped the lungs, she said." His last words were more of a wheeze than words, and he soon descended into a coughing fit. Glancing at the side table, Stephen grabbed a cup of tepid water and helped the old man drink, his heart twisting within him at the nearly fleshless feel of the solicitor's heaving shoulders.

It was another five minutes before the man could speak, his voice paper thin, though still filled with his own dry humor. "Could use some of that witch's brew now."

Stephen nodded politely, completely uninterested in his uncle's old scandal. His thoughts were on Amanda. "Sir, is there anything you can tell me about Miss Wyndham? What do you remember of her?"

The old man frowned, screwing up his lips in distaste. "Not much to remember. Last time I saw her was a little over two years ago. Bitter, sickly little thing all encased in white. Said it made her feel more holy. I thought it made her look like a shriveled-up mummy." His next cackle brought on another, more severe coughing fit that left the man gasping for breath, too pale to do more than blink his watery eyes.

The interview was over, Stephen realized with an inward sigh. Though he wanted to press for more information, he could see that the elderly gentleman would not stand the strain. Standing, he hastily summoned the woman and took his leave.

Five minutes later he was once again outside, frowning at the beautiful London day. The solicitor had described Amanda as bitter and sickly, two adjectives he himself would never choose. Then there was that odd reference about her being shrouded in white, and yet Amanda professed a hatred of the color.

Clearly something momentous had happened to the girl to change her into the generous, vibrant woman she now appeared. A religious conversion, maybe? Stephen shrugged. Whatever occurred, it must have been dramatic.

Perhaps he should take a trip to York just to look around. A few discreet questions, perhaps a guinea or two, and he would surely know the whole tale.

Stephen squinted at the sun, noting its position in the sky. He still had time to leave today. He could be in York tomorrow night. Unfortunately, his other estates required his attention more than the Yorkshire properties. His father had neglected too much during his long illness. And his brother Harry had left things in chaos. Stephen simply could not spare the time for a trip to York.

With a sigh, Stephen pulled out his pocket watch and planned the rest of his day. He had lost so much time tracking down the elder Mr. Oltheten that barely a half hour remained to make his appointment with Perry, Viscount Derbarough, his sheep-farming mentor. With a muffled groan, Stephen kicked the sides of his black stallion while trying unsuccessfully to push his young ward from his mind.

She was an odd one, strangely intriguing, infuriatingly forward, and hopelessly direct. A mystery surrounded her, and he was determined to solve it. Perhaps he could get the answers from the girl herself. She certainly was not hard to read. Little more than an hour of his directed attention should get the information he sought.

Stephen smiled as he felt his spirits lighten for the first time in a week. Yes, he thought, just a little more time with the intriguing Amanda, and he would possess the key to handling the puzzling spitfire.

Gillian stared out the window at the gentle night. More than anything she wanted to disappear into the darkness, wandering the wild moors of her childhood, trying to quiet the restlessness within her.

But she could not. This was London, and despite her urge to throw off the earl's restrictions, she was not completely stupid. To go out alone into a London night would be foolish—not to mention useless. She could not think of anything less quiet, less soothing than the city.

When she had conceived her plan to impersonate Amanda, she had dreamed of ardent suitors, elegant ball gowns, a few months of the joys and laughter that came with being rich—and legitimate. No one had mentioned corsets, prune-faced maids, and restrictions designed to frustrate any sane person.

White! She had to wear white. She could not walk alone. She had to wear a hat and speak softly and only about polite inconsequentials. Yes, she had heard the earl list these ridiculous rules last night, but she'd given them little heed. They were the result of his pique and not really intended to be followed.

Then she'd discovered to her shock that the countess firmly supported each of his wild dictates, not to mention adding some of her own. Gillian might have pushed those aside as well—after all, Lady Mavenford seemed to enjoy Gillian's discomfort—but the modiste was frankly shocked that anyone would question the rules.

"But of course you must wear white," the modiste exclaimed in a thick French accent. "Did not your mama tell you this?"

"Her mother died in childbed," the countess responded in her usual haughty tone. "I fear Amanda did not learn the niceties of polite society."

"Ah," the modiste responded, nodding her head in condescending understanding. "Then you are fortunate to have Lady Mavenford to teach you the ways, *non*? She is very wise and never mislays a step."

The countess, of course, smiled beatifically at the compliment, and the modiste bowed while Gillian nearly choked on her disgust. The modiste's overflowing admiration was merely to ingratiate herself with the countess. Any fool could see that. Once, Gillian would have laughed at the display, but the flattery solidified the two women's mutual admiration, and Gillian lost any hope of enlisting the dressmaker's aid for at least one bright ball gown.

All too soon, Gillian gave up trying to make

her opinions known. She even stopped paying attention to the myriad fabrics held up to her face or draped across her body. She became a human doll. She closed her eyes and pretended she was in York in her secret place by the old tree.

Nothing else existed. Not even her dreams.

Gillian and the countess returned home after what seemed like years of shopping. The older lady took immediately to her rooms for the night, pleading exhaustion. Gillian took one step into her own room, met the prune-faced stare of her new maid, and fled downstairs. There she ate a solitary dinner, oddly piqued that the earl had not deigned to return.

At nearly midnight, she had passed hours of solitude in thought. Never suppressed for long, her dreams returned full force, along with a new determination to make them come true. If the real Amanda could not daunt her spirit with constant insults, then how could the earl's absence be anything more than relief? If Reverend Hallowsby could not shame her with entire sermons devoted to the taint of illegitimate blood, then how could the gift of an ugly maid be anything more than a godsend?

She would not cower or be ashamed. She was Amanda Faith Wyndham, she reminded herself, not a self-effacing by-blow surviving on the grace of a bitter girl. And as Amanda, she would truly and totally get her way. But first she needed to have a frank discussion with the earl.

Assuming that he ever returned home.

He did, at nearly one o'clock. And by then Gillian had worked herself into a fair temper.

"Good evening, my lord," she said from her window seat in the salon. "I suppose this is what you mean by town hours." She winced at her own shrewish tongue, but seemed unable to help herself.

"Amanda! I thought everyone would be in bed." Despite his quick recovery, Gillian did not miss his brief flash of chagrin at meeting her.

"Did you perhaps stay away just in that hope?"

Stephen gave her a rueful smile, making her heart beat double time.

"You have found me out." He crossed into the salon and poured himself a brandy. "I have learned in matters of female interest that it is best to hide until the fireworks fade to a dull roar."

"Your mother has tortured other girls before me?" Gillian's surprise softened her tone.

He grinned, and she looked away for fear her anger would fade under the power of his charm. "I have a sister, and believe me, before Catherine became Lady Waterson, this house was a pitched battlefield. They were the most stubborn pair of pugilists I ever met. It's a wonder I survived."

"You are incorrect, my lord."

He raised an eyebrow in inquiry.

"You have now met me."

He grinned. "Yes, but I have not yet survived your struggle. Let us hope we find you a husband soon, thereby shortening the war in my once peaceful household."

Gillian winced at his blunt words, wondering all the while why they should pain her. This was, after all, her intended goal—to find a husband and in one masterful stroke not only save her mother, but also become one of the peerage that had both created and spurned her. Except when Stephen said it aloud—that she was here just to find a husband—it chilled her blood and made her ashamed.

And that, of course, made her all the angrier.

Watching the emotions play across his ward's beautiful face, Stephen barely restrained a groan. He recognized the martial light in her eyes and knew he was in for a battle.

"My lord," the girl began, "I have some questions for you."

"I tremble with curiosity."

"Do not mock me," she snapped. "I want to know where Tom is. No one will tell me anything. What did you do with him?"

"I did not throw him into Fleet, if that is what you feared."

"Then where is he?"

"Asleep in the mews, dreaming of Cook's blueberry tarts, no doubt."

"The mews!" She practically bristled with outrage.

"I hired him as a stable hand in the mews. Simpton will keep a good eye on him, and at least out there I have less to steal."

"If you think you can hide him away for a few days, then toss him aside when you think I am placated—"

"I hired him as a coachboy," he snapped, feeling his temper rise. "He knows one false step will put him back out on the street. The rest is up to him."

"Oh, really," she said with a sneer. "And how long before something accidentally goes missing or perhaps a tack is damaged? How long before you find some excuse to throw him away?"

Stephen narrowed his eyes. "You have a cynical mind, Miss Wyndham."

"Am I wrong?" she challenged.

"Yes. And were you a man, I would call you out for what you just implied."

"Were I a man, I would not be here in your charge in the first place!"

He stared into her eyes, trying to see deeply within her, trying to guess the secrets driving this volatile woman. "Is that what upsets you, Amanda? That you are under my protection?"

She bit her lip and turned away, her movements impossibly stiff. "I lived under my own care for many years, my lord—"

"Please call me Stephen," he said, startling himself with his own comment. His title preserved some measure of authority with her, something he desperately needed. But already he could see how she chafed under the restrictions of polite society, a sentiment with which he readily sympathized. So he gave her his first name as a token of friendship.

She turned toward him, her eyes drawn wide with surprise at his friendly overture. "Very well," she said slowly. "Stephen."

He smiled, feeling suddenly happy.

"As I was saying, my—Stephen, I cared for myself for years. I do not need a servant constantly hovering about me, nor someone watching my every move. And I certainly do not need a prune-faced maid telling me which slipper to put on which foot."

"Ah!" Stephen leaned against the high table, crystal brandy decanters clinking with the movement. Now he understood some of his ward's frustration. "Has Mother assigned Hawkings to you?"

"She did if that is the name of the sour crone in my bedchamber."

He nodded, reaching again for his glass. "Sad case, that. She was very ill as a child. Obviously she recovered, but the sickness destroyed her looks. Mama brought her in, trained her as a dresser, and now she knows more about fashion than most modistes. Why, even my valet consults her, and in time, one gets used to her looks."

"Apparently not. The countess has assigned her to me."

Stephen shrugged. "Mother does not need the advice of an expert. Clearly she thinks you do."

Amanda spun around, pacing the room, her nimble body moving gracefully past the furniture. "But I do not! That is what I am saying. I have dressed myself since I was a child."

Stephen did not move, but suddenly his senses pricked as his mind spun back over everything he knew about her. "I thought your half sister maided you."

Amanda slowed, her slippers catching in the carpet. "She maided me until she grew ill. And then I was forced to handle my own affairs."

He could not miss the sudden wariness in her voice. "That must have been very difficult for you," he said.

She shrugged. "I did what I had to."

"Of course. But you said you maided yourself since you were a child. Mr. Oltheten visited you a little over a year ago, and he said you were very ill."

She turned toward him, her eyes wide with surprise. "You have seen Mr. Oltheten?"

He nodded. "Early this afternoon. Unfortunately he himself is very ill, and he could not give me detailed instructions on your estate."

Amanda looked slightly distracted, as though her thoughts turned elsewhere. "I can tell you all you need to know about the Wyndham legacy. Was he very ill? Is it his cough?"

"I believe so. A coughing fit ended our interview."

Amanda nodded, her gaze shifting to the window. "I see," she said softly. "He was a nice man. I am sorry he is so ill."

Stephen fell silent as he studied the woman before him. Two minutes ago she was in a towering rage. Now all traces of it were gone, lost in her compassion for a dying old man.

Suddenly the mystery became too much for him. He needed to know the secret behind his strange ward. He took a step closer to her, forcing her to look up into his eyes. "Amanda, Mr. Oltheten said you were very ill the last time he visited York. You were sick and encased all in white. And yet I cannot imagine a healthier person than you, and you voiced a strong distaste for white. What happened?"

She winced, but he touched her arm, preventing her from turning away. When she at last spoke, her gaze wandered over his shoulder to the dark night. "I healed," she whispered, "and formed a severe distaste for my sick-clothes. There is nothing unusual in that."

"He also said you were very bitter."

She shrugged and made to draw away, but still he held her, now with two hands resting gently on her shoulders.

"You seem sad for Mr. Oltheten."

"He is a kind man who is dying of a horrible, wasting disease. I have seen many people carried off by such an ailment." Her thoughts were clearly turned inward to sad memories. As a gentleman, he should leave her alone, Stephen thought. But he wanted more information. He needed to understand.

"That is not the reaction of a bitter woman, Amanda," he said. "Was Mr. Oltheten wrong about that?"

She bit her lip, and the sight of her even white

teeth distracted him for a moment. "No," she finally said on a soft sigh. "He was not wrong." She took a deep breath. "The Amanda in York was angry and jealous. She wanted . . ." Her voice trailed away.

"What? A Season? A husband?"

The girl shook her head. "She wanted everything she did not have. Little things would infuriate her. A smile. Laughter." She stepped away from him, putting a single hand on the windowpane as if reaching for something but barred from having it. "I tried to be understanding. I tried compassion, gentleness, even friendship. But always there was anger. And jealousy."

"But you changed."

She turned back to him, her eyes hard and challenging. "A new vicar came to our little village. He was responsible."

His eyebrows raised in skepticism. "A religious conversion?" He'd thought as much earlier, but somehow it did not match his image of her.

"Religion is a powerful force, my lord. If it were not for Reverend Hallowsby, I believe I would still be in York, sitting by the fire, counting sins."

Stephen frowned, trying to picture the scene she described. It did not fit.

"Reverend Hallowsby preached, my lord. He preached obsessively, fervently. And if he felt you had sinned, he would punish you."

He stiffened, his senses suddenly wary. "What manner of punishment?"

She stepped backward into the shadows, but he followed her. He did not touch her, but angled himself so he could see her expression reflected in the window.

"He punished in public first, cataloging sins before the entire congregation. And then later he would visit in private, finding me alone so he could suggest ways to redeem my soul."

Her words chilled him, but more than that, it was her face. Her expression was cold and hard, and for the first time he saw the bitterness within her. Then suddenly she spun back toward him, her expression washing away into a blank facade.

"He did not succeed in his intentions, my lord. In fact, I should be grateful to him. If it were not for his actions, I would never have resolved to come to London. I would not now be standing in a warm home about to embark on the greatest adventure of my life."

Her statement should have reassured him. Her words should have rung with optimism and hope, but instead he heard a fierce determination that defied all who opposed her. She should not be this way, he thought. She was too young to have such anger within her.

Instinctively he reached out to comfort her. She was stiff, shying away from his touch. But he persisted, not with firmness, but with a gentleness that seemed to crumple her resolve.

"Whatever our differences, Amanda, know

that I am your friend. I will help you." His words were a whisper, and as he spoke, he drew her closer until he could feel the brush of her breath across his face.

"I do not trust you." She said the words, and he believed she meant them. But rather than pulling away from him, her body relaxed, swaying forward as if part of her wanted to trust. Part of her, he knew, needed to believe what he said was true.

"I am your guardian," he responded. "You can trust me with anything."

He thought to comfort her, and truly for a moment he saw a need to confide shimmering in the dark green of her eyes. Now he would know what secrets she guarded so closely. But even as that thought entered his mind, other wholly irresponsible thoughts crowded them out.

She was so near, her lips so close. His body tightened, responding with eager delight to the soft feel of her beneath his fingertips, the heady scent that was uniquely hers.

Oh, how he wanted to kiss her. He knew it was impossible, but the need burned within him, startling him with its intensity. She looked at him, her eyes growing soft, her pupils dilating as he lowered his head.

"Amanda—" It was half groan, half plea.

"No!" Suddenly she twisted away, her hands clenched at her sides as she whirled out of his reach. "I thought you were different, but now I can see you are all the same! Reverend Hallowsby, you, every man, and I despise you all!"

He pulled back, hearing the accusation in her words, knowing now with a sick horror exactly what punishments the Reverend Hallowsby had tried to mete out.

"No," he said. Then he repeated it more firmly, denying both the thought and the accusation. "No, Amanda, it is not true." And yet, even as he said it, he knew it was true. Had he not just been thinking of kissing her? And when he had first seen her on the coach yesterday, wasn't his first thought a plan for when and how he would bed her? "I am not like that!" he exclaimed, both to himself and to her.

She lifted her chin, her entire stance one of furious defiance. "It is the nature of man to sin, my lord. It is his nature to lust and desire and covet. Isn't that what the church teaches?"

He matched her tone, making his voice as hard as hers, trying to show her he meant what he said. "I do not know of every man, Amanda. I only know that I am your guardian, and I will protect you. Whatever the circumstances, whatever your past sins, whatever you choose to confide, Amanda, I am pledged to protect you."

"Confide, my lord?" Her voice fairly dripped with sarcasm. "What is there to confide? I am here for the Season to catch myself a rich husband. I will wear my bonnet in public, I will spend your money on ugly clothes chosen for me by a shriveled crone of a maid, and in the end I will be rewarded with some old ogre of a husband so I can spend his money and adorn his arm. Years ago this was beyond my wildest dreams. Now I am living it. Confide, my lord? What could there possibly be to confide except that I am thankful for my opportunity?" Her voice rang with an anger that cut at him, tossing aside his offer of understanding, pricking at his guilt.

He raised an eyebrow. The natural disdain that came with his new title surged forward. "Very well, Amanda. I concede to your greater understanding. You have nothing to confide. But let me tell you one thing. . . ." His voice lowered with threat. "There is nothing I despise more than a liar. If you are hiding anything—a scandal maybe, no matter how small—you will wish you had never been born."

She lifted her chin, her raised eyebrows the perfect picture of haughty disdain. "I have wished that countless times already, my lord. Such a threat has no meaning to me."

Then with a swirl of her shapeless skirts, she disappeared, leaving him to curse his foolish brother for bequeathing him a defiant ward and a mystery all wrapped up in an enticingly beautiful package.

She'd almost told him!

Gillian ran up the stairs and dashed into her room, remembering out of long habit not to slam her door. She closed it silently, then sank to the floor, her back pressed into the hard wood.

She'd almost told him!

After months of planning, years of degradation and self-effacing humiliation, she had almost told the earl the truth. Here she was on the verge of her whole future, hers and her mother's, and what had she done? Weakened! Her mother's life depended on her success; how could she have just melted?

It was bad enough she'd nearly fallen into his arms. He was so powerful. The urge to let go was so strong, so alluring. She could give over her burden to him.

But that was madness. So she'd reached for her anger, using it to back away from him. Then he, too, had become cold and angry, seeming to tower over her even though he had not moved. And despite his fury, she had still wanted to confess!

How could she be such a fool? Stephen Conley was no different from the other pumped-up, arrogant popinjays of the ton. He was kin to the man who had sired her, then threw her to the likes of Reverend Hallowsby.

What would Stephen do if he liked a maid's smile? If that little scene was anything to judge by, he would act just as her father had. Just like the old baron, he would lie with her, creating another bastard, then forgetting her, leaving the child to a life of humiliation and degradation.

To tell Stephen the truth would be like handing him the torch to light the fire by which to burn her at the stake. He would never understand what had brought her to such lengths. He would never even try.

She knew all this, and yet barely one day in his house and already she felt vulnerable around him, susceptible to his charm and mesmerized by his sheer presence.

It was insane!

Gillian let her head drop back against the door, her heart heavy. What did it matter why this was happening? For some reason, she was weak around the earl. For her own sake, as well as her mother's, she must find a way to stop his heinous influence. She must remain strong around the man.

Her only hope was to avoid him. True, he would pursue her. She saw that her past intrigued him. She would have to be very careful. Thank heaven Gillian knew how to fade into the woodwork when necessary. With any luck, the Season would keep both her and the earl so busy she would never see him except in passing.

Then if God smiled on her, she would be safely married before anyone discovered the truth.

Yes, she decided, it was a good plan. She could manage it.

She must manage it.

Feeling better, Gillian stood and stripped off her dress, taking time to wash the perspiration from her face. She needed an ally. Someone quick, part of the earl's household, and totally loyal to her. Someone not strictly moral who would help her achieve her goals.

Only one person fit that description.

Tom.

Perhaps it was time to visit the mews.

Chapter Four

A lady does not run barefoot after cutthroats.

Gillian went straight to the window and looked out to judge the distance to the ground. Although not an expert climber, she had extensive experience working her way over the rough Yorkshire terrain while looking for herbs. She would have no difficulty managing the trellis, assuming she could swing out through her window far enough to grab it.

She could, of course, try to sneak out of the house through the servants' stairways, but Stephen was still awake and about. She could not risk him finding her.

It would have to be the trellis.

Gillian eased open the window and squeezed her way through headfirst and backward until all but her legs were outside. She sat there a moment, breathing deeply of the London night, then abruptly changed her mind. She was used to moonswept moors, the near silence of the country, and the sweet, fresh scent of heather. By comparison, London felt crowded, noisy, and choked with noxious odors. The buildings seemed to huddle together, trapping the stench inside. Even the moon had no room to peep through. The only illumination came from gas lamps, which shed tiny pools of greasy yellow light.

It was very much like those gothic novels Amanda had so loved, and Gillian repressed a shudder of mixed fear and excitement.

Then she shook her head. She was in a perfectly respectable area of London about to cross a cobbled back alley to sneak into the mews. There were no mad Bedlamites or hideous ghouls lurking about, and it was foolish to even imagine such things.

With calm resolve, Gillian pulled herself upright to stand on her windowsill, one arm hooked inside to anchor her. The sill was slick from the evening rain, so she quickly kicked off her slippers. Her bare toes would maintain a better grip than the flimsy footwear. She braced herself for the swing to the trellis, but before she could move, a low whistle cut through the night.

She froze. It was clearly a signal, but by whom and for what? The sound came from down the alleyway, but she saw nothing except gray shadows. She waited, her body tense as she half hung out her window.

Nothing.

Then it was repeated, this time more shrill, more insistent.

Twisting, Gillian watched the doorway to the mews open and a small figure slip out. The person carried something large and heavy, but he still managed to move smoothly and silently through the night, slinking from shadow to shadow. It took a full minute before the figure crossed a slim finger of moonlight and Gillian recognized his face.

Tom. Carrying one of the earl's saddles.

Gillian did not stop to think. She managed the slight leap to the trellis and climbed nimbly down, heedless of the flower buds she crushed along the way. She could not let Tom escape. She needed him. And from the looks of things, he needed her, too. Only a fool would run away from an opportunity in the earl's household, and Tom was no fool. That meant he was in trouble—whether from the earl's servants themselves or from someone else.

Whatever it was, Gillian was determined to stop it.

She jumped the last couple feet to the ground, landing with a soft thud on the chilly cobblestones. Now she wished she wore her slippers to shield her toes from who knew what slimy things she stepped in.

Suppressing another shudder, this one from the cold seeping through her feet into her very bones, Gillian slipped around the corner following Tom's path. She caught up to him quickly. The huge saddle was heavy and slowed him down considerably. She glanced around, looking for the person who had whistled.

No one.

She took a breath to call out to Tom but stopped as a large, hulking figure stepped out of the blackness. Tom stopped and dropped the heavy saddle with obvious relief.

" 'At all?" The two words were gruff and businesslike, their very callousness sending chills up Gillian's spine.

"Couldn't carry . . . nothing else," came Tom's panting response.

The dark figure bent down and easily hoisted the saddle. "I got this. Git some flash from the 'ouse."

"No," came Tom's urgent response. "The earl's still awake."

"Do as I say, boy. Quick-like."

"No—Ow!"

Gillian had been creeping closer, trying to hear better, but Tom's cry of pain launched her into action. She surged forward, landing a swift blow to the huge man's midsection as she bellowed at him.

"Let him go, you brute!"

She threw another punch, and like her first blow, it landed solidly and squarely in the man's chest—to no noticeable effect.

With a saddle in one hand and Tom's ear in the other, the huge man could not defend himself, so he merely stood still while Gillian tried to hurt him.

"Well, well, wot 'ave we 'ere? A little mouse for my den?" In one swift movement, he released Tom and grabbed hold of Gillian's upper arm, hauling her backward far enough that she could not kick him any more.

"Let go of me!" She tried to spin out of his hold, twist or drop in unexpected ways to loosen his grip, anything, but he was too strong. She succeeded only in hurting herself as his fingers dug deeper and deeper into her arm.

"Pipe down, little mousy, afore I squash ye."

"Run, Tom!" she cried. Then the brute dropped the saddle and clamped his meaty hand down over her mouth and nose. The scents of dirt and gin were overwhelming as he hauled her backward against his body. Then, abruptly, he released her mouth, wrapping his meaty forearm across her throat, giving him both a better hold on her body and a way to choke off any of her cries.

She tried to struggle, but as before, he was too large, too overwhelming, and Gillian experienced a moment of sheer panic. She could not even stand straight, since her feet kept slipping on the slick cobblestones.

Her one hope was that Tom had escaped, but the brute's next words killed the thought. "Get me somethin' to tie 'er up with, Tom. She'll fetch a prime price—"

"Let her go." Stephen's low voice cut through the night air, and Gillian nearly fainted with relief. Now she would be released. But the monster did not act as she expected. He simply shrank back a little into the shadows and dragged her closer to his massive body.

"Ain't none of your affair, mister. She be my wench and 'e's our brat, so's go about your business, afore you get 'urt."

"You will release her or I will put a bullet between your eyes." Stephen's voice was soft, but it carried the full weight of deadly authority. That and the flash of moonlight on the barrel of a pistol was enough to make the villain pause.

Which gave her her chance.

Planting her feet as best she could on the slick stone, Gillian threw her elbow backward straight up and under her captor's rib cage. It was no more than a minor annoyance to the huge man, but it surprised him enough to loosen his hold while she dropped to the ground, easily slipping out of his grasp.

The man bellowed in rage, but the roar died abruptly as Stephen's lightning-fast fist connected with his jaw. The brute stumbled backward, and Stephen followed, landing more well-placed blows until the man collapsed on the ground.

Gillian felt her mouth grow slack with astonishment. She knew Stephen was muscular, even athletic, but never had she thought him that powerful, that brutal with his fists.

"Listen closely for I will say this only once." Though he was slightly out of breath, Stephen's voice carried easily through the murky night. "I am the Earl of Mavenford. This boy is in my employ and this . . . wench is under my protection. Touch either of them again and I will kill you. Now get out before I decide to use my pistol after all."

At first she thought the villain too dazed to understand, because he did not move. But then the moon peeped out from behind a cloud to catch his bloodied face in a look of pure hatred. Gillian gasped in shock, not because of the expression, though it was horrifying enough. She was stunned by its target.

The man did not direct his malevolence at Stephen, but at Tom, who shrank around the corner of a building, his small face ghostly white. She stood up from her crouch, her feet splashing in a puddle as she took a step toward the prostrate man.

"You horrible bully! He is just a child!" She would have advanced farther, but Stephen yanked her roughly backward.

"Shut up, wench," the earl said in a growl.

Gillian started to spin. "Wench!" she exclaimed, but Stephen's tightening hold cut off the rest of her words as he shoved her behind him.

"Get out of here now," he said to the fiend, his voice filled with deadly threat. The man needed no further encouragement. He stumbled to his feet and ran to the shadows before Gillian could remember to breathe.

"Is he gone?" she asked as she squinted into the darkness. "I cannot hear or see anything in this city. There is too much noise. How do you stand it?"

Stephen turned, his eyes glittering focal points in the shadows. "I wear shoes and carry a pistol."

It took a moment for his words to sink in, but when they did, she felt the rising heat of a blush flood her face as her bare feet twisted beneath her. "Yes, well, I would, too, except it would make it difficult to climb up and down the trellis." She flashed him a triumphant grin. "You did not think of that, did you?"

He made a strange choking sound, but when he spoke his voice was dry and controlled. "No, Amanda. I must confess I did not think of that."

She nodded. "And they say men have superior minds." Then she glanced around, looking for Tom. She found the boy inching his way around the neighboring house. "No, Tom. Pray do not run away, not after I went to all this trouble just to save you."

Stephen turned to stare at her. "*You* saved him?"

"Well, we saved him. I delayed that beast until you could finish him off." She turned long enough to send him a grateful smile. "You were magnificent, by the by. Wherever did you learn to fight? And will you teach me how?"

Stephen gaped at her. "I most certainly will not!"

Gillian shrugged as she turned back to Tom. "Oh, well. Perhaps I can find someone else."

"*Amanda—*"

"Oh, do not start lecturing me now," she interrupted. "It is Tom we should think of."

Stephen paused, clearly torn between scolding her outside or hauling her inside to rake her over the coals in private. She never gave him the chance as she addressed Tom.

"Well, what have you to say for yourself, young man?" she asked.

The boy shrank even farther into the shadows.

"Do not try to hide from me, Tom. Stand up straight and tell me he was a horrible, mean brute, and he frightened you."

"But—"

"Say it."

" 'E. . . . 'E was a 'orrible brute, and 'e—" The small voice slid away.

"He frightened you into doing things you never would have done on your own."

Tom appeared to think. Then, when he spoke again, his voice contained a good deal more earnestness. "I never would, mum, never, 'cept 'e frightened me 'orrible."

Gillian nodded, sparing a glance over her shoulder to see if this little speech had any effect on Stephen. It did, but not in the manner she hoped. Even in the pale yellow light, she could see the rigid clench of his jaw and the still-tight balls of his fists.

Hastily she turned her attention back to Tom. "And . . . And now that you are safe from him, you swear you shall not do anything like that again. You will not sneak off in the middle of the night, you shall tell me immediately if you see him again, and you will serve the earl to the best of your ability."

"Oh, I will, I swear it! I will."

Gillian smiled as the color came back into the child's dirty cheeks. Not daring to look behind her at the earl, she flashed Tom a reassuring smile and shooed him toward the mews.

"Very good then, Tom. You may go back to bed."

Not one to miss an escape, Tom scampered away, disappearing into the mews before she could draw a second breath. Now if only she could manage a similar disappearing act. She turned to the earl, giving him her best smile. "Well, that is taken care of. I believe I shall be off to bed as well. I am still adjusting to these town hours."

Stephen made no answer, and Gillian felt a surge of hope. She might actually escape unscathed. Then she felt his hand on her chin, tilting her face upward with hard, uncompromising fingers.

"You will come to the library in ten minutes." He glanced significantly down at her bare toes. "After you have suitably attired yourself." Then he hoisted the saddle onto his shoulders and walked away, his heavy tread ringing on the cobblestones.

He stopped at the servants' entrance, holding the door open wide as he waited for her. She followed him slowly, pausing briefly at the base of the trellis, but he cut off the thought before it fully formed.

"Through the doorway, Amanda!"

His bellow gave her feet wings. She scampered past him up the stairs before the echoes died away.

"Do you know I am accounted a generally good judge of character?" Stephen did not stop to hear her answer, but continued to pace behind his desk, only occasionally glancing up to make sure Amanda maintained her demure pose. "Well, I am. So when you promised to behave as a lady, conducting yourself as would befit the ward of an earl, I judged you to be honest and forthright. I took you at your word. Was I incorrect? Did you not indeed intend to behave like a lady?"

He stared at her as she sat so sweetly, with her hands folded in her lap. She looked remarkably pretty for an incorrigible, recalcitrant hoyden. She had brushed the leaves out of her hair and scrubbed the dirt smears off her face. Her feet were once again shod in pale pink slippers, and her dress was a fresh white and pale yellow confection that covered the essential parts of her anatomy. In fact, the only remaining indications of her ordeal were the rapidly darkening bruises on her forearm where the cutthroat had restrained her.

He glared at those dark splotches as though they were to blame for the fear still pumping through his body. Good God, when he thought of what might have happened if he had not heard her climbing down the trellis . . . Thank heaven the library was situated just below her window. She had been quiet slipping down the wall, but there were enough soft scratches for him to go investigate with his pistol.

"Are you quite sure you are unhurt?" he asked for perhaps the fifth time.

"I am fine, my lord. Really, I cannot see what the fuss is about. Tom is safe. I am safe. You have a marvelous right hook, and it is late. Can we not just go to bed?"

He whipped around, nearly sputtering as the last of his fear translated to anger. "No, we cannot just go to bed! You promised to behave as a lady, and yet not twenty-four hours later, I find you climbing out the window to apprehend a cutthroat nearly twice your size!"

"I could not very well let him have Tom."

"Why did you not call for me? Your lungs are certainly capable of it."

Amanda glowered at him for that cutting remark, but it did not deter her. "I could not go find you because he might have escaped. If I screamed, it would only alert him, and he would disappear that much faster."

"So you chose to confront him yourself, barefoot and weaponless?"

She bit her lip and looked away, a puzzled frown on her face. "In my experience, bullies back down when confronted. And failing that, a few well-placed punches have always served me well."

"And you have a lot of experience with London bullies who prey off of young boys and run thieving rings?"

A faint tinge of red colored her cheeks. "Uh, no. London does seem to grow a particularly nasty form of bully. He seemed remarkably impervious to my jabs."

Stephen felt his blood run cold with shock. "You punched him?"

"Oh, yes. Repeatedly, but he only sneered at me. That is why I wish you to teach me how to fight." She looked up at him, her green eyes wide and hopeful.

He reached for his brandy and swallowed it in one gulp. Then he swiftly opened his desk, drew out a few sheets of foolscap, a pen, and ink, and shoved them forward to his odd ward.

"My lord?"

"Write this down, Amanda. In large print so that it will be the first thing you see in the morning and the last thing you read before closing your eyes at night."

"But—"

"Write the following at the top: Rules for a Lady." He glared down at her until she obediently scratched the appropriate words. "Number one. A lady does not run barefoot after cutthroats."

"But slippers were too unsafe on the trellis."

"Write!"

She obediently set his words to paper. "Does not run barefoot after cutthroats," she murmured.

"Number two. A lady does not climb up or

down trellises." He paused, waiting for her to catch up to him. "Number three. A lady does not punch people."

She glanced up. "Even when they are villainous brutes?"

"A lady screams or calls for help so a sufficient number of men can come and knock out the villainous brute."

"Seems remarkably inefficient to me," she commented. "Especially when I could do it just as well." She glanced up, her mouth turned down into a distinct pout. "Or rather, I could if someone would teach me how."

Stephen groaned. "Number four! A lady does not brawl!"

"I thought that was number three."

"You seem to need it twice."

She sighed and continued to write.

"Number five. A lady does not ride on the top of a stage."

"You never forget anything, do you?"

"Some things are etched upon my memory," he said dryly. "Especially since it occurred only yesterday."

She shrugged and quickly wrote the words. Then, when she finished, she glanced up, her face set in an expression of long-suffering patience. "Is that all?"

"For the moment. Though I am sure I will find occasion to add to your list."

"No doubt," she commented, her voice as dry as his. As she sanded the page, Stephen could not help but stare at her. This small woman climbed barefoot out of windows, punched villains twice her size, was nearly choked to death, and yet she acted as if it were all perfectly normal. Was she a lunatic or merely so lacking in sensibilities as to be a threat to herself and everyone around her?

Or both?

She finished sanding the page and sat back in her chair. "May I go to bed now?"

"Amanda, you were nearly killed tonight! Have you no sense of what could have happened to you?"

She lifted her chin, her eyes steady as they met his gaze. "I could not leave Tom to fend for himself against that man. Calling for help would only have alerted the brute and delayed me."

"So you climbed barefoot down a trellis—"

"Why do you keep harping about my feet?" She waved her hands in agitation. "It was the safest way to reach the ground. True, I should have brought something to hit the man with, but I had no idea he was so large."

"Amanda, you had no idea at all. You endangered yourself and Tom without the least chance of success. If I had not heard you climbing down the trellis, you would have been killed or worse." He reached for his brandy, not wanting to think about what would have been worse. Then he discovered his glass empty, and he set about refilling it. Only after he took another few gulps did he chance to look up and see Amanda staring at him with naked shock on her face.

"What?"

"You really are upset."

"Of course I am upset!" he bellowed.

"But why? Because I climbed down the trellis? Because I was barefoot? Or because I defended a street orphan from a bully?"

He set down his glass with a click and crossed to stand directly in front of her. "It is because you could have been killed. My God, woman, have you no fear of dying? Of being hurt or sold into slavery?"

She rose slowly from her seat, and he watched her every movement from the slight tilt of her head to the gentle press of her fingertips on his forearm. "My lord. Stephen. I have seen many people die in my life. They have died suddenly or slowly, some in accidents, others eaten up bit by bit from drink or disease or plain bitterness."

"What has that to do with—"

"I have told you before, I wished myself dead a thousand times. Death holds no terror for me. What terrifies me is living without meaning or purpose."

He stared at her, seeing the earnestness in her expression, the conviction in her voice, and could think of nothing to say. She seemed much too mature for a girl of twenty-one.

"I am tired, my lord." She sketched a brief curtsy. "Good night."

And with that, she slipped out of the room, abandoning her list of rules to him.

Chapter Five

A lady does not pick locks.

Gillian peered around the hall door, then
ducked back as she saw Greely, the earl's
starched butler, standing guard by the front
door. Oh, this is foolish beyond measure! she
scolded herself. She had never in her life been
willfully stupid, but here she was, lurking in a
back parlor waiting to break into the earl's library.

Stupid, stupid, stupid.

And if she were caught, who knew how many
more rules he would add to her list of ladylike
behavior? He had added another four in the last
week alone and continued to post the sheet beside her bed no matter how many times she
ripped the silly thing down.

It had been horrible these last few days. Between interminable fittings, shopping for stiff undergarments, not to mention tea lessons, dancing lessons, and deportment lessons, she was hard put to catch her breath, much less disappear for some solitude. She'd never realized how much she enjoyed her dawn walks along the harsh Yorkshire moors until she came to London and such moments seemed an impossible dream.

So what did she do when she finally found a scant few minutes of peace? Was she upstairs, stretched upon her bed with her eyes closed as she imagined the scent of heather and sweet moss beneath her feet? Was she slipping out of her tight new undergarments or pretending to study her French verbs as the countess ordered? No. She lurked in a dark room, probably smearing dirt all over her hideously white new gown, while she waited for Greely to disappear so she could risk everything on a foolish errand for Mr. Oltheten.

Madness. Total madness.

Gillian sighed. What did she care about a sick old man who had once been nice to her? And he had not truly been kind, merely fair, treating her as a person rather than a bastard. He'd complimented her handling of Amanda's estate and was quite reasonable when she asked for funds to repair some of the crofters' huts.

But that did not demand this idiotic escapade on her part.

Gillian tensed as a footman entered the hallway. If he came to the parlor, he would find her. She hunched down, wondering what excuse she would give for hiding in this back parlor. Then to her surprise, the young servant stopped and spoke to Greely in low, urgent tones. From the expressions on their faces, it was probably another altercation with the temperamental cook. With a muffled curse, Greely waved the footman toward the back stairs, and they both disappeared toward the kitchen.

Now was her chance.

Gillian slid out of the back parlor and tiptoed around the corner. The library door whispered softly against the thick carpet, but then she slipped inside, pushing it shut while the frantic beat of her heart pounded in her ears.

She went straight to the earl's desk. A huge mahogany masterpiece, it was bliss to look at. Unable to resist, she traced the gleaming top, luxuriating in the slide of polished wood beneath her fingertips as she settled into his chair.

The red leather was molded to fit his larger, harder frame, making it feel slightly awkward as she sat, but then it gave beneath her, seeming to enfold her in a sensuous caress. She began to tingle as she felt his scent rise up to greet her, filling her mind with odd thoughts and images of him.

Disconcerted, she fumbled slightly as she drew out a thin wire and inserted it into the desk lock. It took her longer than usual. She was years out of practice, but eventually she heard the satisfying click as the lock released. Within seconds she opened the desk drawers and carefully scanned their contents.

The interior of a person's desk was a strangely intimate place. Whereas her papers at home were often strewn about on top or haphazardly tossed inside, the earl's were tidy, ordered, placed with military precision in neat stacks. She would have to be very careful to place everything back just where it belonged.

Gillian worked quickly, but she searched for something relatively obscure. She wanted the elder Mr. Oltheten's address so she could send on a recipe for a potion for his lungs. She had considered asking the earl, but then he would wish to know why, and that was dangerous ground. The real Amanda had cared nothing for herbs and plants. She'd wanted only laudanum to help her sleep.

Then, too, there was the added risk of seeing Mr. Oltheten. Of anyone in London, he was the only soul who knew her on sight. He would surely recognize her. Better to find the address, then send the recipe anonymously. She dared not risk more.

So she scanned the papers looking for Mr. Oltheten's address. He had been Stephen's father's solicitor. Surely Stephen had his direction somewhere.

Gillian worked at a feverish pace. She pulled out a stack of ledgers, thinking Stephen might have recorded the address in there. She scanned the neat columns, stunned at the numbers she saw. Why, the earl was in command of

a vast fortune! No wonder Amanda's tiny Yorkshire estate was neglected. It was only one pitiful place among a richness of land and other
ventures.

Gillian carefully replaced the books, then
turned to the bottom left-hand drawer, her last
hope. Quickly sliding it open, she was frankly
surprised by what she saw. The pistol and
money box were startling, but not really unusual. No doubt many gentlemen kept both in
their desks. What drew her attention were four
small, worn leather books. Picking one up, she
knew it immediately as a journal.

The starched Earl of Mavenford kept a diary.
What a find!

Unable to resist learning anything about her
forbidding guardian, Gillian opened it to the
first page. There, in a childish scrawl, the young
Stephen recorded receiving this journal for his
eighth birthday.

Quickly turning the pages, she saw regular
entries chronicling his young life. There were
delightful essays on the nature of sour-faced tu-
tors, a clearly much-belabored love poem to a
woman named Betty, and the results of a sci-
entific study into the perfect fishing techniques.

The next three books continued as the first,
recording the days of his life. Her original goal
forgotten, she quickly flipped through the
pages, searching for the day she had first arrived. What could he have written about her?

"Find everything you wanted?"

The earl's low voice cut through her thoughts,

and she nearly jumped out of her seat. One hasty glance over her shoulder revealed Stephen—it was impossible to think of him as an earl after reading his poetry—looking elegantly austere in black, his dark eyebrows a heavy slash of anger across his face.

"Uh, I beg your pardon?" she asked sweetly, knowing there was no way she could brazen her way through this, but nevertheless determined to try.

He stepped inside the room, his eyes reminding her of a winter storm at sea—cold, fierce, and deadly. Behind him, Greely shook his head in dismay, then discreetly pulled the library door shut.

"Why are you in my desk, Amanda?"

"I was looking for a direction, actually, but got quite distracted." Gillian looked down and began returning his journals to their place in his drawer. Then, giving in to a sudden impulse, she discreetly slipped the last book into her pocket, where it lay heavily against her thigh.

"Distracted?" Stephen repeated as he crossed to the sideboard to pour himself a brandy. "Is that what you call reading a man's private thoughts? I call it a violation of privacy, and a very, very serious crime."

Gillian carefully shut his desk drawer and stood, keeping her hands folded demurely in front of her. Then she spotted her lockpick wire on the desk and nearly panicked. He should not see it. He would think she made her living picking people's desks.

But it was too late. Even as she touched the wire, he was there, wrapping his large hand around hers, lifting it up so he could inspect the lockpick.

"My goodness, Amanda, it seems I underestimated you. You appear to be quite experienced at thievery."

"I was not thieving! I told you, I needed a direction." She tried to jerk her hand from his, but she might as well have tried to pull out a tree, roots and all. She was held fast and would remain so until he chose to release her.

"A direction, you say? Whose?"

Gillian hesitated. To tell him would be to expose herself to all kinds of problems. But what could she say that he would believe? Perhaps a distraction would work.

"Who is Betty?"

Stephen blinked. "I beg your pardon?"

"Betty. The woman you wrote that poem to." But as the words left her lips, she realized the depth of her mistake. No man wanted his youthful foibles exposed, and Stephen Conley was more private than most. His grip tightened painfully on her wrist, and she bit her lip to restrain a cry of alarm.

"How much did you read?"

"Uh—"

"*How much* did you read?"

"Only bits and pieces: Actually," she said on a tremulous laugh, "I had no idea you were such a scapegrace as a child. It quite gives me hope."

"That I will forgive your latest transgression?

I fear you are sadly out on that thought, my dear."

Gillian lifted her chin, trying to smile brightly despite her fears. "Oh, no, my lord. I know you will punish me, but it still gives me hope that once you settle into your position as earl, you will relax your puffed-up attitude. Mind you, excessive dignity becomes you as well," she added hastily. "I simply meant we shall be much more comfortable together when you cease to demand such high standards of yourself and everyone else."

She smiled at him, pleased her explanation had achieved its desired goal. He blinked dazedly at her, as if amazed by her powers of thought. His next words confirmed her suspicions.

"Your mind quite astounds me, Amanda."

She smiled. "I am counted quite bright."

He glowered at her. "Did it ever occur to you that perhaps an earl should retain an extra measure of dignity?"

"Of course not. If it did, no one would ever want a title."

She felt his grip loosen in shock, but when she tried to back away, she found him quite determined to keep her exactly where she was.

"Amazing powers of logic. Tell me, Amanda, how does a woman who is counted quite bright come to use a lockpick?"

She hesitated. "The nights in York are quite long, my lord."

"So you resort to thievery to amuse yourself?"

"Uh, no. To break into my father's library. He had quite a number of books he believed too, um, delicate for one of my tender years."

"I can well imagine," Stephen commented dryly as he carefully brought her around his desk to stand directly in front of him. "So mine is not the only library to be graced by your presence."

Gillian smiled, relaxing now that she had managed to distract him. "It was years before I received the keys, and by that time I was so proficient I never bothered with them."

"And he never took you across his knee to give you the beating you deserved?"

Gillian looked down, unwilling to relive the memories revived by his comments. "You need not worry on that point, my lord," she said softly. "Others took up what my father neglected." The real Amanda, in fact, had repeatedly ordered the butler to beat her. This he had done with almost clockwork regularity.

"And what about me, Amanda? Shall I beat you for your transgression?"

Gillian felt her heart do an erratic double thump at his comment. She stood so close to Stephen she could feel the power in his lean form, only partially hidden by his fashionable clothes. He could no doubt kill her with just his bare hands, but despite his words, she did not fear he would hurt her.

In fact, the thought of his hands on her body intrigued her as much as it frightened her.

She swallowed convulsively, and for the first

time in her life had no comment. Her mind was consumed by the images conjured by his words.

Then she felt his hand on her chin, tilting her head until she looked directly into his eyes. This close to him, she could see the gold flecks that made them shimmer in candlelight, and as she watched, the dark pupils dilated, expanding into the blue depths until his gaze seemed wholly dark and devastatingly compelling.

"How shall I punish you, Amanda?" His voice was a hoarse whisper, and she felt her own breath catch on her dry lips. His hold on her face was hard, but not hurtful, and she could feel the leashed intensity in the press of his fingers. "When you pry into a man's secrets, there is no telling what darkness you might find."

Gillian felt her world spin out of control. She wanted desperately to break away from the frightening sensations coursing through her body. She felt hot and cold and trembly all over. All she need do was twist away and the world would right itself again. She would regain her strength and control. Yet she felt powerless to do so. Instead she lifted her chin and swayed forward, begging him with her body to explain the secrets she saw burning in his eyes.

"Why were you in my desk?"

"I was looking for Mr. Oltheten's direction." She could not stop the words if her life had depended on it. And perhaps, she thought with an odd sense of unreality, perhaps her life did hang in the balance. But it was too late.

"Mr. Oltheten? But you have—"

"The elder."

"Why?"

Gillian sighed, knowing now he would not kiss her. She jumped a bit, startled by her own thought. Was she waiting for a kiss? Not possible. Why would—

But her thoughts were interrupted by his growled demand. "Why do you want his direction, Amanda?"

She turned away, finally able to break his spell over her. "Because I wished to send him a recipe for his lungs."

"Why not simply ask me for it?"

Gillian shrugged, her excuse sounding feeble to her own ears. "Because you would make me see him, and I . . . I have no desire to visit his sickroom."

He remained silent for a long moment. Her back was to him, her eyes on the smooth planes of his desk. Would his skin be as silken to the touch? Certainly not as cool, for she had felt his heat radiate through the many layers of their clothes.

"How did you learn this recipe?"

"G-Gillian needed it. I made it for her many times." It was hard to say her own name, to speak of her own death even knowing it was all pretend.

Then she felt him draw closer. She heard the rustle of his clothing and smelled the faint sandalwood of his cologne. When he spoke, his voice was low and his breath teased the hair along the back of her neck.

"It must have been hard to watch your sister die. Especially since she nursed you all those years."

"It is hard to watch anyone die. Gillian's death was no worse than another's." It surprised her how cold she sounded. So much like the real Amanda.

"Still," he pursued, "she was your sister—"

"Half sister. And I never felt any kinship with her." That much at least was true, for both Gillian and the real Amanda.

Then suddenly it was too much for her. He was too much for her. So she crossed quickly to the earl's chair, using the movement to escape his disturbing presence. She remembered his desk in detail, so she knew just which drawer to pull open for a sheet of foolscap.

She quickly scribbled down the recipe without looking up. But though she never glanced at him, she was excruciatingly aware of the man who watched her with those hooded eyes.

"There." She pushed the paper toward him. "Please send it to Mr. Oltheten with my regards. Now if you will excuse me . . ." She meant to slip by him and straight out the door, but he stopped her. He grabbed her arm and drew her close until she pressed sideways against him— her shoulder tucked against his muscular chest, her hip flush against the narrow heat of him, and her thigh nestled between his legs.

"My lord?" She hated the breathless quality to her voice, but she could not stop the fluttering of sensation quivering in her belly.

"We still have not discussed your punishment, Amanda."

Her insides trembled and her knees were weak, but she knew she could not stand more of this strange game of his. She did not jerk out of his hold, because she knew he would not release her. So she simply tilted her head up to look directly into his eyes.

"Then what is your pleasure, my lord? Will you cane me? Beat me? Do you wish to send for your whip? Whatever it is, I pray you get it done with now. We would not want the welts to show beneath my first ball gown." Her voice was hard and flat, and from the shock in his eyes, she knew she had surprised him.

"You sound as if you have experienced it before."

"More times than I can count."

Amanda's butler had used his fists, but his wife had chosen the cane. In truth, she did not blame them, though she fired them both without a reference as soon as she took control of the estate. It was Amanda, with her bitter eyes and all-consuming envy, who had ordered the beatings.

She shook her head, hating the memories, taking the anger she felt and directing it at the earl. "Now if you will excuse me," she said, "perhaps I should wait in my room until you decide exactly what you intend to do with me."

She swept out of his hold and hurried from the room, praying she made it to her bed before she burst into tears.

She paused only once, just as she turned the doorknob. He had not moved, but his voice followed her, catching her unaware as she tried to escape.

"Amanda."

She stood frozen, her breath suspended.

"You look magnificent in white."

She picked up her skirts and ran.

Stephen watched her disappear in a silken rustle of white. She was such a delightful mass of contradictions. One minute she challenged him boldly, her eyes flashing like green lightning. The next, she blushed like an innocent even while she tempted him beyond reason. And then there was that last moment, when her eyes clouded with memories and pain.

How could the mistress of the household be beaten regularly? Who had done it? Was it before she had taken sick? Before she had become mistress of the estate?

Questions spun in his thoughts until he did not know what to do. Best get her married off quickly, he decided.

Stephen sighed and walked stiffly to his desk chair, his thoughts turning inevitably back to the present.

How could new clothes make such a difference in a woman's appeal? Even with her drab clothing, he had known she was a beautiful woman with an animated face and rich, luscious hair. But seeing her today in fashionable attire that emphasized her mature body was like seeing a butterfly emerge from a cocoon. When she'd first stood up from behind his desk, his breath had caught in his throat. Her figure was perfect in every sense. Her breasts were outlined in soft ribbons, their points molding the fabric into classic lines. Though fashion dictated high waists, the soft fabric still clung to her body, suggesting a narrow waist, hips with just the right roundness, and a firm bottom.

Stephen groaned as he sat down in his chair, feeling the soft leather readjust to his frame. He should not be thinking of his ward in such a way, so he redirected his thoughts, forcing himself to relive the outrage. She had been sitting in this very chair, at his desk, violating his sanctuary!

My word, she had actually picked his desk lock and read his journals!

With a grim frown, he turned his attention to his desk. What else had she done besides read his most humiliating escapades during his childhood? Starting at the top, Stephen moved meticulously through each drawer. Nothing was out of place, though his instincts told him she had gone through every inch. Finally he reached the last drawer. She claimed she had not touched his cash box, and he breathed a sigh of relief at the unscarred lock and correct amount of pound notes within.

Then he glanced at his journals. *Three* journals. He did not have to open them to know she had stolen the most recent one, the one chronicling his return to London and subsequent weeks. Then he mentally reviewed everything written within the thin volume and a slow smile spread across his face.

How long would it take her to find out? Surely not more than another half hour. She could not resist for longer than that. Dinner was in an hour, and she would have to dress. If she wished to read his journal in private, it would be now or after his mother's evening behavior drills.

Stephen glanced at the clock, folding his arms across his chest as he waited. He was ashamed to admit how much he relished his ward's coming set-down, but it would greatly repay her for her crimes.

In the end, it took only another seventeen minutes. She burst through his door looking like an avenging angel, his journal held high in the air as though it were damning evidence in a trial.

"Five pages on how your horse adjusts to London, three pages on sheep farming, another four on crops, and nothing—not a single word—about me!"

He grinned. She truly was a magnificent woman. "Would you prefer I pen insults?"

She stopped, momentarily taken aback. "I . . . Yes, I think I would. At least then I would know where I stand."

"Is that why you stole my journal? To find out what I think of you?"

She lowered her arm, pulling his diary close to her breast as though cradling something precious. "Well, not just for that."

He raised an eyebrow and waited for her. He found her face exceptionally expressive at times, completely blank at other moments. But right now she frowned at him, her thoughts clearly turned inward as she pondered her answer. Her face reflected puzzlement, frustration, longing, and then abruptly nothing.

"I took it out of curiosity, my lord. I am sorry. It was ill-bred of me. An act completely without conscience. It no doubt serves me right that you wrote nothing about me. Clearly your horse, sheep, and crops are of more importance to you." Her voice lifted into a definite note of pique.

"Incorrect," he said while struggling to keep control of his humor. "I find I prefer to write about pleasant things."

"And I have been most unpleasant?" she challenged.

He grinned. He could not restrain himself. She was so very insulted by the whole thing. "Even you, my dear, could not call our encounters pleasant. Maddening, irritating, astounding, but definitely not pleasant."

She pursed her lips and absently stroked the leather cover of his journal. "Is that what you think of me?"

He was silent a moment, feeling caught beneath her steady green gaze. What did he think of her? He was not exactly sure, and there lay the true reason he had not written about her. She was completely outside of his experience— both seductive and totally innocent, willful but also generous to the point of gullibility. He had yet to settle her neatly into his thoughts, and therefore could not express his opinion in his journal. And now here she was, the cheeky minx, demanding to know exactly what he had not felt comfortable enough to put in his own diary.

"I think you have been neatly served for prying where you do not belong. Now if you will please return—"

"So I am nothing to you. A nonentity, an insignificance."

He grinned at her lack of self-confidence. "Amanda, you are definitely an entity. You have physical mass. You certainly have an effect on your environment—"

"You know what I mean. I . . ." She bit her lip as she struggled for the right words. "I am an annoyance to you, and you will happily dismiss me to think of more important matters."

He took a deep breath, wishing it were true. If he could easily dismiss her from his mind, he would be a much happier fellow. Instead he had done little else these last few days but think of her. Of course, he could not admit that to her. Instead he tilted his head and regarded her with what he hoped was a bland expression.

"Why does it bother you so?"

Her shoulders slumped in defeat as he seemed to confirm her worst fears. She settled onto the nearby couch and stared morosely out of the window. "What am I to do?"

"You will add the following rules to your list

of ladylike behavior: A lady does not pick locks. A lady does not indulge her curiosity with inappropriate behavior. And a lady most certainly does not read private journals."

She frowned, waving away his rules with a distracted air. "No, no. What shall I *do?*"

He blinked. He had not the slightest clue what she meant. "I do not understand."

She sighed, the sound almost tragic. "I am in London to attract a husband. If you, my guardian, do not notice me, then how shall I ever attract anyone?"

"Uh, I did not exactly say—"

"No, you did not, but then you are the soul of propriety. You would not." She dropped her head on her hand and tapped her fingers against her lips as she thought. He was so distracted by the sight he almost missed her next words. "I shall just have to act more scandalous."

"What!" He nearly bolted out of his chair.

"Oh, nothing too outrageous, just a little bolder."

"Amanda, I assure you—"

"No, no, let me think." She was suddenly up and pacing, her white skirts swirling about her ankles in an enticing display. "I could lower the neckline of my dresses, except there are probably enough demireps around that I could not compete—"

"Your necklines are entirely proper!"

She whirled on him, her hands on her hips as she scolded him like a slow schoolboy. "Well, that is just the problem. I am entirely too proper to the point of becoming boring."

"Amanda—" He pronounced her name in a low growl, but she did not heed him.

"Perhaps I could play cards. I am actually quite good."

"There are a few card parties—"

"Oh, quite correct. Probably too tame. Perhaps a rumor, then. The countess says society practically thrives on gossip. What if I suggest I tread the boards?"

That did it. He jumped out of his chair, crossing to tower over her. "As an actress? You will do no such thing!"

"Too much?" She spun away from him, still deep in her own thoughts. "Very well, an aborted elopement? No, no one would believe it." Then she snapped her fingers in triumph. "I have it! I shall pretend to be illegitimate!"

"Absolutely not!"

She turned, her eyes wide, as if she were surprised by his outburst. He ignored her, stomping around his desk so he could impress upon her the absolute truth of his words.

"Believe me, Amanda. You are nothing if not memorable. I have no doubt that only the senile or daft could possibly forget you."

"But—"

"And as I have decided to provide you with a substantial dowry, let me assure you, you will create a stir even if you were cross-eyed and in your dotage!"

For once she did not interrupt him, but her

downcast eyes stopped him. Finally she spoke in a subdued voice. "Are you saying I shall be courted for my dowry?"

He sighed, stepping forward enough to place his hands on her shoulders. "I am saying I expect to be tripping over suitors three deep on my doorstep once the Season begins. So you have no need for outrageous lies or infamous gowns. If anything I need you to behave with excessive dignity—"

"Oh, I doubt I could achieve that—"

"With appropriate dignity then, and the men will fall over themselves to propose."

She remained silent a moment, considering his words. And while she focused on her inner thoughts, he allowed himself to revel in the silky texture of her arms and the heated blush his touch brought to her skin.

Finally she lifted her gaze to him, and he forced himself to think of something other than the urge to draw her deeper into his arms. "What if I said I was illegitimate?"

"I shall boot you back to York and wash my hands of you entirely. You will not bring such scandal to my family."

She nodded once, looking for all the world like a kicked puppy. What was the matter with the girl? he wondered. He had said everything she wanted to hear. She would have a huge dowry and suitors cramming the rafters. What more could she want?

"Amanda—"

"I must go dress for dinner," she interrupted.

"Here is your journal, my lord. I am sorry I read it. I will not do so again. Now if you will excuse me . . ." He reached down to take his journal from her trembling fingers while he searched her face for some clue to her strange behavior. But her face was once again empty of all expression.

"Amanda—" he began.

"Good evening, my lord." Then she dropped into a deep curtsy before slipping out the door.

Chapter Six

A lady does not listen at doorways.

"*Non, non!* Please, Miss Wyndham, you must try to concentrate."

Gillian sighed and tried to focus her attention on the thin dance master. "I understand, Mr. Flauterre. A figure eight, a curtsy across, and then we pass down a step."

The countess dropped wearily into the couch and glared at her. "If you understand, Amanda, then why do you forever get it wrong?"

Gillian folded her hands in front of her and tried not to let her eyes tear. She felt stupid and awkward and so very, very disappointed. Her Season was supposed to be fun, but it felt more like jail than the longed-for dream of her childhood. And as each frustration followed yet another disappointment, she was hard put to keep her tongue civil, much less remember who took what in their tea or where to put her feet next in some inane dance.

"Mademoiselle, you have such grace, such style, if only you would apply yourself." Mr. Flauterre practically scraped the floor as he begged her to pay attention.

Gillian smiled at him, feeling sorry for the poor man whose livelihood depended on forcing girls like her to attend. "You are very kind, Mr. Flauterre, if a bit given to exaggeration. Very well, shall we begin again, and I will try to put my big, clumsy feet where they belong?"

"Oh, *non, non*, your feet are petite, *ma chérie*, and very skilled. It is only your will—"

"Stephen! Thank heaven you are here." The countess's voice cut a cold fear through Gillian's heart, and she spun around to see the earl lounging in the doorway, looking very handsome in a dark coat and tight-fitting trousers.

Ever since the debacle in the library, Gillian had worked extra hard to avoid him. She could not look at him without remembering the way she had stormed into the room, piqued because he had not written about her in a diary she should not have read in the first place.

What was it about the man that made her lose all reason?

And now he regarded her with those steely blue eyes, and she wondered what stupidity she would commit next in his august presence.

"Pray, do not just stand there, Stephen. Do

something!" The countess dropped backward against the couch, her hand pressed to her brow in a very fragile and tragic sort of picture.

"Just what would you suggest I do, Mother?" Stephen's voice was rich with humor as he gazed at Gillian, clearly inviting her to share his amusement. But Gillian felt too awkward and too stupid to enjoy the countess's foibles, so she dropped her gaze to the carpet and sighed.

"I fear, my lord, that unless you can magically transform me into a pixie, there is little hope for my skills on the dance floor."

"Nonsense," he commented, stepping forward. "I agree with Mr. Flauterre. You are quite graceful, just perhaps a bit . . . bored?" Gillian did not realize he was so close to her until she felt his finger beneath her chin, gently urging her to look up into his eyes. "You do not seem happy, Amanda. In fact, you seem so different from the girl who two weeks ago stormed into my breakfast room speaking of crypts, I begin to think you an impostor."

Gillian jumped at his words, a surge of fear coursing through her despite the innocence of his remarks. Surely he did not know the truth? He was merely saying she seemed changed from two weeks ago.

"Amanda?" he asked, clearly surprised by her suddenly panicked expression.

She hastily looked away. "My apologies, my lord. I am merely somewhat tired."

She could tell he did not believe her. The extended silence felt charged with his curiosity.

117

But then he spoke, his words barely above a whisper.

"Tell me what is the matter."

Gillian tried to keep her eyes averted, tried not to be drawn into the soft blue of his gaze. She knew one look into their depths and she would tell him anything. So, she chose to look at the countess instead, noting the woman's tragic pose as she reclined on the settee and sipped a glass of sherry.

"You need not fear," Stephen continued. "I want to understand."

It was impossible to resist such gentleness, and so she nodded and spoke in a near whisper, choosing to confess what she could and hide what she could not. "All my life I have dreamed about this, about dancing and attending balls. But now . . ." Her voice trailed away, but Stephen would not let her stop.

"But now . . . ?" he prompted.

"Now I find myself completely bored," she finally admitted. "I have no time to read or simply be by myself. I am to practice silly conversations about empty topics. I cannot play cards except for a few paltry pennies. Even the dances are dull."

Behind her she heard the countess sniff in shocked disdain, but Stephen silenced his mother with a pointed look before turning back to Gillian. "The dances are merely opportunities for eligible ladies and gentlemen to converse."

"Converse? How can one converse sensibly

while being constantly interrupted to walk in a circle or curtsy? If we are to dance, then let us dance. If we are to talk, then we should talk."

"You see!" exclaimed the countess from her position on the couch. "You see what ridiculousness I am forced to deal with?"

"On the contrary, Mother, I find Amanda's ideas eminently reasonable. Perhaps the problem is the choice of dance." Taking Gillian's hand, he guided her to the center of their makeshift floor. "Mr. Flauterre, a waltz, if you please."

"A waltz!" exclaimed his mother. "But Stephen—"

"Three steps, Amanda," he said, effectively silencing her. "Like this." Then he pulled her into his arms, and the music began.

It started awkwardly as she tried to adjust to the strange rhythms of the dance, to their constantly shifting direction, and to the overwhelming sensation of being in Stephen's arms. But then he leaned closer, whispering into her ear.

"Do you trust me?"

She was so startled by his odd question that, for a moment, she forgot everything but the gleaming light in his eyes, daring her to refuse.

"You think I cannot do it," she challenged.

If anything, his eyes turned even bluer as they sparkled with mirth. "You are doing it. The question is whether you trust me enough to truly relax and enjoy yourself."

"I . . ." But she had no opportunity to answer

as he spun her into a dizzying turn. It was so fast she clutched on to him to keep from falling. Then it was as if she really had fallen, for suddenly she felt herself spinning along with him. She felt the strength of his thighs, which propelled them around and around the floor, the heat of Stephen's arm as he pulled her ever closer, and the mesmerizing beauty of his blue eyes as they focused wholly on her.

She smiled up at him, and he returned the gesture, his face softening into almost boyish lines. Then they spun again, and for the first time in her life Gillian completely relaxed, trusting Stephen to keep her from falling flat on her face. She gave herself totally to the music and completely to him.

They spun and whirled in glorious abandon, and she laughed from the sheer pleasure of it all. She never felt so free, yet she was totally dependent on Stephen. His arms tightened around her until the two of them seemed to be one person, one body, one glorious expression of joy.

Until the music ended.

He guided her to a stop, gently slowing their bodies until they stood, still touching, their gazes locked together. His eyes seemed impossibly blue, incredibly intense. She was breathless and her pulse pounded through her body, but her heart still soared with his, and she could do nothing but stand and stare at his chiseled features and his dark, masculine lips.

"Well, I certainly think we have had enough

dancing for one day." The countess's clipped tones felt like a bucket of chill water in their faces, and Gillian felt Stephen start in surprise. He abruptly dropped his hands from her sides, and Gillian stumbled slightly as she suddenly supported her own weight.

"Thank you, Mr. Flauterre," continued the countess. "I shall contact you when we next require your tutoring."

"Of course, madame," agreed the thin dancing master. Then he and his assistant quickly bowed their way out.

"As for you, my girl—" The countess rounded on her, but could not continue as Stephen interrupted.

"I believe Amanda is entitled to a rest, Mother. And as I have promised her a trip to the crypts, now is a perfect opportunity."

"But—"

"I shall call around to the mews for Tom. Amanda, can you be ready in—"

"Five minutes," Gillian said with a gasp. "Just five minutes to get my wrap." Then she dashed up the stairs, still breathless, her head spinning with a kind of mindless joy. The waltz was the most fabulous dance ever invented! And now she would go to the crypts!

What a wonderful day this was!

Oh, she knew it was dangerous to spend more time with Stephen, especially after that incredible, heart-stoppingly scandalous dance. But how could she regret anything so wonderful?

And how could she resist spending time with the one person who made her feel so free?

"Stephen, have you taken leave of your senses?"

"I beg your pardon, Mother?"

"We have only a week left before the Season begins. Surely you cannot mean to take her on such an expedition now."

Stephen brushed an imaginary fleck of dust from his coatsleeve while covertly studying his agitated parent. Her hands clutched her glass of sherry, and her eyes narrowed, seeming almost frightened.

"Mother, I do believe you are distraught about something."

"Do not be ridiculous, Stephen. I am merely concerned about how it might seem."

"A guardian taking his ward on an outing? Whatever is wrong with that? We will bring along her maid and everything shall be fine."

"Do not be obtuse, you stubborn boy. I am concerned about Amanda. You must see how she looks at you."

"Me?"

"Gracious, Stephen. Use your head. She has spent her entire life in the country. Likely the only men she has known are farmers and vicars. You overwhelm her."

"Really," he drawled. "I rather thought she was too willful by half. A stubborn chit who has not the intelligence to pretend otherwise. That is what you said last evening, was it not?"

"Do not throw my own words back at me!"

She stood and grabbed his arm, forcing him to look at her while she drove her point home. "The girl is falling in love with you, and if you cannot see that then you are more daft than the thieving boy you are so fond of."

"I have found Tom quite intelligent."

"You will find your ward turning down every eligible offer this Season because she has convinced herself she is in love with you."

"Surely you exaggerate," he drawled, but he could not deny the icy chill gripping his spine at her words.

The countess narrowed her eyes. "Do I? Or perhaps I underestimate your feelings for her."

"Me!" he exclaimed, plainly shocked. "She is my ward, for God's sake, and a childish scapegrace to boot. How could I fall in love with her?"

His mother nodded, satisfaction relaxing her grip on his arm. "Good. I rather had a better bride in mind for you. Lady Sophia Rathburn, last year's incomparable. She is elegant, sophisticated, and everything a countess should be."

"I hardly expect to be setting up my nursery this Season, Mother." He kept his voice firm, hoping his tone would have some effect on his mother.

He was singularly ineffective.

"Piffle," she said with a dismissive wave. "Just make sure you recall your obligations to your title and do your best not to encourage your countrified burden."

Stephen sighed. "You can count on me to do what is proper by my name," he said stiffly.

Then he looked up as Amanda stepped into the room. Her face was unnaturally pale, and suddenly he had a panicked thought. Could she have heard their conversation?

"Are you ready?" he asked too brightly.

She smiled back, her features shifting into a demure, if somewhat lifeless smile. "Yes. Thank you for waiting, my lord."

She had heard. Stephen nearly groaned out loud. Deliberately forgetting to summon a maid, he counted the seconds until he could speak with her alone. He needed to explain his mother's words, perhaps—

He cut off his thoughts with a sigh. What would he say? If she were indeed falling in love with him, then his mother was correct. It would be best to dash her hopes now. And if she had not set her cap for him, she would find any explanation extremely embarrassing. *He* certainly would.

No, he suddenly decided, he would not speak to her. Instead he made an effort to keep the conversation moving, albeit along safe, mundane lines. Amanda responded in kind, slipping easily into the polite chatter she had disdained only minutes before. And all the while, Stephen watched her face for betraying hints of distress.

There were none. And yet she seemed so flat and dull.

"Are you feeling quite the thing, Amanda? We could postpone this if you are tired."

"Oh, no, my lord. Unless, of course, you would prefer to do something else."

"Of course not. I suggested it in the first place."

"Yes."

"Good." Stephen regarded his ward. "You will tell me if you tire."

"Of course."

"Good."

And that was that. Clearly she could not have heard any of his mother's absurd comments; otherwise she would be prostrate with distress, he told himself. Except that Amanda was not a typical girl. In fact, he realized as he let his gaze linger on her tight bodice, Amanda was not a girl at all, but a woman who kept her thoughts hidden deeply within herself.

Which only served to tell him she might or might not have heard his comments, and she might or might not be dying of mortification inside.

Unless, of course, his mother was totally out and Amanda had no tendresse for him whatsoever. For some perverse reason, that thought disturbed him most of all.

Gillian stared unseeing out the carriage window. She had waited an eternity to escape into London, and now she passed buildings and monuments with barely a sidelong glance. Beside her, Tom chattered about everything he had learned and done in the mews, but all she could hear were the countess's scathing comments and Stephen's shocked disdain.

Countrified burden. Stubborn chit.

Obviously he knew nothing of how she had changed, of all the things she had learned.

Childish scapegrace.

That one hurt the most. She had been a fool to think he would ever notice her. He was to marry Sophia Rathburn, a woman born to elegance, no doubt as different from plain, illegitimate Gillian as silk from sackcloth.

Gillian sighed and let her forehead drop against the window. At least she had one reason to be grateful for that little scene. The countess was right: Gillian had begun to fancy herself half in love with her handsome guardian. More and more when she dreamed of her first balls, Stephen was the one leading her onto the dance floor, dropping at her feet in admiration, showering her with tokens of his affection.

She snorted in self-disgust. What a foolish child she was. But now the illusions were gone from her eyes. She saw that whatever kindness or generosity of spirit she thought he possessed was in reality a lie. Beneath the urbane exterior, below the expert tailoring and muscled form, underneath his sensuous words and deep voice, Stephen was simply another callous, cruel member of the aristocracy.

How could I fall in love with her? She could still hear the shocked outrage in his voice.

Thank God she knew the truth now before the Season began, or she might have thought the gentry almost human.

But no more.

She rededicated herself to her goal. She

would find a wealthy husband. She would become legitimate, titled, and revered. If that required endless rounds of French verbs, empty prattle, and haughty disdain, then so be it.

Countrified burden.

She would show him and his Sophia Rathburn. Bastard or not, Gillian Ames would create a future brighter than anyone could ever imagine.

Having made her resolution, Gillian felt immeasurably better. She lifted her head off the window and took stock of her surroundings. Nothing had changed, except perhaps the view outside. Tom still chattered away beside her, but when she turned, she saw Stephen's troubled gaze on her.

Suddenly a picture flashed through her mind. She recalled the countess giving a cheeky footman a set-down with a single look. Striving for just that air of disgust, Gillian tilted her head and sent Stephen an arch look followed by a superior smile.

She nearly laughed when she saw the flushed expression of surprise color his cheeks.

Feeling better than she had in two weeks, Gillian settled back against the squabs and gave her attention to Tom. Then, five minutes later, the carriage slowed to a stop before St. Mary-le-Bow church.

"We are here," Stephen commented unnecessarily.

"Yes, we certainly are," she answered. Then, without waiting for his assistance, she swept out of the carriage onto the street—and stopped dead, the view surprising a gasp out of her.

The church was larger than she had expected, with soaring stone arches and a huge, beautiful bell tower topped by a weather vane in the form of a griffin. It seemed to loom over the surrounding buildings, dwarfing them and the pitiful humans below into near insignificance.

"They say only those born within the sound of these bells are true Cockneys."

Gillian jumped at Stephen's low voice just behind her right ear. She had not realized he was so close until she felt the heat of his breath stirring her hair, sending shivers of delight down her spine.

How could she remain stiffly correct when he was so close it made her knees tremble?

"Shall we go inside?" he asked.

Gillian nodded, furious with herself for being so weak around the man she had just sworn to put in his place. He raised his arm, his expression congenial, his smile warm. Gillian sighed inwardly. Despite her current feelings, she knew it would be dangerous to be too rude. Besides, she intended to be excruciatingly correct, which meant enduring the earl's company no matter what she thought of him.

With a cool smile, Gillian placed her fingertips on his forearm and told herself quite forcefully not to enjoy the ripple of muscle she felt beneath his coat.

As they entered the church, Gillian dropped her gaze out of habit. Bastards did not raise their eyes to God, or so Reverend Hallowsby had repeated over and over to her. So she focused on Tom running along beside her. The boy had filled out in the last two weeks. A steady diet of healthy food as well as a regime of regular bathing had dramatically changed his appearance. His brown curls were now orderly and clean, his face alight with curiosity, not that sallow tinge of desperation. But as dramatic the change, some things remained the same. His eyes still sparkled with a lively intelligence, absorbing and evaluating everything he saw.

"Coo, but don't it look big without the gents stuffing themselves inside?"

"You have been here before?" Gillian asked in surprise.

Tom turned and grinned at her. "Best pickings on Sunday."

"Do you mean to tell me, young man, you came to church to cut purses?" She tried to sound stern, but totally failed in the face of his impish grin.

"Best pickings when the morts try to impress 'is neighbor with the weight of 'is purse." Then he shrugged.

"Tom!" She gasped, awed by his audacity. "Were you truly here cutting purses?"

Slowly the boy's face fell as he shifted awkwardly away. "Naw. They don't let the likes of me in 'ere."

Gillian grew quiet, still keeping her gaze on the boy. She knew exactly what he meant about not being wanted, could see the hurt in his stiff little shoulders despite his demeanor. And in her memories, she relived every single sermon, every echoing word of condemnation that Reverend Hallowsby had heaped upon her head.

All because she had beaten him with his own cross until he bled. He had caught her right after Sunday services his first week in the vicarage. He had pulled her into the back room while whispering about sin and atonement.

And then he had touched her.

She had not stopped to think of the consequences. She had not realized how vindictive the man might be when thwarted. She had merely reacted, grabbing a wooden cross from the wall and striking out until she could escape.

And that was when her nightmare had begun.

Sighing, she reached out to ruffle Tom's hair. "The morts never liked me either," she said softly, and was rewarded with a flash of understanding far beyond his tender years. "But," she added with a grin, "we are here now. And with an earl!"

Tom grinned back, and she knew they had formed a bond. Whatever became of her, she would not forget Tom. And whatever he could do for her, he would. Their loyalty toward one another was assured, and it gave her such comfort that Gillian finally gained enough courage to look up at the church itself.

It was certainly impressive. Large windows threw checkered patterns across the floor, lighting long rows of rich, dark pews. The floor was made of stone, and her walking boots clicked ominously on the gray floor. But it was the altar that drew her attention the most.

Even before Reverend Hallowsby had come to York, church had never been a happy place for her. Though Reverend Crane had always been kind to her, he always said she would have to be extra good, to walk an extra tight line before God because of her unfortunate parentage. Now, despite the distance adulthood gave her, she still felt a tiny bit of panic as she entered the church. Would God strike her dead because she was a bastard pretending to be legitimate? Would Reverend Hallowsby's hellfire and brimstone rise up and burn her alive for her audacity?

In her mind, she knew it was all foolishness, but still her heartbeat accelerated and her fingers clutched Stephen's arm as she raised her eyes to the cross.

Nothing. She saw a gilded cross sweeping upward above the altar. Then, before she could catch her breath, the sight was replaced by a fleshy visage with an obsequious smile.

"Good afternoon, my lord. Welcome to St. Mary-le-Bow church. Have you come to hear the bells?" Gillian blinked and focused on the overly round face of a minister scurrying forward.

"Actually, Reverend," commented Stephen from beside her, "we have come to see the crypts."

"The crypts! My goodness, but—"

"I believe my solicitor contacted you earlier in the week regarding this visit."

The man's face underwent a dramatic change. Where before it was merely ingratiating, it now became positively overflowing with toadying adoration. "Oh, my, yes, my lord. Of course. I had not realized you were the Earl of Mavenford. Please, please, follow me."

Gillian glanced up at the earl. His face was impassive as his gaze wandered over the flowing stone arches.

"You arranged for a visit earlier this week?" She thought their excursion merely an afterthought of their incredible dance. But now, knowing he had actually planned ahead for their outing made her unaccountably pleased with the world.

He glanced down at her, smiling warmly. "I promised you I would. Did you not believe me?"

"No," she answered. "I did not. I apologize for misjudging you."

His face grew pensive as he slowed their progress through the sanctuary. "Not many people have kept their promises to you, have they?"

Gillian's mouth went dry, and she glanced away. How could she forget how very much this man saw even in polite chatter? This was just another example of how easy it was to make serious mistakes around him, how one false word could give away everything before she even began.

She must be doubly on guard today.

"Oh, Reverend!" she suddenly exclaimed.

"This is absolutely amazing stonework. How was it done?" She knew Stephen was not fooled. She had no true interest in masonry. It was merely an excuse not to speak to Stephen. And from the weight of his gaze, he was not happy with her distraction.

Still, he said nothing, allowing her to encourage the minister into long soliloquies of rapture on the construction details of the church. She listened politely, as did Stephen beside her. But all too soon Tom grew bored, wandering about, poking into one niche or another, pocketing a dropped coin when he thought no one saw. Meanwhile, Gillian pretended fascination with the cleric's words while Stephen's hooded gaze remained trained on her, as though she were some puzzle he needed to decipher.

The thought should have frightened her. Instead it gave her an odd surge of excitement knowing she was the center of his thoughts. It was perverse of her, she knew. But she could not deny the thrill she experienced whenever she caught him looking at her.

Gillian sighed as the reverend began another long speech about the details of preparing stone for carving. If only the Season would begin. She must find a husband quickly or she would give her secret away entirely.

"I say, Sophia, is that Mavenford?"

Gillian twisted around at the cultured tones echoing through the sanctuary. From the corner of her eye, she saw Stephen also turn and Tom shrink surreptitiously behind a pillar.

There, sauntering calmly down the center aisle, was what must be a tulip of the ton and an incomparable. They were clearly brother and sister, with the same dusty blond locks curling artfully about their faces. Like Stephen, the woman's eyes were blue, although the tulip's were gray and had the cold gleam of a stone; the incomparable's eyes were more brilliant, flashier, like a rare sapphire.

Both were clothed in the first stare of fashion, although along completely different lines. The man preferred a colorful style Gillian found a trifle effeminate, especially when compared to Stephen. His pantaloons were yellow and his waistcoat gray and gold. This was topped by a dark green coat that flattered his narrower shoulders and emphasized the lean, trim lines of his almost lanky body. All in all, the effect was pleasing if not endearing, fashionable in a way the overwhelmingly masculine Stephen could never achieve.

"Goodness, my lord," said the woman as she neared Stephen. "I heard you were in town. I am so pleased to meet up with you today." The woman's voice fit her appearance perfectly. It was mellow, echoing with a seductive richness in the large sanctuary. Her tone spoke of wealth, sophistication, and most of all supreme confidence in her beauty and position in society. She wore a stunning silver and sapphire walking gown that cast Gillian's dull white dress into the shade.

While Gillian was occupied with envy, Stephen bowed solemnly over the incomparable's hand. "It is always a pleasure, Lady Sophia." He dropped a polite kiss to her fingers, then straightened. "Geoffrey. You look capital, as always."

The other man smiled with a distinctly world-weary air. "One does try." Then he raised his quizzing glass to the earl. "Nice to see you have made the effort."

Stephen returned the smile, his expression almost self-mocking. "As you said, one does try." Gillian tried not to stare at Stephen. He seemed all that was correct, but something in his demeanor told her he was not pleased by this interruption.

The thought quite cheered her.

Then it was Gillian's turn to be introduced, and all thoughts fled as Stephen took hold of her hand and drew her forward.

"Amanda, please allow me to introduce you to Geoffrey Rathburn, Lord Tallis, and his sister, Lady Sophia Rathburn. Tallis, Lady Sophia, this is Miss Amanda Wyndham."

Lord Tallis bowed over her hand, his fingers caressing her palm as he moved. "My pleasure indeed, Miss Wyndham."

Gillian curtsied and was grateful she did not fall flat on her face.

"Oh, my, this must be your little ward," Lady Sophia said with a serene smile. "You are quite lovely, my dear. I am sure you will take this Season."

"You are too kind, my lady," Gillian answered

dryly as she met the frankly appraising glance of the woman. How could she ever have thought to be like this woman, to show Stephen she, too, could be sophisticated and elegant?

Where Lady Sophia's movements were graceful and unhurried, Gillian felt every jerk of her breathing, every awkward shift of her short, clunky body. Where Lady Sophia wore colorful fabrics with style and maturity, Gillian was trussed up in a childish white that already sported dirt smudges along the hem. Even Gillian's hair, her absolute best asset, could not compete with the other woman's fashionable coiffure.

She felt and no doubt looked a slightly scapegrace child. If it were not for the appreciative gleam in Lord Tallis's eyes, she would have given up altogether. As it was, she focused her gaze on Lord Tallis, the one man who seemed friendliest toward her.

"How odd to have met you here, Lord Tallis," Stephen said, interrupting her thought. "I had not thought the crypts especially fashionable these days."

A strange gleam entered the man's eyes as he glanced at Lady Sophia. "True, my dear. But then who knows where my sister's interest will lie from one day to the next. One minute she is happily anticipating a shopping expedition; the next moment nothing will do but to go visit the crypts. Of course, she must drag me along." He shifted into a martyred pose. "And all because of some correspondence from your mother." He glanced significantly at Stephen.

Now Gillian understood why the two had so providentially appeared in the church. The countess no doubt sent around a message telling Lady Sophia to join them here just to make Stephen more aware of Sophia's assets and Gillian's failures.

Well, she thought with an angry sniff, she would just show the arrogant witch exactly what Gillian Ames was made of. She might not be a highborn lady, but she, too, could act haughty, cold, and so reserved she would put the cool Lady Sophia in her place.

So began the most painful lesson of her life.

Chapter Seven

A lady does not play with dead bodies.

They wandered through the upper part of the crypt for a half an hour as the minister more than exhausted the subject of Norman architecture. Gillian's interest did not pick up until he paused at a heavy doorway.

"And this, of course, is the entrance to the lower chambers."

He made to move on, but Gillian stopped him. "But can we not go down there?"

"There?" The man's eyes bulged with shock. "But those are the lower chambers."

"I know, but—"

"Perhaps," Stephen interposed smoothly, "if we could just open the door and look in."

"But—"

"Please." Stephen's voice was firm.

The balding cleric hesitated, clearly reluctant, but he was no proof against Stephen's weighty stare. With a ponderous sigh, he used a large key to unlock the heavy doorway. Then, with Stephen's help, they pushed it open to reveal a cool, musty blackness resembling nothing more than a gaping black maw. Even Tom shrank back from his first glimpse, but Gillian knew what to expect. She had, in fact, been anticipating it.

She realized most people did not share her morbid fascination with burial practices. She glanced disdainfully at Lady Sophia's shrinking form and could not repress a grin. Perhaps this was not what Lady Sophia wanted to see, but then, Gillian had not asked them along.

"As you can see," continued the minister, "the lower crypts can be somewhat, uh, gruesome."

"Oh, I do not mind," quipped Gillian as she reached for a torch resting nearby for those entering the chambers. "The gruesome has always held a particular fascination for me."

"Why am I not surprised?" Stephen drawled.

Gillian flashed him a grin. "Because you know one can learn a great deal about a culture from the way they treat their dead. The ancient Egyptians, for example, used to . . ." Gillian let her voice trail away as she caught sight of Lord Tallis's horrified face. It did not bother Gillian a whit that Lady Sophia backed away from the lower chambers, but to have Lord Tallis staring at her as though she had just grown two heads was enough to give her pause.

She must appear hopelessly odd to him. Gillian bit her lip, indecision making her nervous. She was exceedingly curious about the crypts. So anxious, in fact, that it graced the top of her list of tourist locations. But she did not wish to look completely beyond the pale with her first gentleman acquaintance.

"Oh, Stephen," Lady Sophia called in a breathy voice. "Do stop her. It just is not done."

Gillian arched an eyebrow, suddenly decided. She wanted to be rid of Lady Sophia's infuriating presence. And the best way to do that was to enter the crypts. So she lit her torch off a wall sconce and flashed another grin at the wilting incomparable. "You will find, Lady Sophia, that I am hopelessly countrified. I often find myself doing things that just are not done. But"—she started to descend the narrow stairs—"if you would rather stay behind, I am sure I shall not come to any harm alone."

She shot another look over her shoulder, desperately trying to keep her expression innocent. Her efforts were rewarded by Stephen's exasperated sigh. "Minx," he said softly. "You know I cannot let you wander around there alone. Who knows what sacrilege you might commit? Then legions of old ghosts would come haunt me for allowing you to wander about unchaperoned."

"Nonsense," she replied as Tom joined her on

the steps. "I would desecrate only one or two. You need not fear whole legions."

Stephen groaned, his eyes shifting uncomfortably between herself and Lady Sophia. "You are determined?" he finally asked Gillian.

"Absolutely." At that particular moment, Satan himself could not have prevented her from descending the stairs.

Stephen shrugged at the still goggle-eyed cleric, then lit his own torch. "Have at it then, brat."

Gillian grinned, pleased to have won out over the shrinking Lady Sophia. "Excellent." Then, just to make sure the elegant interlopers stayed behind, she continued to prattle in a seemingly innocent manner. "You know, I wonder if any of the raiments are still on the bodies or whether they will all have decomposed."

Beside her, Stephen groaned, but Gillian could not restrain a giggle. Her last glance at Lady Sophia showed the fashionable incomparable literally trembling on the threshold as she tried to steel herself for the descent. It would take only one last comment to make sure the lady stayed above. Gillian lifted her torch high, pretending to shine it about the large alcove, looking for a body.

"Oh, look," she called up. "The finger bones on this one are still intact. It seems as though he is reaching for something. Or could it be someone?" In truth, it was nothing more than a rats' nest. The bodies were kept deeper in. Still, it achieved its desired effect. High above them, she heard Lady Sophia's horrified gasp.

Then just behind her left ear, she heard Stephen's low voice, sending chills up her spine. "That was not well done of you, brat."

She did not answer at first, choosing instead to focus on her footing as she gained the main chamber. Stephen was seconds behind her, but that gave her enough time to make sure her back was to him.

Still, she knew she was acting shrewish, and a sharp stab of guilt coursed through her.

She squelched it, giving rein to her anger as she did her best imitation of his mother at her most annoying. "Oh, la," she said in an overly sweet tone. "It is not as if we invited her to join us."

"No, we didn't," he responded, his voice still low. "But my mother did, and it behooves us both to act civilly."

"Perhaps it behooves you," she snapped, throwing the words over her shoulder. "But your *little ward* does not feel nearly so charitable." Why she was so put out by his defense of Lady Sophia, she had no idea. But she was given no time to think about it as he grabbed her arm, spinning her around to face him.

The crypts were dark, the only light from the flickering torches. They cast a reddish glow over his face, giving him an almost demonic appearance as he stared at her. Then, with one firm hand, he gripped her chin, tilting her head upward, forcing her to look directly into his eyes. The flames danced there as well, mesmerizing her even as she felt a sudden fear chill her bones.

She stopped all pretense of a struggle.

"Listen well, brat," he said, his voice reverberating eerily against the stone walls. "Good manners are more than saying please and thank you. They are about being kind. About bringing out the best in people rather than the worst. And if you cannot do that, then you'd best go back to York now, for you will disgrace us both with your spite."

Gillian felt her chest compress with mortification.

He was right. In her effort to be sophisticated, she had acted as the very worst of the gentry rather than the best. Dropping her gaze, she murmured a soft, "You are correct, of course. I am sorry."

She watched in amazement as a smile pulled at the corners of his mouth. Chucking her under the chin, he placed her arm on his. "Come on, then. Let us go see your dead bodies."

But in that they were forestalled, as Lady Sophia, with more pluck than Gillian would ever have given her credit for, teetered down the steps on the arm of her brother, her face so pale as to be nearly translucent. Behind them came the minister, carrying another torch, his round forehead slick with worry as he glanced nervously at Lady Sophia.

"Praise be," called Lord Tallis with a relieved sigh. "I was afraid you had gone on. Come help her, Mavenford, while I light my torch."

With an irritating quickness, Stephen disengaged himself from Gillian and crossed the chamber to the base of the stairs. He reached out one hand, and Lady Sophia nearly tumbled into his arms as she tried to half run, half fly down the remaining steps. Then she attached herself to Stephen as though he were the sole barrier between her and the Great Beyond.

In her disgust Gillian nearly said something caustic, but mindful of Stephen's lecture, she kept her tongue firmly between her teeth. Not so Tom, who kept close to her side.

"Looks like a plucked chicken with that scrawny neck and pasty skin o' hers."

Gillian looked down in surprise, nearly choking on her laughter. "Tom, that was not kind."

He shrugged, clearly showing that the earl's lecture had no effect on him. "Want I should draw 'er feather?"

"What?"

"That geegaw. Should I pluck it fer ye?"

Gillian glanced back at Lady Sophia. The woman had regained some of her composure and now stood nearly candlestick straight, except for her decided lean toward Stephen. They conversed in low tones while the cleric rambled on again about the stonework.

It was not until a flash of torchlight caught the gleaming gold of a cross resting neatly between Lady Sophia's breasts that Gillian understood Tom's question.

"You cannot mean to lift her cross, Tom. Why, she is wearing it in plain sight."

Tom stiffened at what was apparently an insult to his pickpocketing skill. "I can. Just watch me."

He made to slip away, but Gillian grabbed him, holding him back. "Do not dare, Tom. Just think what would happen if you were caught. You would lose your position with the earl. Besides, he would have my ears on a platter for letting you try."

"But—"

"No, Tom." She gave him a hard stare until he finally gave in with a dramatic sigh. She grinned and ruffled his hair as they passed through a stone archway into another chamber. "Thank you for the thought anyway," she whispered. "It would have been nice to see that superior little smile wiped right off her face. Ah, well," she said on her own mournful sigh. "I am respectable now and must not think such things."

"Don't know why you take on so." He grimaced at the earl and the woman who was now so close to him she seemed suctioned to his hip. "Plain as piss you have twice as much bottom as she."

Once she translated his comment into understandable English, Gillian felt her spirits lift. Yes, she still wanted to scratch Lady Sophia's eyes out, but at least Tom remained her friend. "Thank you, Tom. I think."

"Yep." He nodded. "You and me, we's cut from the same cloth. Don't go trying to ruin it by becoming one of 'em." He spat disdainfully toward Lady Sophia, then caught sight of the first corpse-filled recess. "Blimey, think they has any geegaws left on 'em?" Then he dashed off to inspect it, carefully blowing away the dust as he no doubt tried to find something to steal.

Gillian slowed her step, her eyes trained on the boy while her heart beat hard in her chest. He'd said they were cut from the same cloth. Could it be that apparent? Could everyone see her baseborn roots as clearly as Tom?

She knew he meant his words as a compliment, but Gillian saw them as another example of just how far she must go to pull off her charade. If one little street boy could figure her out in two weeks, how long before someone else did?

How long before Stephen did?

She would have stood there in shock, her confidence failing her with every breath, if not for the sudden appearance of Lord Tallis by her side. "Save me, sweet lady, from dying of boredom. It would seem our cleric is intent on relating everything ever recorded on stonework until I quite want to drop some of these exquisite examples on his head."

Gillian blinked, refocusing her thoughts with an effort. "Uh, I am sorry if this bores you, my lord. Perhaps you could go above and find—"

"You misunderstand, Miss Wyndham," he interposed smoothly. "I said the prosy cleric bores me. You, however, do not. Do you truly find these bodies interesting?"

They wandered over to a room filled with dusty piles of bones laid out in recessed alcoves.

Kneeling down, Gillian brushed some of the filth away from ancient lettering carved into the rock. "Yes, Lord Tallis," she finally confessed. "I do find this interesting. I know that makes me hopelessly odd, but there it is."

He stepped closer, apparently to inspect one of the higher bodies. "Say unusual rather than odd." He turned so he looked nearly straight down at her. "Unusual and most intriguing."

Gillian stood up and backed away, not liking the way his gaze seemed to center on the curve of her breasts. When she spoke, she kept her tone hard, but not cold. "You will find, my lord, I am most immune to Spanish coin. I know the true reason you are speaking with me is to free up Stephen for your sister."

His light eyebrows raised a fraction of an inch. "Stephen, is it?"

She felt herself blush and was furious with herself for such a stupid gaffe. "The earl is my cousin and my guardian. We have become somewhat familiar."

"Indeed." There was a wealth of subtle intrigue hidden within the word, and Gillian found herself angry despite the fact that an innocent debutante might not understand any of his implications.

"I find your tone offensive, my lord."

Suddenly the slightly debauched courtier disappeared as Lord Tallis grinned with boyish impudence. "My apologies, Miss Wyndham. It is just that Mavenford is such a handsome devil. You would not be the first young chit to find herself in thrall to him, even before he got the title. I just needed to be sure—"

"My lord! He is my guardian!" Her tone was stiff with outrage even though her face felt like an inferno of embarrassment.

"Gently, Miss Wyndham. Gently," he soothed, and they glanced over at Stephen and Lady Sophia, who both regarded them with mixed expressions of curiosity and disapproval. Lord Tallis smiled and nodded at them; then he reached over and gently took her hand, placing it on his arm. Though reluctant, Gillian did not resist, and when she looked back up at her guardian, he was leaning down to catch something Lady Sophia felt necessary to whisper into his ear.

Irritating biddy, Gillian thought with rancor. She should just speak up so everyone could hear. Then she looked over to see Lord Tallis watching her closely.

"Is it my sister's attention or Mavenford's neglect that bothers you?"

Gillian flushed guiltily, then glanced away. Were all the men in London so astute? "Neither," she finally said. "It is just that she is so beautiful and well mannered, I find myself completely put out with jealousy."

"But Miss Wyndham, you are ten times as intriguing as my poor sister. Surely you realize that?"

Gillian flashed him a wry grin. "Because I like looking at old bones and centuries-old carvings? If you find that intriguing, then I fear you are as odd as I."

"Perhaps." He shrugged, and though the movement dislodged some of his carefully arranged cravat, she found him all the more attractive for it. "I do not think so, though. In fact, I am so sure of it as to lay a wager on it."

She hesitated. "A wager? But is that proper?" Gillian frowned, trying to remember if wagering with a gentleman was on her list of things a lady should not do.

"We shall keep it our little secret. Now, I wager you will shortly become this Season's original, which will make you decidedly fashionable."

"Surely you exaggerate—"

"And my forfeit," he continued, "shall be what?"

Gillian bit her lip, excited by the thought of both an illicit wager and becoming an original. "You shall take me on another sight-seeing trip. My choice of location."

"Excellent. And your forfeit?"

She hesitated. "Your choice of location?"

He grinned, and for a moment she reconsidered her offer, wondering at his motives. But then it was too late as he exclaimed, "Done!"

They continued to walk deeper and deeper into what felt like catacombs beneath the London streets. Gillian began to enjoy herself, pausing to inspect one body after another while Lord Tallis entertained her with amusing *on-dits*. He turned out to be a wonderful companion, and she soon forgot his real purpose was to free Stephen for his sister.

In the end, she found she was having quite a marvelous time. But then they came to the end of the crypt and were forced to turn around. The two of them were almost halfway back before Gillian chanced to remember their other companion.

"Why, what happened to Tom?"

No sooner were the words out of her mouth than she heard a strange moaning sound. It was almost intelligible, but given the echo in their dark surroundings, it was nearly impossible to understand or locate its source.

It never occurred to her this was a haunting. She was a practical girl, not given to flights of fancy. Lady Sophia, however, was clearly not as levelheaded. She clutched the earl in a deathlike grip, her mouth parted in a delicate O of horror.

Then another moan cut through Gillian's thoughts as she finally recognized the sound.

"Tom!" She hastily scanned the next chamber. Loose rock lay everywhere, not to mention rats' nests and other hazards. He had probably fallen down and hurt himself. She had to find him.

His moan became louder and stronger as she clamored into the next alcove. She knew from the sound that the boy was close by, but she could not discover where.

"Tom!" Her sharp word echoed through the rooms, seeming to run down the chambers only to bounce back and confuse her.

"Iiieeaaaa."

Gillian heard Lady Sophia cry out, and Gillian spun around, following the pale girl's shaking gesture. Then one of the bodies shifted. Out of the dust rose a single skeletal arm. The bones were complete, narrowing down to a clawed hand from which dangled Lady Sophia's gold cross necklace.

Even though Gillian could guess what was happening, the sight was gruesome at best, horrifyingly sick at worst.

"Laaady Soooophiiaaaaa," came the moan, only this time with a distinct Cockney accent.

Behind her, Gillian heard a thunk and a clear oath. Turning, she saw Lady Sophia prostrate on the floor in a dead faint. Stephen had only half caught her and was trapped beneath the woman as he tried to settle her gently on the floor.

Whipping around, she glared at the skeleton. "Thomas—" She paused when she realized she did not know his last name. "Tom, you get out here this second or I swear, I will have you tied to that corpse and left here to rot with it!"

Almost instantaneously, a dirty head popped up from behind the body. "I was only trying to give her geegaw back." He grinned.

"I thought you were dying!"

"Naw! I was just taking a little nap when wot do I see but this 'ere corpse filching Laidy Sophia's geegaw." He neatly lifted the cross off the skeleton's finger and spun it around in the air.

Just to her left, Lord Tallis began choking.

She might have been alarmed if the sound had not quickly descended into a hiccup that grew into a belly laugh that had him leaning against the wall to keep from falling over.

"By God." He gasped. "That is the best laugh I have had in years. Laaady Soooophiiaaaaa!" he mimicked, his Cockney accent overly thick.

Gillian stared at him, and slowly she felt a smile tease at the corners of her mouth. Truly it was rather funny, now that she thought about it.

"Really, my lords!" exclaimed the cleric, his balding pate a beacon in the gloom. "I must protest such disgraceful behavior!" He practically quivered in outrage, looking so much like an orange jelly dessert Gillian began giggling in earnest.

It was then she chanced to see Stephen's face, and her delight faded like the morning mist. Her guardian was definitely not amused. In fact, he appeared furious. She could see it in the hard blue chips of his eyes and the angry clench of his jaw. Then he spoke, his words soft and low, but with the bite of steel.

"I quite agree, Reverend. I assure you the culprits will be punished. Severely." He focused his blue stare right on her, and Gillian felt herself wilt inside.

"Oh, nonsense, Mavenford," answered Tallis, stepping forward. "Sophia faints all the time. Most wilting female I have ever known."

Not for one second did Stephen shift his angry glare from Gillian. "Your sister's delicate

152

sensibilities are to her credit. I could only wish others were so refined."

Gillian swallowed, feeling her stomach clench in anger. She had never told Tom to pull this silly prank. In fact, she had told him specifically not to, but it seemed her guardian had decided to lay everyone's sins at her door.

Well, if that was the way he saw it, then so be it. She lifted her chin and fixed him with a heated stare. "It is lucky for you I am not nearly so *refined*." She nearly spat out the word. "Otherwise you would have two delicate females to lug up the stairs. Fortunately I have enough intelligence to leave my sensibilities at the door when entering a place like this."

Then she spun away, torch held high as she stomped up the stairs.

"I have never been so embarrassed in my life! To think my ward would behave with such reckless abandon. It was irresponsible, reprehensible, appalling—"

"Have you sacked Tom?"

Stephen felt his words dam up in his throat as he stared at his unfathomable ward. They were in his library, where once again he attempted to instruct her on appropriate ladylike behavior. And once again his words seemed to have no effect whatsoever.

"I believe, Amanda, we were speaking of you."

She sighed and waved away his lecture as though it were nothing more than an irritating fly. "Yes, yes, I am a disgrace to the Mavenford name, a reckless hoyden, a countrified chit, and all that." He turned quickly, catching the overtones of his mother's harangues in her words, but she pushed on, not allowing him the luxury of questioning her further. "But the question is, my lord, what have you done to Tom?"

He remained silent for a moment, watching her anxious face. The truth was, he had not decided what to do with the boy. "He has not been dismissed. I have yet to discover how much of this latest debacle was his idea."

Amanda lifted her chin, her expression completely blank. "None of it. It was all my idea."

Stephen watched her closely, amazed at how easily she lied. It had been obvious she was surprised in the crypt. How far would she go, he wondered, in her defense of one mischievous street urchin?

He stepped forward, forcing her to tilt her head backward to look at him. "You planned the whole thing? From beginning to end."

"That is correct."

"Why?"

She did not even pause. "To get even with Lady Sophia for spoiling our trip."

"I see. You must know that if that is true, I will send you straight back to York on the next coach. I cannot sponsor such a spiteful woman into polite society." As expected, Amanda paled, swallowing nervously while her hands clenched in her lap. He leaned against his desk. "Care to rethink your answer?" he asked.

Much to his surprise, she shook her head, her eyes wide with apprehension. "No," she said softly. "No, it was all my idea, and I am sorry."

Stephen shifted his weight against the desk, stalling for time as he tried to puzzle out a woman who thought more of a street boy than her own Season. She was a piss-poor liar, he thought, although not in the usual way. It was as though she shut down emotionally, boxed up her feelings when she lied, and suddenly he wanted to push her out of her self-sacrificing complacency, forcing her to confront him with her usual frankness.

He looked up, needing to watch her face as he caught her in her lie. "And when you screeched at him, saying you thought he was hurt, that was your idea too?"

She nodded as she spoke, but her voice remained bland, almost empty. "Most definitely. It was . . . part of the plan. To make it seem more authentic."

"I see."

Finally he saw a change in her expression. She looked up at him, her huge eyes imploring. "Please, my lord. Will you keep Tom on? Truly, he is a good boy. And . . . and he did it only as a favor to me."

Aha, he thought with an inner smile. Now they were getting somewhere. "What favor was that, Amanda? Perhaps to see Lady Sophia drop like a sack of meal to the dirty floor? Or to humiliate me before members of the ton?"

"Oh, no." She gasped. "I would never embarrass you."

"But you seem to do it with increasing regularity."

She frowned, finally throwing away her earlier bland exterior. "Well, it was her own fault, you know. She should not have gone down there in the first place. She only went so she could make sheep eyes at you."

He stood up from the desk, needing to pace off some energy. "Her motives for going are none of your affair."

"Of course they are when they spoil my outing!" She jumped up from her chair, standing with her hands clenched right in front of his desk. "If your mother wants to marry you off to some fashionable princess with more style than sense, let her do it at a ball and not on my one trip out of this house!"

He stared at her, finally understanding where all her anger came from. In truth, he had felt much the same way when he first saw the immaculate Lady Sophia and her brother gracefully wending their way down the line of pews. How could he blame her for wanting to tweak the interlopers just the tiniest bit?

"Still, that is no excuse for frightening the woman into a faint." He spoke with less heat than before, sounding more grumpy than angry.

She blinked at him, clearly startled. Her green eyes grew lighter as she widened them in what he hoped was sincere understanding of her crimes.

"You are not sending me home!" she said, breaking into a grin. "You are not angry anymore, and you will let me stay."

"I most certainly will not!" he exploded, even though he never had any intention of sending her back to York.

"You are! I can tell!"

"Do not be ridiculous." He resumed pacing, furious with himself for becoming trapped in this foolish situation.

"Admit it. Inside, you thought it was just as funny as I did."

He stiffened. "I most certainly did not. It was disrespectful, spiteful, and downright mean."

"It was a boyish prank in terrible taste." Except for her smile, he might have thought she agreed with him.

"It was a good deal worse than bad taste." He rounded on her. "Do you know I had to give the cleric ten guineas just to soothe him about his poor disturbed brother? That was a priest, you know, whose bones Tom so cavalierly manhandled."

"Nonsense!" she quipped, her smile widening into a grin. "I am quite sure there was nothing cavalier about it. Actually, it was a most well-thought-out plan, do you not think? Not only did he have to steal Lady Sophia's necklace, but he had to crawl into the burial spot and wait the longest time. And his moan was quite good, too.

If it were not for the Cockney, I am sure I would have thought him an evil spirit—"

"Do not try to distract me, brat!" he sputtered, more appalled at the tickle of humor she sparked within him than by anything Tom did.

"I am not distracting you." She blinked at him. "I merely point out that although Tom should be severely reprimanded for his prank, he should not be sacked."

Stephen folded his arms across his chest and tried to look stern. "And why not?"

"Well," she began, her expression serene as she ticked off her reasons. "This was actually sort of a holiday for him. And since it was his holiday, he is not answerable to you for how he spends his time."

"He most certainly is. As long as he wears my livery, he is expected to act appropriately." The words sounded pompous even to him, and she punctured his pretensions with one word.

"Piffle." She folded her arms and challenged him stare for stare. "He was not in your employ during his holiday, so he cannot be sacked for misbehaving. And since I did not really know about it in the first place, you will not send me back to York." She nodded as though she just solved a mathematical problem.

"I thought you said the whole thing was your idea."

She shrugged. "Well, of course I said that when I thought you would sack Tom. But now I see you will let him stay on, so I feel free to confess my absolute nonparticipation in the entire affair."

Stephen raised an eyebrow in an effort to look intimidating. "I have not said Tom could stay on."

"But of course you will, because you are an eminently fair man. Despite your wounded vanity and that"—she wrinkled her nose—"earl air of yours, you know Tom was on holiday and could do whatever he liked."

"Earl air! What the devil does that mean?"

She pointed her finger directly at his chest. "Exactly, my lord. Earl air."

Stephen took a deep breath and tried to restrain his temper. "The boy was with me, and whenever he is with me, he must act accordingly."

Amanda nodded, smiling serenely as if she were soothing a petulant child. "Well, of course he must, my lord. But Tom was not with you. He was with me. And I have graciously decided to forgive him his transgression."

Stephen felt his eyes bulge at her audacity. "You have!"

"Absolutely, my lord. Because I, too, am a fair and reasonable person." And with that she flashed him a devastating smile and sailed out of the room.

Stephen stared slack-jawed at the door long after her flowing white skirts disappeared around the corner. Of all the impossible, incorrigible, managing females he had ever met, Miss Amanda Wyndham took the cake. She was . . . He took a deep breath. She was . . . His mind boggled at the attempt to find a suitable adjective for the woman.

To think to tell him *she* had decided not to sack Tom. That *she*—

He collapsed into his chair and suddenly, abruptly, burst into a rolling gale of laughter that lasted a full five and a three-quarter minutes.

A Special Offer For Leisure Historical Romance Readers Only!

Get Four FREE* Romance Novels

A $21.96 Value!

Travel to exotic worlds filled with passion and adventure—without leaving your home!

Plus, you'll save at least $5.00 every time you buy!

Thrill to the most sensual, adventure-filled Historical Romances on the market today…

FROM  LEISURE BOOKS

As a home subscriber to the Leisure Historical Romance Book Club, you'll enjoy the best in today's BRAND-NEW Historical Romance fiction. For over twenty-five years, Leisure Books has brought you the award-winning, high-quality authors you know and love to read. Each Leisure Historical Romance will sweep you away to a world of high adventure…and intimate romance. Discover for yourself all the passion and excitement millions of readers thrill to each and every month.

SAVE AT LEAST $5.00 EACH TIME YOU BUY!

Each month, the Leisure Historical Romance Book Club brings you four brand-new titles from Leisure Books, America's foremost publisher of Historical Romances. EACH PACKAGE WILL SAVE YOU AT LEAST $5.00 FROM THE BOOKSTORE PRICE! And you'll never miss a new title with our convenient home delivery service.

Here's how we do it. Each package will carry a 10-DAY EXAMINATION privilege. At the end of that time, if you decide to keep your books, simply pay the low invoice price of $16.96 ($17.75 US in Canada), no shipping or handling charges added*. HOME DELIVERY IS ALWAYS FREE*. With today's top Historical Romance novels selling for $5.99 and higher, our price SAVES YOU AT LEAST $5.00 with each shipment.

AND YOUR FIRST FOUR-BOOK SHIPMENT IS TOTALLY FREE!*

IT'S A BARGAIN YOU CAN'T BEAT! A Super $21.96 Value!

LEISURE BOOKS A Division of Dorchester Publishing Co., Inc.

Get Four Books Totally
FREE* —
A $21.96 Value!

(Tear Here and Mail Your FREE* Book Card Today!)

PLEASE RUSH
MY FOUR FREE*
BOOKS TO ME
RIGHT AWAY!

Leisure Historical Romance Book Club

P.O. Box 6613
Edison, NJ 08818-6613

AFFIX
STAMP
HERE

Chapter Eight

A lady does not enter conversations uninvited.

"I warned you, my lord. I told you, but you would not listen."

Gillian paused outside the library door, her curiosity piqued by the sound of someone who actually dared speak to Stephen in such a superior, condescending manner.

"At the time, Wheedon, you said it was a bold, aggressive move." Gillian stepped closer to the door to hear Stephen's comment, though there was no mistaking the deadly restraint in his voice.

"Of course, my lord," responded the unknown man, clearly oblivious to Stephen's dangerous tone. "It was a move so like an aggressive military man, but as I told you before, farming is not a war—"

"Of course it is!" the earl snapped. "You fight insects, bad weather, poor soil—"

"You nurture the land, you bless it with your tears, you tend to its animals as you would your own children. . . ." Gillian stifled a giggle at the image of Stephen trying to nurture a slobbery little calf. Clearly the speaker did not know much about the earl.

Apparently Stephen thought so, as well. "You are being ridiculous."

"I am being honest, and you refuse to listen." Gillian gasped at the speaker's audacity, even as she leaned closer to the keyhole. "You must forgive my presumption, my lord, but your brother, God rest his soul, placed a great deal of confidence in me, and I grew accustomed to speaking my mind. This crop change idea, like your coal mining improvements, is another example of how unfit you are to handle the decisions involved in a large estate."

Gillian felt her jaw go slack at such insolence from a man who must be Stephen's steward or maybe his man of business. She did not understand why the earl did not boot him out the door. But Stephen remained stubbornly silent while the obnoxious man continued to rant.

"It is no shame to you, of course. You are a military man. You view the world from that perspective."

That at least was true. There were times when Stephen tried to literally command her and others into a parade-ground precision. One look at the various unique personalities in this household would have told an imbecile that military order was simply not possible. And yet Stephen persevered.

"Perhaps, my lord, I may be so bold as to suggest you attach yourself to the Home Office. They must have something for you to do."

"Then you would be free to do whatever you like with my estates," Stephen said, his voice low and cold.

"That is what your late brother hired me to do."

Stephen remained silent, and Gillian held her breath, waiting for the coming explosion. Whoever this man of business was, he certainly needed a set-down, and Stephen was just the man to do it.

She could well imagine the earl slowly rising from his chair, hunching down over the desk until nearly nose-to-nose with the weaselly man. Stephen would take a deep breath, dragging out the moment until the little man began to sweat under the strain. Then Stephen would say it, those cutting words that would effectively slice the pompous steward in half.

Gillian waited, fairly tingling with anticipation.

"As you may have noticed," he said with a faint tinge of amusement, "I am not my late brother."

"What?" Gillian burst through the door, her outrage clouding all reason. "You cannot possibly mean to let him," she sputtered, "remain in your employ after what he has said to you !" She turned and glared at the man, then felt her jaw go slack in astonishment. Contrary to what she expected, the steward was not a small, weasel-faced man. *Enormous* would be a better description. *Huge, muscular,* and *hatchet-faced* would be even better.

This man was certainly not a solicitor. He looked like a man who worked hard beneath the sweltering sun, a man who daily fought with the trials and horrors of a farm. He must be a steward on one of Stephen's many estates, she decided.

"Mr. Wheedon, may I present my ward, Miss Amanda Wyndham," Stephen commented in an icy tone. Gillian glanced at her guardian. He was impeccably dressed, as always, but this time the afternoon sun seemed to highlight not his exquisite form, but the faint lines of strain bracketing his angular face.

"Miss Wyndham." At her name, Gillian turned her attention to the intimidating man. He rose from his seat and executed a proper, if somewhat awkward bow, given the constrained space between his chair and the earl's desk.

"Mr. Wheedon," she acknowledged, lifting her chin with clear disdain. Perhaps he was a huge bear of a man, but that certainly did not give him the right to speak to Stephen that way.

"Did you want something, Amanda?" Stephen's voice indicated he was coldly furious, which was not the least bit surprising. What did startle her was that his anger appeared directed at her, and not his steward, who even now waited impatiently for her to leave.

Gillian floundered. "I . . ." Her gaze shifted between Stephen and Mr. Wheedon. Then suddenly she straightened and challenged the earl. "I most certainly do, my lord. I want to know why you allow this man to speak to you in such a discourteous way."

"I see." Stephen folded his arms across his chest. "And the reason you feel entitled to this explanation is . . . ?"

She stared at him, momentarily stymied by his question. Then she gave him a brilliant smile as she settled herself in a nearby chair. "Because, my lord, you are neither unfit nor stupidly aggressive. Many people view farming as a war, what with the blights and all. As for the thought of *nurturing* a ram into a frigid stream for his cleaning, well—"

"Just how long were you listening at the door?" Stephen exploded, finally losing his maddeningly cool exterior.

"That does not matter." She gave him an airy wave as she spoke. "What is important now—"

Stephen stepped forward to tower over her. "*I* will decide what is important, my girl."

She nodded and flashed him her best smile. "Precisely my point, my lord. You should decide what to do on your estates, and not be dictated to by people who should know better than to speak in such an insolent manner." She slanted an accusing glance at Mr. Wheedon and noted with surprise that he flushed with embarrassment.

But Stephen did not allow her the luxury of intimidating his steward. Instead he leaned down, fixing her with an imperious stare. "And why is it I should make all the decisions? Merely because I have the title?"

"Goodness, no!" She gasped. "My father had a title and, as you no doubt are aware, he was a complete idiot when it came to anything but drinking and wenching."

Mr. Wheedon choked at her frank speech, but Stephen, more used to her, merely glowered. "Whereas my experiences with cannon fire and the finer points of killing make me eminently qualified."

She frowned at his sarcasm. "Your determination and discipline make you eminently qualified. And if Mr. Wheedon has not the patience to teach you the rest instead of trying to fob you off on the Home Office, then perhaps you ought to find someone else who is."

She was gratified to see Mr. Wheedon's ruddy complexion pale beneath her steady regard. And for once, Stephen surprised her by staying silent, apparently lost in his own thoughts. He straightened, his gaze abstract as he returned to his desk while both she and Mr. Wheedon waited for his attention.

Fortunately for Gillian's strained patience, they did not have to wait long. Stephen blinked; then after a brief glance at her, he turned to his steward.

"Thank you, Mr. Wheedon, for coming today. I realize as this is spring, your time is extremely short. Please return to Shropshire and implement the changes we have agreed on. I hope to visit there in a fortnight."

The man rose swiftly despite his large size. He bowed to Stephen, gave a curt, triumphant nod to Gillian, then exited the room.

"But . . . but you are not going to sack him?" she asked as the door closed behind the insolent man.

Stephen waited until they heard the muted thud as the front door closed. Then he turned his attention slowly, imperiously to her.

"I decide how I am addressed by my employees, Amanda." He voice was deadly cold as it pierced her like tiny needles of anger.

"Well, of course," she stammered.

"Mr. Wheedon speaks out of love for the land he manages. He is honest and forthright, qualities I highly prize. He would never dream of doing anything disrespectful or dishonorable, such as eavesdropping or bursting in on things he knows nothing about." He punctuated his words with a frosty stare that made her blood freeze.

Naturally she expected him to be angry. She had belatedly realized one did not typically burst into a man's conversation with his steward without warning or preamble. But Stephen was accustomed to her. Other than perhaps a mild scolding and another rule on her list of ladylike behavior, she had not expected anything truly horrid.

She certainly did not expect the implacable fury lacing his deadly voice or the frightening power of his barely leashed temper.

"You have exactly one minute to explain your appalling behavior, Amanda."

"I . . ." she began, her mind spinning furiously. "I was trying to defend you."

"Defend me?" he said, his voice still low, like the soft hiss of a blade coming out of its sheath. "So you thought I needed your protection?"

"No, of course not—"

"Or perhaps you believed you could help me by humiliating me in front of my employee?"

"No—"

"By bursting through a closed door and showing you have no decorum?"

"No—"

"By then sitting down, uninvited, pushing yourself forward in the most unseemly, disgraceful fashion?"

"I thought—"

"Thought! Amanda, you had no thought whatsoever!"

Gillian looked down at her hands, a lump forming in her throat. She only now began to realize how hasty and ill-conceived her actions were. "I am sorry," she whispered.

Stephen did not respond, leaving her to wilt beneath his implacable scrutiny. Eventually she could not stand staring at her white knuckles any longer. She glanced up, and then wished she had not. His face seemed haggard, his shoulders stooped as he regarded her.

"Stephen?"

"I hoped," he began, his voice once again tight with control, "between my mother and I, we would see you on the path of social decency. I even pictured myself presenting you to the regent himself."

Gillian stared at him, her heart sinking with his every word. "The crown prince?" she whispered.

"Do you know what these are?" He took quick strides around his desk, pulling open his bottom drawer and retrieving, one by one, her crumpled "Rules for a Lady." It had become a game to her in the past weeks, ripping down his signs, tossing them out the window, then dreaming up ways to prevent him from putting up another. She had tried everything from locking her door when she left it to blocking her room at night, but still, each evening when she went to her room and each morning when she awoke, she found yet another one of his supercilious little lists hanging on her wall.

Now, one by one, he brought out her discards from his desk. She had not realized there were so many. And that did not count the ones she had burned. She looked down at her hands, unable to face the growing pile.

"Are you happy here, Amanda?"

Gillian started, confused by his abrupt change of topic. "My lord?"

He settled into his desk chair with a heavy

sigh. "You have been restricted these past weeks, jailed in the house while my mother attempted to teach you how to go on."

More like terrified me into submission, she thought sourly. Then she chastised herself silently for her ill thought. The countess tried her best to make Gillian into a proper lady. It was just her methods that were singularly heavy-handed.

Though she did not speak aloud, Stephen must have read the emotions that chased across her face. "She and I have used every means available to us—pleas, anger, threats—everything short of violence. But it now occurs to me it may be impossible for you to change a lifetime of habits in barely a month."

She looked up, hope kindling within her. Could he possibly be about to forgive her? To ease up on the thousands of ridiculous rules hedging her in from every direction? She could barely contain her glee.

"I think, Amanda, you would be much happier back in York. You have an adequate competence, your own home, and servants you have known for a lifetime. You would never lack for anything."

All her spiraling hopes came crashing down upon her. "You are sending me back?" She gasped.

He sighed, holding up his palms in a gesture of futility. "Surely you can see now how much happier you would be there."

She shook her head, panic making her heart

beat triple time. "No! I have waited nearly my whole life for a Season."

"If I let you come out now, your Season will be a disaster. You are much too wild. Perhaps you could return in five or ten years when you are more settled."

"But—"

"I cannot present you now. You will be completely ruined, Amanda. No one in London will ever receive you. At least this way, you retain the option for the future."

"No!" She pushed out of her chair, her hands pressed tightly together to keep them from clenching into fists. "It would be years too late. I must make my come-out now!" She turned to him, pleading with him to understand. "Please, Stephen, you cannot mean it."

But she saw in his face he did indeed mean it. She was to be sent back to York, her plans in ashes.

"A spinster's life is not such a terrible fate," he said softly. "I will make sure you are well provided for. You may even grow to appreciate it."

She shook her head, thinking of her sick mother, knowing she could not return to York without the protection of a husband's name and money. "Please, Stephen, I beg you—"

"Go to your room, Amanda. There is nothing else to discuss."

She would have stayed, she would have gotten down on her knees and kissed his feet if she thought it might help. But she saw it was too late. His mind was made up, and the earl was nothing if not steadfast in his decisions.

But it did not matter what he thought. She would not leave. She could not leave.

"I will never go back, Stephen. Never."

Then, choking back a sob, she ran from the room.

His mood was quite foul.

Nothing had improved his temper since the moment Amanda had burst unannounced into his meeting with Wheedon. Not seven hours, a congenial dinner, whist with his mother, or even the nighttime solitude of brandy and Aristophanes in his library.

He poured himself another brandy and sank slowly into his mother's library chair. He could not sit at his desk, in the chair molded first by his perfect father, then by his brilliant brother. He sat in a different chair, one not so touched with memories or the tinge of failure.

This chair was new. It was hard and uncompromising and very fashionable. Everything he wished he could be right now.

He must send her home, he told himself. Even now his blood burned with anger at the memory of her storming into his library this afternoon. No one, not even his sister at the height of her rebelliousness, had ever dared defy his father in such a way. He could not allow Amanda to do so either.

He was the new earl. And he was right, damn

it. She was much too wild to foist off on polite society now.

The irony of the situation, of course, was that she'd thought she was helping him. Heedless of the consequences, she had rushed to his defense, just as she'd rushed to Tom's defense in the coaching inn and later in the dark alley behind the house.

It was one of the qualities he liked most about her. It was also the one quality he could not allow to continue unchecked. She must learn proper manners, not to mention good sense. Otherwise she might run after some damned puppy and end up in the wrong area of London with her throat cut or worse.

It was much safer for her in York, where everyone knew her, and her savior instincts could continue with relatively little danger. If worse came to worst, he would simply hire someone to keep a protective eye on her. She could not stay in London, where her heedless attitude would expose her to too many dangers—both in society and outside the haut ton in the darker areas of a deadly city. She must go home to the country.

Taking a sip of his brandy, he waited for the familiar burn to ease the ache in his chest.

He was draining his fourth glass when a slight tap interrupted his thoughts. He knew who it was immediately. Not his mother—she had already retired—and no one else dared disturb him when the library door was closed.

No one but Amanda.

Pouring another glass, he studied the candle-light as it filtered through the amber glow.

The tap came again, louder this time. Then louder again.

He could not help but smile. He'd best let her in, he decided, or she would soon bang on his door with a mallet.

"Come in, Amanda."

She slipped through the doorway, shutting it quietly behind her. She was as beautiful as ever, her hair coiled like burnished copper about her face. Her movements were graceful and, for once, a bit subdued. It took her a moment to find him in his mother's chair, situated as it was in the corner, away from the spill of moonlight from the window. But eventually she saw him, and her green eyes widened with surprise.

"Am I disturbing you?"

"You know you are," he said without heat. "But that has never stopped you before."

Even in the dim gloom of evening, he could imagine her blush. Seeing the slight duck of her head, hearing the way her breath seemed to catch on a sigh, he knew her cheeks would be brushed with that soft tinge of rose he found so enchanting.

This was torture. She had become achingly familiar in the last weeks. He had not realized how much he liked her here, how much he longed to hear her soft tread or her saucy voice each morning.

And now he must send her away.

He turned to look out the window. "You must

know it is too late, Amanda. I will not change my mind."

"I know." Her voice was a whisper, but he caught the note of disappointment, and he grinned.

"Minx," he teased, his gaze drawn inevitably back to her. "You know, but you mean to try anyway."

He expected her to grin impishly at him and continue with her campaign, but she did not. Instead she brought out a piece of paper from behind her back.

"I brought you something," she said, stepping forward. Slowly, almost warily, he took it from her hand. What did she think would sway him? A written note of apology? Some watercolor or sketch meant to be a last tearful good-bye present? Would any of those change his mind?

He rather doubted it, but whatever her choice, it would make their parting that much more painful.

"Please look at it," she said, her voice slightly strained.

Reluctantly he held the paper up to the candlelight. It was a neatly copied version of her "Rules for a Lady." All fifteen of them were there, plus two more that read:

16. A lady does not listen at doorways.
17. A lady does not enter a room or conversations uninvited.

"Very nice, Amanda, but what is your point?" His voice was unnecessarily harsh to cover up the emotion that sat like a cold stone on his heart.

She knelt beside him, and he did not miss the submissive posture. Neither did he appreciate it until he realized she had placed herself there not to plead with him, but so she could look out the window at the clouds drifting past the moon.

"I used to look out my window at night, and I would pretend I was a bird, winging my way to London, my journey lit by the soft light of the moon." She glanced back at him. "Daylight was much too cruel, you understand. I had responsibilities during the day, jobs and tasks. But at night I was free, and I would fly to London, where all my dreams could come true."

"London is not a haven, Amanda. It is a place, just like any other place, with its own special rules and dangers." He spoke harshly, his heart beating faster as he watched the moonlight limn her features in silver.

God, she was beautiful.

"I know, Stephen. It was just such a shock to discover that everything I dreamed of for so long was nothing like I expected." She turned and gently pulled the list out of his hand, smoothing down the edges. "I wrote these down so you would know I did learn them. Up until today, I thought they were silly restrictions you made up just to plague me."

"Silly restrictions!"

She bristled slightly. "Well, yes. Rules like I cannot go to the lending library without someone to accompany me. Literally hundreds of books just within reach, and I cannot go because your mother took the carriage and you did not trust me out from under her eye."

He winced, remembering the argument following that particular dictum. He was sure it had been heard all the way in Cheapside. "So you ignored my rules because you thought I was motivated by pique?"

She shrugged, confirming her unflattering image. "That or perhaps you were too narrow-minded to see reason."

"How flattering to know I am not just a creature of spite," he commented dryly.

She did not answer, running her long fingers down the list, as though she counted each item or perhaps committed them to memory once again. "Except now I know is not true. I see your rules are there for good reasons."

"I see," he said. "And this great revelation came in a flash of insight? Is it perhaps because I intend to send you home?"

She shook her head, her hair shimmering in the candlelight. "Because I spoke with Tom."

He started slightly, surprised by her unexpected confession. "Tom? When?"

"This afternoon."

"But you were in your bedroom all afternoon with the door locked."

She flushed under his intent stare, and this time he was close enough to see her cheeks turn rosy. "Surely, my lord, you recall my most excellent skill with a lockpick?

177

"You unlocked your door, then sneaked out through the back stairway?"

She nodded. "I would have used the trellis except it was broad daylight and someone surely would have seen me."

He sighed and reached for his brandy. "And yet you swear you are a reformed soul."

She pressed closer, letting the list drop to the floor in her need to explain. "I spoke with Tom for a very long time, Stephen. Mostly, I complained about you, but then . . . Then he started saying things."

He set down his brandy untouched. "What things?"

"Stories. Terrible things, really. About young girls from the country, kidnapped into unspeakable horror. Or rich young men with a reforming spirit, robbed and murdered by the very people they sought to help."

Stephen felt his stomach clench at the thought of what she must have heard. He remembered things from Spain best left buried behind a wall of brandy and polite banter. Horrors no young girl should ever hear. "He should not have spoken about that to you."

She turned to look at him, her eyes awash of silver and green, her sympathies making her appear all the younger and more vulnerable. "How can you stand it? How can you not try to stop it?"

He shook his head, wishing he had an answer. "They happen everywhere, Amanda. Not just here, but everyplace men reside." He paused, hoping he was wrong. "Surely you have seen it in York."

"Yes." Her voice was soft, filled with a pain that cut straight through to his soul. "But somehow I thought London would be different. Instead, it is worse." Then her expression changed. No longer did he see confusion and sympathetic pain for those unnamed people in Tom's stories, but a hope and a trust in him as she leaned forward, touching his arm in her eagerness. "Surely you can do something for them."

"Do something? Amanda, I am only one man."

"But you are an earl. And you have a seat in the House of Lords. Surely something can be done for the innocents who are not so fortunate as to have a guardian to protect them."

He stared down at her earnest face. He had expected her to plead for her Season, to beg for a reprieve from banishment. Instead she was petitioning for London's innocents, the hundreds or thousands she could not help from the wilds of Yorkshire.

"Oh, Amanda." He sighed, feeling his resistance melt away. "What will I do with you?"

It took a moment for her reaction to set in, but all too soon her eyes widened with surprise and hope. "Does that mean you will say something in the House of Lords?"

Stephen shook his head. "It is not as easy as that." Then he looked down at her sparkling green eyes and knew he could not disappoint her. "Yes, I will raise the issue. And since it is your idea in the first place, I suppose you ought to stay in London long enough to hear me at it."

"But the next meeting of the House of Lords is in . . ."

"Two weeks."

"Two weeks?" She frowned, but he was not in the least bit fooled. Her eyes were too bright with mischief. "Two weeks is much too soon to prepare properly, what with the Season and the business of the estate. Really, my lord, you must wait until the session after that."

"Oh, must I?"

"Absolutely." She smiled hopefully. "And that is . . ."

"Six weeks away."

"Goodness." She gasped with feigned shock. "Such a long time for me to sit in the house. I am sure I shall drive myself and everyone around me quite mad."

"Quite," he commented dryly, amusement pulling his cheeks upward into a smile.

"Well, perhaps you will allow me to escape a bit. Maybe to a card party. Or perhaps a ball." She looked up at him, her eyes shimmering emeralds in the moonlight.

He chuckled, amused and enchanted despite his noble intentions. "Truly, Amanda, you are the most manipulative female I have ever met."

"Does that mean I may attend a few parties?" She gazed up at him, her lips quivering with suppressed excitement.

He grinned. "It means if you faithfully remember every single one of your rules . . ." He paused as she grabbed the paper off the floor and clutched it to her heart. "And write them down every day—"

"Every day," she echoed.

"Then perhaps I can see my way through to allowing a ball or two."

"Oh, thank you, Stephen." She launched herself up from the floor and wrapped her arms around his neck, her list of rules once again forgotten as it fluttered to the floor.

Catching her at the waist, he struggled to remain detached, desperate to keep her tempting softness at arm's length. But he could not hold out. He smelled the lilac water she sprinkled in her hair, heard the gentle whisper of her muslin skirt, and most of all felt her pliant, womanly body pressed so close. Even knowing she was old for her come-out, he was not prepared for the maturity of her body—the ripe curves begging for a man's touch, the heady press of her thighs against his, and the lush swell of her breasts so close to his fingers.

This was no young girl, but a woman whose body tantalized him as no guardian should be tantalized.

"Amanda!" He set her away from him, his body shaking with the need to draw her closer even as he let her go. "Do not do that again!"

She took a step back, shock catching her breath in a soft "Oh!" He could see the hurt clouding her eyes, darkening the green to the color of bruised moss. But what could he say to her? How could he explain his behavior when he himself did not understand it?

He turned away, his expression grim.

"I . . . I am sorry," she stammered.

"Amanda—"

"I did not mean to offend you."

"You did not off—"

"I had better go to bed now."

Her words conjured an image of her in his bed, stretching out on cool, crisp linens, her hair a sensual halo. . . . He clenched his teeth against his body's instantaneous response.

"Stephen?"

"Good night, Amanda," he said in a growl, hating himself for the cruel sound of his words.

"But—"

"Go."

He could not watch as she jumped away, nearly running from the room, but he heard her. He heard the soft patter of her feet as she dashed down the hall and up the stairs. He flinched at the abrupt clap of her door as it slammed shut above him, echoing in the still house.

Then he heard himself curse—long and fluently as he had not done since Spain.

Chapter Nine

A lady does not hide in closets.

"Do not be nervous, Amanda. It is just a ball, and you will go to hundreds of balls this Season."

"Yes, my lady," Gillian answered automatically, her voice wooden as she stared at her reflection in the mirror. In her hands, just out of sight beneath her dressing table, she held her thin maid's cap, twisting it around and around in her fingers while the countess continued to prattle.

"You look absolutely perfect. That green netting is just the right touch. Hawkings, twitch that curl in place!" The old crone obediently tugged at Gillian's twisting, curling coiffure.

"Yes, absolutely perfect. See? There is no reason to be nervous."

"No, my lady."

"Just remember to use your fan the way I taught you."

"Yes, my lady."

"And do not dance with anyone more than twice."

"No, my lady."

"And for heaven's sake, mind your tongue!"

Gillian tossed a weary glance at the countess's reflection in the mirror. "I will make sure to leave my intellect behind."

The countess nodded until Gillian's comment sank in. Then she gasped in outrage. "You see! That is exactly the type of insolent remark I mean. You have been allowed entirely too much head, my girl—"

"Are you sure that tiara matches your gown, Mother?" interrupted Stephen's low, smooth voice. "Perhaps you should check it one last time before we leave."

All three women spun to look at the earl as he entered her room. Indeed, thought Gillian a little enviously, how could they not? She had never seen Stephen in his finest evening wear, and he literally took her breath away. Unlike her reflection, he appeared the perfect aristocrat. His dark blue dress coat and gold-trimmed waistcoat were the perfect complement to his twinkling blue eyes. His nearly black pantaloons hugged his muscular thighs while providing a striking contrast to the snow white linen of his shirt and the dark silk of his cravat.

Next to him, Gillian felt like a drab bird, washed out in white, her only color in the wispy green netting covering the silk slip.

His mother, of course, wore an elegant pearl gown that accentuated her dainty figure and creamy complexion. Stephen's comments notwithstanding, the pearl tiara was the perfect accessory. Gillian, however, did not say that as the countess suddenly touched her hairpiece with a startled gasp.

"Do you really think so? I could not decide between . . ." Her voice trailed off as her eyes suddenly narrowed on her son. "Well, you might have just said you wanted to be private with her, Stephen."

Her son bowed his head slightly. "My apologies, Mother. The tiara is perfect."

"Oh, piffle," returned his mother. "Come along, Hawkings." Then, with a disdainful sniff, the countess left the room, the maid trailing silently behind her.

Stephen watched them depart, a fond smile curving his lips. "I never could outfox her. She always found me out in the end."

Gillian did not answer. Her mind was too scattered to think.

What was wrong with her? Here she was, about to embark on her first society ball, and all she could do was stare at her reflection in the mirror. She expected butterflies, nervous agitation, anything but this empty dread dulling her mind.

She was not afraid, she told herself. This had nothing to do with last night's impulsive embrace with the earl. Stephen was formal to a fault. If he did not wish to be touched by her, it made little difference to her.

But it made an enormous difference, her heart whispered. If Stephen did not like her, then what about the others? What about the rest of the ton?

So she had sat in her room all afternoon, trying to talk herself out of a prime case of nerves. As for the cap she still clutched beneath the dresser, she had no clue why she had dug it out from its hiding place at the back of her wardrobe. She had never intended to see it again. But for some unknown reason, she retrieved it two hours ago, needing to feel it in her hands.

"Amanda?"

Gillian came back to the present with a startled blink, her gaze catching the earl's handsome reflection in her glass. "Y-yes?" she stammered.

"I, uh, I wanted to apologize for my behavior last night."

She stiffened, not wanting to hear what he said, but unable to stop him.

"I have been off balance lately. It was such a shock, you know, suddenly becoming an earl. There were so many more restrictions and expectations. Suddenly I needed to think about my duties to the title, about which clothes I wear and what I say, when I truly just wanted to lie back with my shoes off and blow a cloud."

For the first time in nearly two hours, Gillian twisted away from her dressing table mirror to stare directly at someone else. "What must it be like?" she asked in excruciatingly dry tones. "To be suddenly hemmed in—your every word, every action, every thought carefully watched and criticized?"

Stephen glanced at her in surprise, then had the grace to flush. "Ah, well, yes," he murmured. "I suppose you women have it a bit more awkward than the men."

"Do you truly think so?" she said with exaggerated innocence. Then she turned back to her mirror, not because she wanted to look at herself, but because there was nowhere else she could go while still holding her mobcap.

She hoped he would leave now, but he remained, coming up behind her, his blue eyes clouded with confusion.

"I am sorry," he said softly.

"I know."

Their gazes caught and held in the mirror. His eyes were confused and embarrassed, but mostly they were sad as he silently asked for her forgiveness. But she could not give it because she wanted more than an apology; she wanted more from him than just words.

She wanted his acceptance. His affection. His l—But her mind balked at the word that came to mind. She did not want that. Surely she did not want *that*.

"What is the matter?" he asked.

"Nothing."

187

"Are you sure?"

With a frustrated sigh, Gillian twisted around, needing to confront him face-to-face. "Of course I am sure," she snapped. "I am not one of those whey-faced girls who cannot connect one thought to another! If I say I feel fine, then I am fine! If I tell you nothing is the matter, then nothing is the matter! Lord, but I am tired of people not trusting me to know the simplest things." She paused to take a breath, only then focusing on Stephen.

He had taken a step backward, folded his arms across his chest, and watched her with an expression of tolerant amusement. "Oh, good," he commented. "Just so long as there is nothing the matter."

Gillian felt her mouth go slack in horror. Had she truly just screeched at him like a madwoman? She looked down at her feet, suddenly feeling very foolish. "I am sorry. I do not know what just came over me."

He simply raised one eyebrow, waiting for her to continue.

"I-I mean . . ." Her voice trailed away.

"I know what you mean. You mean that between my mother and your imagination, you have worked yourself into a fine state of nerves."

"No, I—"

"Come here." He took her hand and pulled her over to the bed. It was only then she remembered the mobcap, and it was already too late.

He saw it and lifted it out of her hands.

"What is this?"

"It is . . . Gillian's cap."

"Your half sister's?"

She nodded, frantically scrambling for an explanation. "I do not know why I kept it. It is silly really." She tried to draw away from him, but he held her still, keeping her hands encased in his.

"Why would you keep Gillian's mobcap, Amanda?" His voice was low and deceptively casual. Gillian sighed. She could not get around it now. He would not let her escape without some explanation.

Gillian pulled her hands away from him, releasing a half laugh that sounded strained. "I . . . I used to wonder about her at night. What would it be like if I had been born her, and she me."

"Truly? What did you decide?" His tone gave nothing away, and Gillian found herself slanting looks at his face as she struggled with her words.

"I . . . I do not know. At times I thought one life would be easier—gathering herbs, tending to the sick, polishing the silver. It was not a bad life. Then again, maybe living in Wyndham Manor was better. There were servants and fine things. She—I never worried about starving."

His gaze remained hard on hers, and for a moment she was afraid. Then his expression gentled as he urged her to continue. "Now you wish you were Gillian. That you did not have to worry about what to say, how to hold your head, what to dance and with whom?"

She nodded, agreeing with him, but not for the same reasons. She wanted to be herself again, to walk the moors and not have to double-think every word, every action, wondering if she were revealing her true bastard nature.

Wondering if she embarrassed or betrayed Stephen every time she spoke or did something ill-bred.

She looked down at her hands, twisting the cap around her wrists until it felt like manacles. "I . . . In York, I knew who I was and what was expected of me. But now I say and do things I do not recognize. I look in the mirror and see someone entirely different. And I wonder if . . . if . . ."

"If maybe it would better if you just left and went back home?"

She sighed, surprised by her own confusion. She had been swamped with guilt all day. All she could think of was Stephen's anger and frustration last night in the library. She had done that to him. She came into his life and totally disrupted it. Yet he and his mother had still taken her in and trained her for a position in society. It was enormously generous of them, and yet how did she repay them? By committing a fraud, lying to them about who and what she was.

If her perfidy ever came to light, they would be severely compromised. In fact, they would never completely recover their social standing.

The haut ton never forgave a hoax as deep as hers.

"Amanda?"

Gillian came abruptly back to the present, only to be buried under another wave of guilt. She looked up at his handsome face, feeling her chest squeeze with anxiety. Now was the perfect moment. He was waiting for her to speak. She could confess all, make a clean breast of it right now before it was too late.

But looking into his dark blue eyes, she saw the concern swirling there. He had the most changeable eyes, darkening with anger, turning gold in sunlight, sparkling with amusement.

How would they look after her confession?

Probably hard with fury as he unceremoniously threw her out of his life and his house.

She could have withstood an ignominious return to York. But not the thought of leaving him, or that their last moments together would be angry and bitter. She could not do it. She could not tell him the truth.

"Amanda? Do you truly wish to be back home?"

She took a deep breath, ruthlessly pushing her doubts aside. "No, my lord. I will not go back to York."

He nodded, and she narrowed her eyes as she studied his face. It was cast half in shadow, emphasizing his harsh angles and dark eyes. But what she noticed most was his expression—or rather lack of one. If ever there was a moment she wanted to read his emotions or understand

191

his thoughts, now was the time. But there was nothing to see.

Nothing to read.

Then suddenly he stood up, drawing her with him. "Come with me."

"What?"

He tugged the mobcap out of her hands and tossed it carelessly onto the dresser. "I have something for you."

He drew her to the doorway, and then, after a quick glance to make sure no one was about, he pulled her down the corridor to his room. Then they ducked inside, and he quietly shut his door.

It took a moment for Gillian to realize she was in his bedroom. She felt a tingle course down her spine. If she thought looking through his desk was intimate, it was nothing compared to standing in the center of his private chamber. She gazed around her, turning slowly as she absorbed the details. She did not know what she expected—something grand, maybe a little pompous. A great, huge bed with a raised platform and gilt posters. Maybe rich draperies with the earl's crest emblazoned all over them.

But there was very little of that here.

He had a large bed, one probably handed down through the generations, but the draperies and extra pillows were stripped away, making it seem bare, almost austere. There were the usual accoutrements of any modest bedroom—a wardrobe and a dresser—but both were bare of knickknacks, coins, or even a hairbrush. In fact, the only thing in the entire room that seemed uniquely Stephen's was a large leather chair pulled close to the fire, and a stack of books beside it.

She crossed to it, running her fingers along the top of the chair, noting the unmistakable indents in the seat and back cushions. Like his desk chair, this one already bore his mark. It was all she could do to resist folding herself into his chair just to feel herself surrounded by his presence and the heady scent of leather and man.

"Here."

Gillian looked over to see him pull out a small box from a drawer of his dresser.

"I intended to wait until your come-out ball, but perhaps it is more appropriate now." He held out the package to her, and she reached forward, gingerly lifting it from his hand.

It was small and very light with a pretty silver ribbon, which she tugged open. Then, almost with a sense of dread, she pulled open the lid. There, nestled on a piece of white silk, was a delicate gold filigree necklace twisting around green stones shaped like leaves. Above them rested matching ear bobs. The jewelry was so beautiful and delicate she felt her chest constrict in awe.

"Those are emeralds," she said softly.

"Yes." He leaned over, reaching past her fingers to lift the necklace off the silk and hold it up to her face. "Almost a perfect match for your eyes," he said softly. "Except you sparkle more than they." Then he stepped behind her and brushed aside her hair to fasten the necklace. His fingers sent a tingle of awareness through her body, and she gasped as she felt the cool caress of the necklace contrasted with the hot press of his fingers.

"Exquisite," he murmured, his gaze holding hers in the dresser mirror.

Gillian raised her hand to touch the beautiful creation about her neck. He had given her emeralds.

What was she, Gillian Ames, bastard and lowly housemaid, doing wearing emeralds? She should be thrilled at finally starting on the path to her dreams. She had wealth, support, and most of all, the opportunity for a fine marriage that would establish her and her mother for the rest of their lives.

She should be dancing on the rafters in excitement.

Instead, all she could think was that she was a thief and a liar living someone else's life. Her breath caught on a sob, and she felt Stephen's hands tighten on her shoulders in surprise, turning her around so he could look directly into her eyes.

"Amanda? What is wrong?"

"I . . . I do not belong here," she said, then felt her eyes widen in shock. Why on God's green earth had she said that? "I . . . I mean—"

"Shhh, it is all right. You are Amanda Faith Wyndham."

"No—"

"Yes. Amanda, listen to me. You are an earl's ward and a beautiful woman who has already become an original even before your come-out."

"No, I am not who you think—"

"Shhh." He pressed his finger against her lips.

She shook her head, trying to clear her thoughts. Then she felt his hands drop to her shoulders, drawing her closer to him as he tried to caress away her trembling.

She meant to move away from him, to escape somewhere, anywhere. But her body would not obey her mind. Then he touched her, lifting her chin until she looked directly into his eyes, and she knew she was lost.

"I believe in you," he whispered. "I believe that after tonight, all of society will be at your feet, and I shall be stepping over suitors three deep in the hallway."

She blushed at his foolish image. "Do not be absurd," she whispered.

"It will happen," he said, his voice unnaturally rough. "Then what will I do?"

She did not understand the husky timbre of his voice or the almost desperate sound of his words. The mesmerizing golden flecks in his eyes filled her thoughts, and she felt her heart beat faster as he drew a ragged breath.

He leaned down, his dark hair brushing against her forehead as his breath mingled with hers.

"So beautiful," he whispered, and then without even realizing that she was the one who moved, she found herself in his arms, straining upward as his lips descended to hers.

Their first touch was achingly tender, lips to lips, and through them she felt him shudder as if he struggled with himself and lost the battle. She opened her mouth to him, not knowing what to do, only wishing somehow to have him closer.

He claimed her mouth with a groan, wrapping his arms around her and crushing her against him as his tongue invaded her. She let her head drop back, opening herself to him as he plumbed her very depths.

She heard him groan. It was deep, guttural, almost animal, and it thrilled her to her toes. She felt the power of the sound, and strength in his arms, and, most important, the fierce, possessive way he explored her mouth.

She mimicked his movements, learning from him even as she trembled from the wonder of it all. As he held her close, she arched even further into him, pressing intimately against him, feeling the heat from his form along the entire length of her body.

And still she wanted more. So very much more.

"Amanda!" The countess's strident tones pierced the air. "Where are you?"

She and Stephen froze, their breath suspended, their lips less than a breath apart.

"Stephen, have you seen that dratted girl? Stephen?"

With a muffled oath, he pushed her away, and

she nearly fell as she was forced to support her own weight. "Quickly," he rasped. "In here."

She looked at him, her thoughts whirling, her mind in a daze. He pulled open the doorway to the corridor linking his bedroom with his future wife's, urgently gesturing her through.

Gillian nodded, forcing her wooden feet to the dark hallway, stopping only after she was well hidden in the darkness.

"Amanda?" he whispered.

She turned, her gaze flying to his haggard features, framed in the doorway.

"I . . . I am sorry," he said. Then he shut the door, closing out the last of the light.

A moment later she heard his deep tones, smoothly sophisticated as he called to the countess, "I am right here, Mother. What did you need?"

"Well, I am looking for that ridiculous chit. We should be leaving soon. . . ." The rest of the countess's response was lost to Gillian as the two moved down the hallway, the familiar creak of the stairs telling her they headed downstairs, probably for the front parlor.

Gillian waited another few moments, her heart beating triple time, her breathing harsh and loud in the enclosed space. What had she done? Her stupefied mind played over everything that happened, every sensation and trembling desire that coursed through her as she kissed Stephen.

She had kissed Stephen!

And it was wonderful and frightening and exciting and terribly, terribly delicious. Oh, heavens, she thought with shock. She had loved every moment of it!

Men had kissed her before. More than one of the villagers had used her lowly birth as an excuse to take liberties. Without exception, each kiss had been horrible, starting from the blacksmith with his thick, meaty lips, right through his son's fumbling, wet affair, and most horrible of all, Reverend Hallowsby's sanctimonious cold pecks while his hands . . . his hands roamed places that had made her run to wash in the cold bite of the mountain stream.

But this was different.

With Stephen, she'd felt as if she flew, soaring through the stars like a fiery comet. Even now, after he left her dazed and trembling in a dark corridor, she still wanted nothing more than to run to him and throw herself at his feet.

I am sorry.

His last words echoed in her mind.

I am sorry.

What was he sorry for? Leaving her in a dark hallway? Or kissing her? Was he sorry his mother interrupted them? Or that he'd given in to his baser instincts and used her for his own pleasure?

Given his horrified expression as he shut the door on her, she strongly suspected the latter. The virtuous and oh-so-correct Earl of Mavenford had given in to lust and kissed his ward.

Scandalous.

Gillian bit the inside of her cheek for the

umpteenth time today, and cursed herself for the tears threatening to spill down her cheeks.

I am sorry.

Was she sorry? Did she wish it had gone on forever? Or had never even begun? Did she want him to lay her down and teach her so much more of what went on between a man and a woman? Or did she want to scratch his eyes out for the audacity of his touch?

She did not know.

I am sorry.

So was she. So very, very sorry, and she did not even know why.

But she could not cry. She gripped her hands. She was about to go to her very first ball. She would soon be presented to the ton. This was what she had wanted, had dreamed, had prayed for.

She would not cry.

She would go downstairs and step into her dreams.

I am sorry.

Very well, she decided. He was sorry. And so was she. It should not have happened, and never would again.

It did not matter the reason for their kiss, she decided. It did not matter if he had been swept away by her beauty, overwhelmed by love for her. If he even now was aching for her as only a lovesick swain could.

Stephen would never break with society's strictures so much as to marry her. He was destined for Lady Sophia Rathburn in a brilliant match appropriate for an earl. For her part, Gillian did not want a man who made her knees go weak and her thoughts scatter. It made her too vulnerable to sudden confessional urges.

Above all things, she could not have that.

So the answer was clear. His feelings and motives made no difference. For that matter, her emotions and feelings were equally irrelevant.

Gillian had to find a rich husband. Stephen would never marry her. Therefore she had to find someone else. She had to find that someone else soon, before this madness with the earl got out of hand.

So what was her next step? She took a deep breath as she focused her thoughts. The next step was to dazzle the ton—tonight—and find a husband soon. Tonight. Perhaps within the first few moments of entering the ballroom.

I am sorry.

Biting back her tears, Gillian whipped her new resolve into a nearly tangible force. Forcing her feet to move, she slipped out of her hiding place and back into the earl's bedchamber. It was nearly dark now, the last of the sunlight giving a slightly reddish gold tinge to the room where she had so nearly been swept away.

She had no doubt his kisses would have progressed to their natural conclusion. She was that weak around the earl. Unable to resist, she stepped lightly to his bed, laying a hand on the soft coverlet. Perhaps it was her bastard blood coming to the fore, but even now, her body still tingled with the memories of his touch.

With a soft curse, she twisted away. She was a weak and foolish girl prone to the same lustful thoughts her mother had succumbed to with the baron so many years ago. Now her daughter was haunted by the same base desires, tempting her to throw away everything she had, everything she wanted, just to lie with a man.

Well, Gillian Ames was made of stronger stuff. She would not give in to her bastard heritage. She would be wise to push all baseborn thoughts out of her mind.

But as she slipped down the stairs toward the front parlor, she heard Amanda Wyndham's mocking laughter following her. Gillian was a bastard, taunted her half sister's ghost. All of her thoughts were baseborn by definition. And no noble intentions would change that.

Or the fact that temptation lurked a scant few doorways down the hall from her own.

Chapter Ten

A lady forgives and forgets.

Gillian's first view of Lady Allardyce's ballroom was enough to make her lose the last of her courage. *Stunning* did not begin to describe the dazzling array of the fashionable haut ton arrayed about the room. From diamonds to dandies, they were all there.

And she felt as if everyone had turned to inspect the earl's willful ward.

Her first response was a sudden urge to grab Stephen's arm and hide in his embrace. But as custom dictated, he was ahead of her on the stairwell, escorting his mother into the ballroom, leaving Gillian to stand alone for a moment at the top of the staircase looking down at the glittering throng. Naturally he could not turn and give her one of his reassuring smiles. Of course, given the strained silence between them after their aborted kiss, a reassuring smile was the last thing she expected from him.

So she stood at the top of the stairs alone, fighting the urge to flee. Then, for once, her miserable childhood came to her rescue. If there was one thing the real Amanda had taught her well, it was how to handle the hostile stares of a jealous tabby.

Suddenly Gillian felt a smile curve her features, her confidence returning tenfold. Let them stare, let them gossip and nitpick. Nothing could change the fact that she, Gillian Ames, bastard daughter of a lowly baron, was finally among them, entering the hallowed portals of a haut ton ball.

She felt her smile grow into a triumphant glow as she began her descent into the humid ballroom.

Gillian Ames had arrived.

At the base of the stairs, Gillian was introduced to her host and hostess. She curtsied first to Lady Allardyce and her daughter, surprised at how easy it was to perform the task. Buoyed by her confidence, she moved with a fluidity that had hitherto escaped her. Her knees did not creak, and her head did not drop too low. In fact, just to her right, she caught the countess's pleased smile.

With a sudden start of surprise, she realized she had mastered the fine art of aristocratic carriage—complete and total arrogance!

Except that Lady Allardyce and her daughter did not seem the least bit enchanted. They regarded her coolly, almost with hostility, barely forcing out their greetings. "I am so pleased you could come, Miss Wyndham," Lady Allardyce said, her tone heavy with sarcasm.

Gillian was so surprised by their animosity she nearly missed Lord Allardyce's comment, though he spoke loudly, almost directly to her nose. "Save an old man a dance, what," he said with a broad wink, "before all the young bucks snatch them up." He completely missed the icy glare his wife shot him.

"I would be happy to dance with any older gentleman who asks," Gillian bantered politely, stretching her neck to see behind him. "But whoever do you mean? I shall give him the dance directly after yours."

Lord Allardyce chortled heartily at her compliment, patting her hand as he shooed her on. Then, just after she turned from him, she heard him say to his wife, "Definitely an original, my dear."

"She is nothing of the sort," snapped his wife. "Just another impertinent mushroom with a large dowry, and you would do well to remember it!"

Twisting back, Gillian gave the pair a quizzical look. Lord Allardyce's comment confused her almost as much as his wife's shrewish response. How could one polite riposte make her an original? Surely what she said was not nearly so unique as to give her one of the most valued female labels. And as for his wife . . .

Unfortunately she was not allowed time to think on it, as Lord Tallis, mercifully without his sister, suddenly appeared at her side and bowed over her hand, neatly preventing her from joining the earl and his mother.

"Ah, my lovely, it is a pleasure to see you. Please tell me you have saved two dances for me?"

Gillian could not help but smile at his soulful look. He always reminded her of a sad puppy dog when he took that pose. "You know I have, Lord Tallis. You have reminded me every day for the last two weeks." She lifted her hand and dutifully showed him her dance card, where his name was indeed already penciled in next to two country dances.

"What?" he said with mock horror. "Not a waltz?"

She grinned. "That would certainly set the gossips' tongues wagging." As a girl in her first Season, Gillian would not be allowed to dance a waltz without special dispensation from one of society's matrons.

"Very well," he said with a dramatic sigh. "I shall just have to be content with two *country* dances with the Season's brightest star." He lowered his voice and winked at her. "It is quite a sacrifice on my part, you know. I had my heart quite set upon a waltz. Not only would it steal the march on my competitors, but it would do wonders for my consequence."

After two weeks of Lord Tallis's daily visits,

Gillian was accustomed to ignoring his teasing comments, but this time it reminded her of what Lord Allardyce had just said, and even more of when Stephen had said she was already an original.

She narrowed her eyes, studying Lord Tallis as he struck a refined pose of casual disdain. It could not be. But then who else did she know with an interest in her success? "My lord," she said with a gasp, "what have you done?"

"Me?" he said, his expression far too wide and innocent. "Why, nothing."

"Have you told everyone I am an original?"

He shrugged, but she saw the laughter in his eyes. "I only set out to win my wager with you."

"But . . ." Her voice trailed away as she looked around her. The men eyed her with speculation, interest, even a few with a naked hunger, no doubt for her dowry. She dismissed them without a second thought, glad for their interest, but not overcome by it.

Right now the women drew her attention. Those who did not pointedly ignore her sent her venomous glares. Try as she might, she could not find even one passably neutral look, much less a friendly expression.

"Sweet heaven," she murmured in shock, "they all hate me."

"Nonsense." Tallis beamed. "They are fascinated—"

"Not the men," she said, still searching for a friendly face. "The women."

He glanced around, as though only now noticing society's flowers. "Well, that is to be expected." He glanced back at her, his expression quizzical. "You know, most ladies would practically swoon with delight at such a wonderful happenstance."

Gillian snapped her fan shut in irritation. "I am not the swooning kind, my lord." But even as she clenched her teeth in anger, she wondered why she was so upset. What did it matter that she was surrounded by a roomful of Amandas all trying to tear her down? The men were interested, and they were the only ones she cared about.

Except that until this very moment, she had not realized how very lonely she was. In York, her best companions were the women—mothers, daughters, servants. Despite her illegitimacy, most of the women gave her grudging respect for her medicinal skills. A few had even become her companions, especially Mrs. Hobbs, the Wyndham housekeeper. Her enemies were always the men. And Amanda.

But now, thanks to Lord Tallis, she was surrounded by an entire roomful of jealous women, damned before she even opened her mouth.

"I have truly upset you." For the first time ever, she saw Lord Tallis's fashionable attitude slip, revealing a startlingly handsome and sincere man. "I thought you would appreciate—"

"You thought I would be just like every one of them." She cast a scathing glance around the room. "You thought I would happily elbow them aside on my way to becoming a diamond or some other such nonsense."

He did not answer, but it was clear from his expression he had thought exactly that. '

"Well, I am sorry to disappoint you, my lord, but I find it distinctly unpleasant to have the entire female population against me even before I make my bow."

"But the gentlemen—"

"Will expect me to say witty things while they are eyeing the size of my dowry." She tried to repress a scowl, but her spirits were suddenly very low. She felt more like an outcast now than she had ever been in York.

Then someone lifted her hand in a gentle caress, jolting her out of her thoughts. She looked at Lord Tallis in surprise.

"I knew you were unique, Amanda," he said softly, "but I did not realize how very special you are."

She felt herself soften toward him. Indeed, how could she not with his gray eyes washed with apology? "What is done is done, my lord. And besides," she said with a sigh, "only a fool would look to the haut ton for a friend."

He glanced around, his sharp gaze no doubt absorbing more details and nuances than she could fathom. "I doubt I can undo my tampering, but let me at least promise you this, Miss Wyndham: I shall always stand your friend. If you need any help or merely a willing ear, I shall move heaven and earth to assist you."

She looked at him, startled by the earnestness

of his offer. She had thought him a shallow fribble, but now she saw the depth of character he hid below his dandified exterior.

"Thank you, my lord," she whispered.

"It is my honor, my lady." He bowed over her hand, his manner exquisitely gracious. Then he raised his head and winked at her, and suddenly she was laughing.

"Oh, you are a complete hand, my lord. I only hope I can carry off the role you have given me."

"I would not worry, Amanda," drawled Stephen's low tones behind her. Gillian twisted around, her heart in her throat. "Trust me when I say you are most definitely an original."

Gillian lifted her chin. Somehow, coming from him, it did not seem like much of a compliment.

"And remember, Miss Wyndham," added Lord Tallis, slipping easily back in his role as a world-weary cynic. "The ton sees what they want. They expect an original in you, and they will see exactly that, even if you never open your sweet lips to say a word."

"Of course, but—"

"Mother is waiting, Amanda," interrupted Stephen. Though his words were for her, Stephen glared at her companion, his eyes hard and cold.

Beside her, Tallis gave her another deep bow. "It appears, Miss Wyndham, that I must release you to the throng. Do not forget my two dances."

"Of course . . ." Gillian began, her gaze slipping between the two men. She could sense the growing hostility between them, but could not understand its source. "What—"

"It is time to move on, Amanda," Stephen practically growled in her ear as Lord Tallis pulled away.

"But—"

"Now." Then he turned her around and took firm steps toward the countess, who was, indeed, tapping her fan impatiently.

Gillian took a deep breath, ready to object to his high-handed treatment, when her gaze landed on the half dozen men loitering around the dowagers, looking as impatient as the countess. Her anger evaporated in surprise. "My goodness," she said, "why are they all standing there?"

"They wait to meet the latest original." His tone indicated he was less than pleased at the thought.

"Surely you exaggerate." But one look at Stephen's grim face showed her he was in dead earnest. More than that, it told her he was not the least bit pleased with her success.

And for some perverse reason, that thought restored her good mood and her confidence. "Truly, my lord," she said airily, "there is not much to becoming a success, is there? After all those weeks of lessons and rules, all I truly needed was Lord Tallis." She flashed a smile at the gentleman in question. He was doing the pretty with an elderly matron, but the sally nevertheless had its effect.

Stephen's voice was harsh in her ear. "Tallis? Is he the silly ass who spread rumors about you?"

"He is the *gentleman* who graciously paved the way for my successful Season."

"Do not overestimate Tallis's abilities on your behalf," Stephen warned. "There are still a great many pitfalls ahead of you."

"Truly?" She glanced at the increasing group of young gentlemen hovering by the dowagers' seats. The countess was clearly torn between smirking at her success and glaring across the room at Gillian. "How many men do you think wait there for an introduction? Eight? No, it looks more like ten."

"Your manner is entirely too forward."

"Nonsense," she shot back with an arch look, purposely slowing their progress across the ballroom to a sedate crawl. "Have you not heard, my lord? Thanks to Tallis, I am an original. Any oddities in my behavior merely enhance my image."

She stopped to flash a brilliant smile at a spotty-faced boy standing awkwardly nearby. Much to her satisfaction and Stephen's obvious consternation, the young man was so shocked he stumbled in his haste to get an introduction. Unfortunately, Stephen dragged her away before the young man found his footing.

"There is a limit to what society will tolerate, Amanda, even in an original." The Arctic could not match the earl's freezing tone, but Gillian was not intimidated. She matched his frosty expression with her own arrogance.

"If this is to be another one of your lectures on proper behavior, my lord, I beg you to save time. Write it down, and I promise to add it to the list in the morning. In the meantime," she said, flashing him another beatific smile, "I believe your mother wishes me to meet some gentlemen." Then she crossed the last few feet to the countess and the dozen men already lining up for her attention.

Stephen watched her go with a growing sense of panic. She was furious with him. That in itself was nothing new, but her anger combined with her beauty to give her a fiery brand of regal disdain that was an irresistible call to men of all kinds. Already the puppies bowed almost to their knees as they were introduced, fawning around her, doting on her every word as they vied to gain her favor. Two scurried off to get her punch while others fought for the opportunity to hastily scribble their names on her dance card.

It was all his fault. Her behavior was out of fury because he'd taken advantage of her innocence, lured her into his bedroom, and made unseemly advances. Worse yet, he had no doubt that if his mother had not interrupted them, he would have taken her to his bed before she thought to protest.

He did not know how it happened. And, to his eternal shame, he could not even guarantee it would not happen again. Something affected his mind when she came near him.

He had learned in Spain to keep his passions tightly leashed. But with Amanda he became weak-willed and confused. He found himself alternately wanting to strangle her or bed her, and neither was allowed. He was her guardian, for heaven's sake, and yet when she flashed her dark green eyes at him and turned with that saucy flare of her skirts, he wanted nothing more than to catch her so close she would never dare leave him.

Stephen clenched his fists and tried to look appropriately genial toward the horde of men bowing over her hand. Good God, she became more beautiful with each passing second. She would certainly become the original Tallis promised, damn his eyes. All too soon, Stephen would receive marriage offers for her from eager young bucks totally incapable of restraining her. They would no doubt give her free rein to take in dangerous strays and punch cutthroats without the slightest regard to her welfare or reputation.

And despite the fact that he was her guardian, he knew there was not a damn thing he could do to stop it. He knew she would marry wherever her heart led her, no matter what he said. In fact, if he ever dared refuse one of her suitors out of hand, she would probably plan a run to Gretna Green just to spite him.

With sudden resolve, Stephen turned his back on the woman who most filled his thoughts and scanned the ballroom for a substitute.

His hungry gaze landed on Sophia Rathburn, and finally the tension in his belly found an outlet. She was everything Amanda could not hope to be—refined and elegant with an aura of delicacy appropriate to a future countess. Where Amanda burned hot with emotion, Sophia was cool, a tempered soul of unmistakable gentility. She would never dream of climbing down a trellis barefoot in the middle of the night or of punching anyone, cutthroat or not. She certainly would not deign to be pandered to by fawning young bucks in such a vulgar way.

No, Sophia had the sensibilities of a lady.

He quickly made his way to her side, almost ruthlessly cutting through the crowd.

And there he remained for the rest of the evening.

"Are you enjoying your first ball, Miss Wyndham?"

Gillian looked up from her seat at Lord Tallis with her first genuine smile in hours. Around her, she could hear the muted groans of more than a few gentlemen as they noted her sudden animation. "Yes, my lord. I have discovered there are distinct advantages to popularity." She beamed at the men around her.

"I am most gratified to hear it," he said as he leaned down, neatly trapping her hand to bestow a gentleman's kiss on her fingers. But when he glanced up, his eyes twinkled with devilment. "Do you know, Miss Wyndham, I have a sudden urge to attend a bearbaiting. Or perhaps a cockfight? Wonderful tourist spot, you know."

She raised her eyebrows in what she hoped was an imperious look. She knew he referred to their improper wager. His forfeit would be the tourist attraction of his choice, but for her to go to a bearbaiting would be a scandalous breach of etiquette. Of course, she would not admit such a silly thing as the fact that society's strictures stopped her from the honorable fulfillment of her wager.

Especially when she knew a much more potent weapon.

"Have I mentioned, my lord, that I like to take Tom along on all but my most proper excursions?" She strove for an abstracted air, but she did not miss the sudden widening of his lordship's eyes. "And Tom is such a scamp, there is no telling what he might do at a bearbaiting."

Actually, she could list quite a number of possibilities, including picking the bear's shackles or fleecing every pocket in the crowd. One glance at Lord Tallis's face told her the same thoughts occurred to him. He could not know the complete truth of Tom's background, but only a fool would underestimate the boy after their trip to the crypts.

Bowing slightly, he sent her an appreciative look. "Perhaps a visit to the Tower would be more suited to my tastes."

"Perhaps it would," she agreed with a grin.

Then she glanced out into the ballroom. "Have you come for your dance?"

"I have waited weeks for it. Nothing short of an untimely demise could keep me from your side."

"Then I shall pray you are by my side each and every evening." She held out her hand, allowing him to escort her onto the floor. While they stood, waiting for the music to begin, she caught sight of another couple just entering the dance floor—Stephen and Sophia.

He had been with that ice princess all evening, his attentions remarked by almost everyone. It was most irritating, especially when he seemed to notice Gillian only occasionally, and then only to scowl. She had, of course, been too busy with her own gentlemen to bother with Stephen's actions. Still, she knew this was not his first dance with the chilling Lady Sophia.

Was this their second dance? Or their third? A second was unremarkable. Gillian herself intended to dance twice with Tallis. But if it were his third dance with the woman, why, that was tantamount to a proposal of marriage!

"Is something amiss?"

Her attention skittered abruptly back to Lord Tallis, and she felt herself flush with embarrassment. "I am terribly sorry; I was only thinking."

Tallis followed the line of her gaze to his sister and Stephen, who chose that moment to scowl back at them.

"Have you perhaps argued with Lord Mavenford?"

"Oh, la," she commented airily as the music began and she moved into the opening steps. "My stiff-necked guardian believes I am entirely too forward."

"I see," Tallis commented, bowing as his first steps began. "And have you been?"

Gillian bit her lip, startled by his perception. Thankfully, the dance separated them, hiding her reaction. But all too soon he returned to her side, his fathomless blue-gray eyes challenging her to answer his question. Had she truly been too forward?

"Yes," she finally admitted, "I suppose I acted a bit outré."

"It cannot be easy," he said softly, "to be the guardian of such a tempting young woman."

"My lord!" she said, blushing to the roots of her hair. His simple statement should not have unnerved her. His was only one of a hundred compliments tossed her way this evening. But it did unnerve her simply because she believed him.

It took another two turns of the dance before she regained her composure. Then he promptly destroyed it by whispering into her ear.

"Listen to what Stephen says, Amanda. He is no fool, for all his military stiffness. There are many dangers of which you are not aware."

Gillian lifted her gaze to his face, seeing not the gentle admiration of a handsome man, but the arrogant assumption that she required his advice. She had thought Lord Tallis different from Stephen, but here he stood, ordering her around as if she had no more brains than a peahen.

"Do you know, my lord, I am entirely too tired of men telling me to behave because of some unknown danger." She glanced over at Stephen as he smiled benevolently down at Lady Sophia. She would bet her last groat that he never warned Sophia of unknown dangers, but for some reason both Stephen and Tallis seemed to take a perverse joy in trying to correct Gillian's behavior.

Her companion must have seen the gathering storm on her face, because he rapidly tried to backtrack. "Uh, Amanda—"

"In fact," she interrupted, "I believe these threats are merely constructions of the male mind, intended to keep women docile." She spun away from him, using the motion of the dance to turn her back on him. Then, when she returned for the final steps, she lifted her head and delivered her last parting shot. "You will find, Lord Tallis, I have a mind of my own. I am not easily frightened by nameless phantoms."

"I never said—"

"Oh, look, it is the viscount." She lifted her fan and waved at the young man to whom she had promised the next dance. As she expected, he rushed forward, ignoring social custom by joining her on the dance floor without the required trip back to the countess.

Lord Tallis stiffened, clearly aware of her maneuvering, and she held her breath, wondering if he would create a scene. In the end, he did not, relinquishing her in silence, though his dark gray eyes spoke volumes.

"A success! An unqualified success!"

Gillian could only grimace as the countess's loud tones continued to fill their carriage with her overflowing enthusiasm.

"Did you see Lady Marston? She practically ate her own liver with jealousy. And her with three indifferent daughters to launch."

Stephen nodded and murmured a noncommittal response.

"I must tell you, Amanda, I had some anxious moments. When you first arrived in London, never did I imagine you could manage at all, much less become an original! We did marvelously, my dears, absolutely marvelously. But now we must make our plans. We have hundreds of decisions to make about the rest of the Season."

Gillian turned from her inspection of the dark London streets to stare at her silent guardian. "Does that mean I will not be banished to York?"

The countess gasped in shock. "Banished? Now? Whatever could you be thinking? You cannot possibly leave now. We must build on tonight. Stephen, tell her she is not leaving. Why, it would be utterly ruinous."

But Stephen did not answer. He merely shifted his gaze until it locked onto Gillian's.

She matched his stare, holding her chin high though her blood rushed painfully in her ears and her mouth went dry.

"Oh," said the countess, cutting into the sudden tension with her own frustrated sigh. "You two have had another tiff."

Gillian shifted her gaze, startled enough to break away from Stephen's mesmerizing face. "Tiff?" she echoed. The countess had called their arguments many things—explosions, tirades, even the onset of Armageddon—but never a "tiff."

"Yes, yes," responded the countess in an exasperated tone. "You two are constantly getting into these childish little spats. Well, go on, Amanda. Apologize, and then Stephen will say all is forgiven, and we can set our minds to our true task—finding you a brilliant match."

Gillian opened her mouth to say something rude, only to be forestalled by Stephen, his low voice filling their carriage as completely as the chill night air.

"On the contrary, Mother, it is I who must beg Amanda's pardon."

Gillian stiffened. He *was* sorry he had kissed her. So sorry, in fact, that he was apologizing in front of his mother.

"Oh," commented the countess in disappointed surprise. "Very well, Stephen. Now, Amanda, say all is forgiven."

"What if all is not forgiven?" Gillian failed to keep her voice even, upset because she could not understand why his apology hurt her so.

"Well, of course everything is forgiven," snapped the countess, clearly at the end of her patience. "He has said he is sorry, and I am certain he promises he will not do it again."

"Most assuredly," Stephen said.

"He certainly will not," Gillian said at the same instant.

"There," the countess said with a gratified smile. "Now all is well." And since the carriage had finally arrived at their home, no one bothered to contradict her.

Chapter Eleven

A lady honors and obeys her parents.

Gillian was miserable.

Nearly two weeks had passed since her confusing entrée into the haut ton, and in that time she had been showered with every kind of flower, danced until her feet were numb, and had every part of her body immortalized in poetry. In short, she was a greater success than she had ever dreamed.

Given her imagination, that was high praise indeed.

Yet she was totally, incredibly miserable.

She was in love.

She did not know how it happened. She was not even sure when, but the facts were inescapable. It did not matter whose hand she held on the dance floor; her thoughts invariably compared the man to Stephen. This viscount's shoulders were not as broad; that lord was not nearly as graceful. This duke was too comfortable, that baron too complimentary.

But even that she pushed aside as nothing more than simple selection. After all, she must make comparisons to keep everyone straight in her mind. It was not until nighttime that the inescapable truth held her in its burning grip.

No matter what happened during the day, when darkness closed about her, Gillian would lie stock-still and fight the desire to run to him. It did not seem to matter that Stephen was clearly destined for Lady Sophia or that he had spent the last weeks either ignoring or scowling at Gillian. At night, all she wanted to do was throw herself into his arms and whisper that all was forgiven.

Yes, she was in love. With Stephen. She sighed and dropped her hand on her chin.

"I see my wit is failing me today," commented Lord Tallis dryly.

She glanced up in guilty surprise. She was so caught up in her thoughts that she'd failed to even notice she and Lord Tallis had already arrived at the Tower for their tourist event and the fulfillment of their wager.

"Thank heaven it is early for the fashionable throng," he drawled. "Otherwise my reputation would be quite done in."

"I am so sorry, my lord. My thoughts have been wandering."

"If I were of a romantic nature, I might think you were a woman in love."

She started, twisting in his curricle to consider him more closely. He was a handsome man in his own cynical way. Whereas Stephen was straightforward and honest to the bone, Lord Tallis was . . . different, almost devious in the way he presented himself to the world. Not as tall as Stephen, he nevertheless had his own aura of power hidden beneath his fashionably dandified air.

And for the last two weeks, he had seemed like her only friend, despite her set-down at the ball.

"My lord—"

"Please," he interrupted, helping her descend from his curricle. "I think the coming confession calls for given names."

She flinched, wondering just how much of her soul he could read with his keen gray eyes. Then she sighed. She must speak with someone, and at the moment he was her closest friend.

Even so, she waited until after he paid their admittance fee to the Tower menagerie and dismissed their guide. She did not speak until she stared at the cage of a particularly sad-looking panther.

"Oh, Geoffrey, the truth is, after all my scoffing at unseen dangers, it seems I have fallen into the biggest trap of them all."

"You have fallen in love." He spoke evenly, his words a statement and not a question, but she could sense his underlying tension when she touched his arm.

She looked away from the panther to gaze at a cage of careening monkeys. "I . . . I seem to be having difficulty ruling a particularly willful aspect of my nature. Despite all logic and reason, I feel . . . pulled toward one man."

He did not answer at first, waiting patiently as other visitors passed out of earshot. "I take it the gentleman in question is unacceptable."

She released a disgusted laugh. "Unacceptable, irredeemable, and cantankerous to boot."

He raised an eyebrow, a sparkle of amusement flashing in his eyes as they wandered on. "How dreadful."

"He has been a thorn in my side from the first moment. The thought of willfully subjecting myself to his tyranny for the rest of my life is insupportable. I simply will not do it."

"Methinks the lady doth protest too much," he commented dryly.

She glared at him. She had never been particularly fond of *Hamlet*. Too much moaning, too little doing. But unfortunately Geoffrey did have the right tack. She was protesting too much, and all the while her illegitimate nature gained a foothold in her heart.

She looked back at the monkeys. "I am undone by my own traitorous blood."

"Not blood, Amanda. Passion. And passion can easily be ruled by the head."

She lifted her gaze to him and knew he, at least, believed it was true. Despite his frivolous air, Geoffrey was a man of control, a man who probably never once let his emotions override his reason.

She suddenly discovered she had a great deal of respect for him. She straightened her shoulders, wanting to copy his example. "Very well, Geoffrey. What do you suggest?"

He was watching her closely, as if gauging her mood. Then abruptly he spoke, startling her with the plainness of his words. "Marry me, Amanda."

"What?" She gasped.

"I like you. I think we would suit admirably. And I must confess, although my estates are quite solid, an infusion of fresh capital right now would not go amiss."

Gillian blinked. "You mean you want my dowry."

He sighed, seemingly apologetic as he nodded. "Yes, I need your dowry. But I also think I could be a good husband." He turned to her, his eyes serious. "I would not object if you took the unsuitable gentleman for a lover."

She gasped. "He would never do that."

She answered without thought, never realizing how much she gave away by such a statement. There were not many men of the ton who, once invited, would turn down a married woman's bed. Add to that her statement that he was a thorn in her side from the beginning, and the list narrowed down to only one man.

Geoffrey was too quick not to understand.

His eyes narrowed. "Your guardian is to

marry my sister," he said, his tone cold.

Gillian glanced away, letting her gaze wander over the rows of cages. "I know."

"Is he aware of your feelings?"

"Good God, no! He thinks I want to scratch his eyes out." She tilted her head in a half smile. "And most of the time he is right."

Geoffrey pulled her along, guiding her to a more secluded spot near a Spanish wolf. She did not speak as they walked, knowing he was thinking. Then suddenly he turned to her, his eyes filled with a careful determination. Clearly he had made a decision, and she held her breath, waiting for his pronouncement.

"I want to marry you, Amanda, but there are a few questions still."

With a supreme effort, Gillian controlled her expression while her thoughts whirled. Here it was. The moment she had anticipated for years. She needed keep her head for only a few more moments; then her future and her mother's would be set.

"First, could you stand seeing Stephen and Sophia at family gatherings and holidays?"

She bit her lip, flinching at the thought of unending Christmases watching Stephen and Sophia together, seeing their children year after year. Could she do it? "I . . ." She took a deep breath. "I suppose I shall have to in any event. He is my family, even if he is not yours yet."

Geoffrey nodded, apparently satisfied by her response. "I shall insist upon an heir first. There will be no lovers before that."

"That will not be difficult." Once away from Stephen, she doubted she could be tempted by anyone.

He searched her face, and she lifted her chin, showing him her own resolve. She did not bother asking about his lovers. As it was for her, this was a business transaction. She would get his title; he would get her dowry. And her mother would get a warm home in the winter.

She felt him raise her hand, and once again she found herself comparing him to Stephen. Like that of the earl, Geoffrey's touch was firm and commanding, but his hand was smaller than Stephen's and somehow did not give her the same sense of security.

It did not matter, she told herself sternly. The dowry Stephen provided would give her whatever Geoffrey could not.

"Miss Wyndham, will you do me the great honor of becoming my wife?"

She swallowed, forcing the words out of her mouth before her traitorous heritage overcame her reason. "Yes, Lord Tallis. It would be my great pleasure."

Then he kissed her, not gently or reverently, but professionally, with a skill that impressed her, warming her blood even as it left her heart cold.

Stephen heard the rattle of carriage wheels and could not stop himself from looking out the window. As he suspected, it was Amanda returning with Lord Tallis.

He glanced at the mantel clock. She would have to hurry if she intended to be ready for tonight's round of balls and routs. His mother intended to take Amanda to no less than three separate establishments tonight.

Since the evening of her first ball, Amanda had indeed become this Season's original. For the past two weeks, he had tripped over posies and calf-eyed young bucks until he thought to convert the front rooms into a dormitory for lovesick fools. They were so thick, in fact, that he hid himself in his room to avoid the sight of yet more young tulips of the ton.

The whole situation was maddening. He could count the times he was alone with Amanda on the fingers of one hand. And each of those three times, it had been an awkward affair in the hallway between engagements. Neither knew what to say and both disappeared to their respective destinations at the earliest opportunity.

They no longer even attended the same functions anymore. It appeared that Amanda planned her evenings intending to avoid him and Sophia.

Stephen glanced back at the carriage and frowned. Amanda was still there, speaking on the doorstep with Lord Tallis. Easing the curtains a little wider, Stephen narrowed his eyes and tried to guess at their words.

He had no clue, of course. But there did seem to be a new rapport between the two. Amanda clearly was not flirting, and yet she lingered on the doorstep with the man. It was as if the two had come to some understanding. . . .

Stephen stepped back from the window in shock, immediately denying the evidence of his eyes. She could not have made her choice already. It was only a few weeks into the Season. No, Amanda was too levelheaded to make her decision so soon.

Stephen settled back into his chair and returned to his reading—a pamphlet on the plight of young boys. But he could not concentrate; his mind was too full.

Amanda and Geoffrey. True, the man had a title, social standing, and enough wealth with the addition of Amanda's dowry. By all accounts, the man was a good match. Why, Stephen was even considering marrying Tallis's sister, as much because of her family status as her inherent breeding.

So why should he have this feeling of dread? Something was definitely wrong.

Setting aside his half-finished notes for his speech to the House of Lords, Stephen rang for his valet. It was time to make some inquiries, not only into the particulars of Lord Tallis's estate, but also to resolve some lingering questions about Amanda. He had put off the task, no doubt afraid to uncover whatever indelicacies her childish passions had thrown her into.

But it was time to face his responsibilities. He was Amanda's guardian. While his solicitor poked into the niceties of Tallis's affairs, he had time to check on Amanda's inheritance, making

sure everything was in order before her nup-
tials.

With a grim expression, he turned to his valet,
ordering the man to pack a small bag for him.
Then he ducked down the back stairs, searching
for some brandy to dull the ache in his gut.

Gillian was still awake. It was past three in the
morning, at least an hour after everyone else in
the household had sought their own beds. But
Gillian was awake, staring out at the overcast
night with nothing but a frail piece of foolscap
to keep her company.

Her mother had written her a letter. It had
clearly been delayed, sent through Amanda's
housekeeper, Mrs. Hobbs, a notoriously forget-
ful woman despite her kind heart. It had arrived
here care of Amanda Wyndham, buried in with
a long series of the manor's household receipts.

Gillian twisted the page in her fingers.
Though there was no light to read by, Gillian
reviewed the page word by word. It was not
hard, for the missive was very short.

*I love yu. Yur father did to in his own way.
Rember yor cap.*

It was not even signed, but Gillian recognized
her mother's shaky letters, the belabored script
and frequent misspellings. She also recognized
the underlying message: *Good-bye*.

Her mother did not expect to see Gillian
again.

Gillian bit her lip, trying to muffle the sobs constricting her throat. How could this happen?

Gillian felt her ball gown rustle beneath her fingers as she crumpled the shimmering silk. The letter came in the post this afternoon, but she had not received it until after she'd returned home from Almack's. What irony, she thought with a grimace. While she danced in society's most guarded ballroom, her mother's last good-bye waited on the front table for her attention. Had she truly been so immersed in her deception that she'd forgotten her own mother?

No. She had not forgotten her mother. When Gillian left two months ago, her mother was healing. With spring's arrival she should have continued to grow stronger each passing day. Gillian never would have left York if there was any hint of a relapse.

But the tone of her mother's letter implied otherwise. Gillian felt her hands shake, her heart breaking as she thought of her sweet parent. Was it possible? Was her mother truly dying?

She had searched frantically through the receipts, looking for anything else, even a note from Mrs. Hobbs telling her some news. But there was nothing—only the certain conviction that her mother was dying, and Gillian was hundreds of miles away.

She dropped her head in her hands and let the tears fall unchecked. But long before her gown grew wet, Gillian dried her tears, dismissing them as a useless waste of time. She must make her decision, and sobbing would not bring her any closer to an answer.

The question now was simple. Did she go back to her mother and forget the future? Or trust her mother was fine and carry on her charade until the end?

Abruptly pushing out of her chair, Gillian began to pace, the crumpled foolscap resting like a white flag on her bed. She was an engaged woman. Although Tallis had not wanted to make their betrothal public until after his sister was settled, their agreement was finished.

She would soon be Lady Tallis.

But would their engagement survive her sudden absence if she disappeared to Yorkshire?

The answer, of course, was yes. Geoffrey would certainly not propose to a woman, then forget it the next evening. The problem lay in his desire to spend more time, not less, with her. Once she decided to visit York, he would undoubtedly offer to accompany her. It would be a natural opportunity to inspect the property that would go with her hand in marriage.

And she could not allow that.

Only her mother and sweet Mrs. Hobbs knew of her deception. Everyone else in York would call her Gillian Ames, bastard daughter of the old baron. Geoffrey would discover her fraud within an hour. So she could not go to York, at least not yet, and certainly not openly. But she still could do something for her mother.

With sudden determination, Gillian stripped

off her ball gown, regretting her decision to allow Hawkings to retire. It was awkward pulling at buttons meant to be unfastened from behind by a maid, and in the end Gillian tore the delicate fabric in her haste. She gave it barely a regretful sigh as she pawed through her wardrobe for something appropriate.

Gillian pulled out a serviceable walking gown. It was much too bright for skulking about in the nighttime shadows, but it was the best she could find under the circumstances. And, best of all, she could fasten it from the front.

Then, taking a deep breath to calm her thoughts, she sat down to compose a letter.

Gillian's first mission was to revive her mother's failing health. That meant a doctor, but the nearest one she trusted lived miles from her mother's small village in York. Though he did not begrudge his services, he usually required some recompense for his time and travel.

Rooting about in the back of her dresser, Gillian retrieved her maid's cap from its hiding place. Folded within the white linen, she kept the last of her pin money and the piddling sum she had managed to win at a card party. She could easily have gotten more, but she had not wanted to be too forward at her first card party. Now she wished she had been ruthless.

Nevertheless, she decided, as she spilled the pound notes out across her escritoire, her small cache would be enough for the doctor. She quickly scribbled her request that the doctor visit her mother immediately. The money was to pay for his time and any medicines he prescribed.

The next step was to see her mother. Since there was no end of difficulty in going to York herself, perhaps she could bring her mother here to London, where she would set the dear lady up in a peaceful room nearby.

That, of course, had been her original plan. As soon as she was married, she would send the money for her mother to move to London. She felt her lips curve at the thought of finding a quiet location nearby where she could visit her mother whenever the society whirl became too much for her. Mary Ames had an extraordinarily simple way of viewing life, and somehow she never failed to even out the worst of Gillian's riot of emotion and action.

The problem was, of course, finding the money for a discreet abode.

She must talk to Geoffrey. She would have to tread very carefully, plan out her exact phrasing beforehand, but she thought she could convince him to loan her the money. She would speak with him when he returned from his estate. He had left this morning, pleading urgent business, but he'd promised to return as soon as possible.

In the meantime, she had to post her letter in secret. Which meant she must give it to Tom.

Just as before, Gillian took off her slippers and climbed out onto the windowsill. Her gaze fell briefly on her list of ladylike behavior, noting especially number two on not climbing up and down trellises.

She sighed, knowing that if Stephen caught her, he would banish her for sure. But this was the safest, quietest way to escape the house, and that overrode any considerations of ladylike behavior.

At least this time she would not be barefoot. She slipped both her footwear and the letter into her pocket.

She stepped past the sill and felt her toes grip the trellis. She climbed safely and silently down to the ground, an involuntary shiver coursing up her spine as her bare feet settled on the cold cobblestones.

Suddenly a hand slapped over her mouth. It was thick and heavy and nearly suffocating. Gillian tried to scream, but all she managed was a muted squeak. Then an arm wrapped around her rib cage, crushing her against a huge, foul-smelling body.

"An' wot 'ave I caught today? Why, it be a wench for Tess."

Two coarse laughs echoed through night air, and Gillian realized there were at least two men against her. If only Stephen had taught her to hit, then she might have had a chance.

But he had refused, and all of her struggles were useless. Her captor was too strong, his hold too secure.

All too soon, a massive fist exploded against her left temple and the world went black.

* * *

Stephen tossed aside his bedcovers in disgust.

He could not sleep. His mind was too full of the sight of Amanda speaking intimately with Tallis on the doorstep. He knew nothing improper had occurred, but he still envisioned all sorts of illicit conversations and meanings attached to their simple actions.

He tugged the bellpull with unnecessary force, summoning his valet. If he could not sleep, he might as well make his way toward York.

He was barely dressed and a message sent to the mews when the commotion began. In what should have been a quiet house, he heard the distant sound of a boy calling.

". . . lordship! Yer lordship!"

Stephen frowned, a cold dread seeping into his blood. "Check Amanda's room," he ordered his valet. Then he crossed the room, yanked open the door, and was halfway down the stairs when Tom stumbled to a gasping halt in front of him.

" 'E's got 'er!"

"Start at the beginning, Tom. And speak clearly."

The boy nodded, his eyes wide with fear, his clothing begrimed, but he took a deep breath and made a valiant effort at speaking precisely. "I was watching. I know ye told us t' stop, but I thought 'e might come back."

Stephen did not wonder what Tom meant. The morning after Amanda's escapade on the trellis, he and the boy had spoken at length about Bullard, Tom's former "protector." Then Stephen had ordered Tom and one of the footmen to watch the house at night in case Bullard returned to make mischief. But he'd canceled the order last week, thinking the cutthroat effectively intimidated. Apparently Tom had decided to continue on his own, and unlike Stephen, the boy had not underestimated Bullard's patience.

"Miss Wyndham is not in her room, my lord." Stephen turned to stare at his valet, his worst fears confirmed. "And the window is open."

" 'E's got 'er!" repeated Tom. " 'E was waiting off to the side. I didn't see 'im until she was already down. And then it were too late."

Stephen felt a cold fury begin to build. "He climbed through the window for her?"

Tom shook his head. "Naw, she was coming down. I . . . I did not think she would, not after the drubbing you gave her afore."

"Apparently I have underestimated a good many things lately," Stephen muttered under his breath, his mind spinning furiously, searching for a plan.

"There was two of 'em. I couldn't get close to help."

"Bullard?"

Tom nodded. "An' Johnny. They grabbed her and knocked her flat."

"They hit her?" All thoughts scattered at the horrifying image of Amanda struck by the two thugs.

"Flat."

Unconscious. Amanda was unconscious and stolen by two brutes. He tried to sort through the rage, fighting for his battle calm as he decided on a strategy. "How long ago?"

"Twenty minutes—"

"Twenty!"

"I followed 'em to make sure where they was going. When I knew, I came back 'ere."

Finally Stephen felt a measure of control return as he found a glimmer of hope. "You did the right thing, Tom. Where did they go?"

The boy's face paled, and Stephen knew the news would not be good.

"They took 'er to Tess."

The name meant nothing to Stephen, but from the boy's terrified expression, he could well guess what was in store for Amanda if he did not find her soon.

"Can you show me where?"

Tom nodded, but his eyes were still pulled wide with fear. "But it won't do no good."

"Why?"

"Tess'll let 'im break 'er in first as payment."

Stephen swallowed, dread mixing with the rage building in his gut. "How long do we have before he starts?"

"He'll start as soon as the chains are on."

Chapter Twelve

A lady never drinks gin.

Gillian woke to a throbbing headache and the raucous sound of male laughter. All her senses seemed dim, as if she struggled through water to consciousness, but she was sure she could smell the stale scent of sweat and gin as if they were right beside her.

She did not move. She did not dare risk inflaming the already overwhelming pain from her temple. So she kept still and concentrated on what she could guess of her surroundings. She lay on her side, presumably on a soft bed, for she felt a mattress and damp sheets beneath her. Except for her head, she felt mostly unharmed, almost whole except for a heavy weight on her wrists.

She cracked open her eyes, flinching at the sudden stab of candlelight. It took another moment for her sight to adjust to the wavering light so she could look at her hands.

Shackles. Someone had fastened cold iron fetters across her wrists. And that someone watched her from a chair directly beside her bed.

"Wakey, wakey, ladybird."

Gillian blinked, the coarse voice jolting her into awareness. She had memories of that voice, fragments of thoughts encased in darkness. Had she been climbing down the trellis?

" 'Ere yer are, tart. Drink up."

Suddenly her head was tilted backward and the hard neck of a bottle clanked against her teeth. Foul-smelling gin gushed into her mouth. She swallowed reflexively, then gagged on the burning liquid, twisting her head in an effort to knock it away.

" 'Ey now! Don't go wasting good rot." He took a swig, swallowing with loud gulps before smacking his lips in satisfaction. Then, with a gap-toothed smile, he settled on the bed beside her. " 'Ave some more."

"No—" The word was a soft gasp, but he would not listen, already intent on pouring more of it down her throat. This time she was ready for him. She remembered what Tom said about people stealing young girls and getting them drunk for days on end until they forgot everything except their next taste of gin. Tom told her how to fool them, how to pretend to drink, but not swallow, letting the gin spill to the side of her neck.

Unfortunately, knowing and doing were two different things, and though she at least did not half drown in the vile stuff, she was forced to swallow a few mouthfuls before spilling the rest.

" 'At's a good girl."

Gillian was still trying to catch her breath, but when she did, she glared up at her captor. "It is vile!"

"Aye. But ye'll soon be beggin' me fer it."

Gillian let her head drop weakly back onto the mattress, only half pretending exhaustion. Her memories finally returned, and with them came the certain knowledge she was in dire straits. She had been abducted by this man and presumably taken to some bawdy house for initiation into her new life. That would explain the soft moans filtering through the walls and the explicit drawings on the wallpaper surrounding the bed.

She searched her still-foggy memory for anything else Tom had told her that might help. Nothing, except what she would have thought of in the first place: drink as little as possible and pretend to be weaker than she was. Fettered and watched, she had little hope of escape before Stephen found her.

"My guardian will be furious when he finds me."

Bullard laughed, the sound echoing harshly

off the thin walls. "Yer guardian ain't gonna find you."

Gillian looked up at her captor, forcing herself to see past his grimy clothing, the matted beard, and his few yellow teeth. She focused on the dull brown of his eyes. "My guardian *will* find me. And when he does, he will kill you." She paused, trying to hold his gaze. "You had best make your deal with me now, before he gets here."

He blinked, and for a moment she thought she might have gotten through to him, but a second later he stood, tugging open his ragged breeches with a harsh cackle. "You ain't got nothing left to bargain with, ladybird."

Gillian felt her breath freeze in her chest as she realized his intention. For the first time since waking up, she faced the possibility that Stephen might not arrive in time to help her. Bullard stepped forward, grabbing the gin as he moved, and she recoiled, her hands moving backward on the sheets.

And she touched something thin and sharp.

A hairpin! She did not know if it was hers or some other poor unfortunate's, but however it got there, she was eternally grateful. It would be awkward, but given enough time she knew she could pick the lock on her shackles.

The problem was finding the time.

She eyed the man Tom had called Bullard, seeing his Adam's apple bob up and down as he poured half the bottle of gin down his grizzled throat. He was half-drunk and liable to get even more so before the evening was over.

Good. She had handled drunken men before—most especially her own father and his cronies. The first step was to gain some measure of authority. Remind them of a stern grande dame, and they all seemed to quiver.

But that meant sitting up, and between the gin and her pounding head, she was not at all sure she could do it.

Bullard set down the bottle and came closer, advancing slowly on her in what he clearly thought was an attractive male swagger. It only made her feel nauseous. She took a deep breath and pushed herself up, neatly catching the hairpin and twisting it into the lock as she moved.

Pain lanced through her head, and the world spun about her. She felt light-headed and hot, then cold and clammy in alternating waves. And still Bullard kept coming.

"I am going to be ill," she said in a gasp.

That stopped him, at least for a moment. He took one look at her face, then twisted away for the nearby bucket. He hauled it over to her, and she felt her stomach roil until it heaved. She prolonged the agony, pretending to rest as she took shaky breaths, all the while twisting her shackles into her skirt to hide her work with the hairpin.

" 'Ere. This'll settle yer stomach." He tilted her head back and poured more gin down her throat. She tried to jerk away, but he held her head fast, and she was powerless to stop the first few swallows. She wished she could get ill again, but the burning sensation in her throat did indeed hold back the nausea.

And he insisted she finish the rest of the bottle.

Ten minutes later, she was soaked through with gin. Although she managed not to drink much, her head still whirled and the world seemed softer, almost fuzzy as her thoughts drifted.

" 'At's better, ain't it?" He sounded almost gentle, and though she knew it was an act, she pretended to accept his newfound kindness. She smiled at him, her movements vague, as if she were lulled into a gin-induced euphoria.

"You want a job?"

He blinked. "Wot?"

She smiled and lifted her head slowly, her words gauged to keep him off balance as she continued to fiddle with the hairpin. "You need not live like this, you know. Preying off of young boys, stealing girls. There is a better life available to you."

He stared at her, his face slowly splitting into his yellowed grin. This time she did not even flinch at the smell of his breath. "Wot, you think Prinny 'as a spot on 'is council fer me? Shall I give 'im advice on 'is tailoring?" His laughter was loud, pounding against her head until she flinched.

"I can get you a job," she persevered. "You can work in the earl's household—"

"And wot would his nibs want with me?"

"You could work in the mews or as a footman. Eventually you might even be butler." She twisted to look directly at him while moving the lock to a better angle. "It would be an honest job and a chance for a better life."

He stared at her, his eyes wide. Then he broke into a deep laugh that had him falling backward onto the sheets. "Wot should I say then? 'Yes, yer nibs, no, yer holy nibs. Bless your bleeding pisser, yer nibs.'"

Gillian lifted her chin, stung by his blatant refusal. "I am serious. I have enormous influence with the earl. I could get you an honest job." She tried not to blanch at so huge a lie.

He sat up, his eyes suddenly cold. "I got yer job all ready fer ye, ladybird. And I don't want no more yammering."

She took a deep breath, striving for a calm she did not feel. "You have to trust somebody sometime, Bullard. You can try for a better life."

He clenched his teeth, his eyes narrow and feral. Suddenly she realized she had badly misjudged the situation. Offering help to a boy Tom's age was one thing, but Bullard was too far gone to listen to her.

And her time had just run out. He leaned over her, trapping her between the thick columns of his arms.

Snick.

The shackles sprang open. She was free.

She did not waste any time. Throwing the heavy irons into Bullard's face, she bolted for the door. The room swam, and she felt heavy and slow, but she staggered forward. Behind her, she heard Bullard howl in rage, barreling toward her with the power of an enraged beast.

She made it to the door a second before him, hauling on the latch only to find it locked. Idiot! she railed at herself. She should have realized it would be secured against her.

Slamming herself sideways, she narrowly avoided Bullard's grasping hands. Her only other hope was the window, and she dashed toward it as fast as her wobbly legs could stumble.

Barred.

The window was barred closed. Then she felt Bullard's heavy fists grab her hair, dragging her backward as she screamed in frustration and fear.

His hands were brutal on her body as he lifted her upward and threw her onto the bed, his face split by an evil grin. "Scream away, ladybird. Ain't none wot will come to you now. Not even yer bleeding, holy nibs."

Gillian scrambled backward on the bed, grabbing the shackles as her only weapon. She held them high, gasping for air as she waited for an opening. Her only hope was to knock him unconscious in a single blow. She would not get another chance.

He grinned, anticipating her move, even relishing the challenge.

CRASH!

The door burst inward, and Bullard spun around, ready for the new threat. Gillian did not wait to see who arrived. It had to be Stephen, thank heaven, but just in case it was someone else, she swung the iron fetters hard, slamming them into Bullard's temple, then waited for him to crumple.

He did not. He bellowed in rage and raised his massive fists toward her. She tried to jump away, but she was blocked in by the wall, her feet twisted awkwardly in the sheets.

Then Stephen entered the fray.

Bullard's massive fists were still in the air when Stephen jerked him off balance and flattened him with a powerful right cross. The villain raised his arms in defense, but he never had the chance. Stephen struck him time after time until Bullard was nothing more than a bloody mass on the floor.

Gillian could only watch in shock until Stephen finally stopped. He stood still, his fists clenched, his breath coming in angry gasps.

Gillian took a deep breath, then let it go on a long, steady sigh of relief. "I do wish you would teach me to do that."

He lifted his gaze to her, his eyes wide. Then suddenly she was in his arms as he gathered her close to him. She felt his long, sinewy muscles, knotted with tension and fear. She felt his ragged breath and the strength with which he clutched her. And she felt her heart swell with love.

"Are you all right?" he whispered against her hair.

She nodded against his chest. "I knew you would come. I knew it."

"Let us go. The magistrate will be here any

moment." She reluctantly pulled away from him, but he would not release her. He lifted her up in his arms and pushed her face against his neck. "Stay still. We will be gone in a moment. Tom, see if there is anything you can tie him up with until the magistrate arrives."

She lifted her head, scanning the room until she saw the boy, his face pale with fright. "Tom? You should not be here. It is too dangerous."

She felt Stephen's strangled cough and looked down at her rescuer in concern. Then she remembered her makeshift weapon and twisted to speak to Tom.

"Use the shackles, but search his pockets for the key." She grinned and held up the hairpin. "I have the lockpick."

Stephen tightened his hold on her, shaking his head in amazement. "I should have known you would find a way."

"Oh, no," she responded quickly, lest he think she did not appreciate his rescue. "In fact, I found it most sad. I could not seem to reach him at all."

"What?"

"I tried everything, Stephen. I even offered him a job as your butler, but he would not believe I was sincere." She watched bleary-eyed as Tom closed the shackles about Bullard's wrists. "He just could not believe."

"Amazing," he replied, his voice hard with sarcasm.

She looked back at him, suddenly feeling very, very tired, wondering why her words sounded so slurred. "Oh, stop it, Stephen," she said. "You would have hired him."

"The man who abducted you and just tried to . . ." He stopped abruptly, his voice rough as he tightened his hold on her.

But she barely heard him. Her head felt disgustingly heavy, and it was so sweet to just surrender all her cares onto his competent shoulders. She snuggled deeper into his arms.

"Of course you would," she murmured. "Just as you shall hire all his children."

"Children? What children?"

She smiled against his chest, letting herself fade into the delightful scent of bay rum and Stephen. "The ones like Tom. The ones he cannot care for now."

Then she let herself slide into a heavy sleep, knowing she was safe in Stephen's arms.

The sudden influx of nearly three dozen young children to the earl's household was remarked upon by many of society's members, though none with any authority. Some believed it had to do with Miss Wyndham's brief illness. Others merely ascribed it to an attack of conscience. The earl, they said, was taking care of his many bastards.

Those closest to the earl's family remained silent, knowing no man, not even one of Stephen's obvious strength and virility, could possibly sire that many children, all between the ages of seven and twelve. They simply believed he had gone mad.

A thought that had Stephen's wholehearted agreement.

Never in his life had he behaved so erratically. One minute he swore he would strangle his maddening ward; then the next second found him giving in to her most bizarre whims.

It had to stop.

Now.

It was time Miss Amanda Wyndham learned who was in charge of this household. It was time she learned to obey the rules.

More important, it was time she learned to obey *him*.

But that meant answering some of the lingering questions he had about her.

He heard a soft tap at his library door. He waited, drawing out the moment before allowing her entry. Finally he folded his arms across his chest and called, "Come in."

The door opened, and he bit back his gasp at her beauty. After six weeks of sharing the same household, he ought to have accustomed himself to her extraordinary looks.

He had not.

What was it about her that drew him so? Was it the beautiful dress she wore or the delightful way it emphasized the sway of her hips? Was it the enthusiastic snap of her temper or the soft melt of femininity when he kissed her? Or perhaps it was the way her lips curved into a mischievous smile that could at any moment become an angry scowl or a wholehearted grin. Nothing about Amanda was halfhearted. She felt and reacted with her whole being, and he always admired such courage. He could never expose himself so easily—not only to the reactions of a cynical world, but to the joys and pains that came of feeling those emotions so strongly.

Amanda was one of the most courageous people he knew, merely because she allowed herself the freedom to be who she was—completely, wholeheartedly, and without reservation.

And now it was his job as guardian to rein in the very temperament he so admired.

Stephen sighed and waved her to a chair. "Good morning, Amanda. I trust you are feeling better after your ordeal?"

Her rosy cheeks lifted as she smiled at him. "It was not such a horrendous thing, you know." She settled into the chair and tilted her head to give him a look filled with deviltry. "I would have managed much better, you know, if you taught me to hit properly."

He raised his left eyebrow, giving her a look that made her flush prettily. "I trust I do not need to express my opinion on brawling again."

She sighed and folded her hands in her lap. "No, you need not. But you cannot blame me for trying one last time."

"I can blame you, and I do," he said without heat, and as expected, she merely shrugged off his reprimand as another step in the elaborate dance the two of them went through on such regular occasion. He sighed and folded his hands before him, turning his steady gaze on her sweet face. "Amanda, I have asked you here to answer a question that has plagued me since your abduction two days ago."

She looked down, no doubt guessing what was on his mind.

"I promise to try to remain calm and understand your reasons, but I will have an honest answer." He paused, making sure she understood he was prepared to be reasonable. Lord knew threats and scolding had no discernable effect on her. "Amanda, why did you climb down the trellis again?"

"At least I brought my shoes this time." She glanced at him, her smile inviting him to share her humor.

He did not.

"You were nearly killed." He abruptly pushed out of his chair, the fear freezing his breath once again. "Do you have any idea what could have happened to you? What *was* happening?"

"Yes, Stephen, I do know." Her voice was low and contrite. "And even if I was not completely aware, Tom was quite vocal on the subject before he left." He turned to look at her, seeing the silent shadow of fear cloud her eyes. Then she blinked, and it was gone as she smiled at him. "And thank you, my lord, for taking care of all those children. I know it was not an easy thing to do."

Stephen returned to his chair, feeling slightly awkward. He was well aware most of the ton thought him mad or criminally licentious, but when he had seen the look on Tom's face upon learning the plan, he knew it was the right thing to do. "They all will have plenty to do on the Shropshire estate. And between Tom, my steward Wheedon, and that dragon of a housekeeper, they should do fine."

She nodded, her gaze drifting downward. "Can we visit them soon? I . . . I miss Tom." He caught the note of loneliness in her voice and realized he, too, felt the same longing to see the young scamp. He shook his head, amazed at himself. The boy had been gone for only three hours.

"I think something can be arranged."

"Oh, good!" She jumped up, her face glowing with delight, and as she made for the doorway, he suddenly realized she had distracted from his original purpose.

"Amanda."

She froze halfway to the door.

"Please sit down."

She obeyed meekly.

"You have not answered my question." She tried an innocent expression, but he forestalled her with one steely look. "Why did you climb out your window?"

He could tell she did not want to tell him. She was no doubt searching for some other distraction. He waited in silence, letting her know his determination to find an answer. Eventually he heard her soft sigh, and knew she finally gave in.

"I wished to speak with Tom. Privately."

"You mean without my knowing."

She nodded.

"Why?"

She looked up, her expression defiant. "I do not wish to tell you."

"Why?"

"Because you would not understand."

"Why?"

"Because you would not."

They were going in circles, and he was surprised by a flash of pain. This was the type of conversation they had had when she first arrived. "Amanda," he said softly. "I thought you trusted me more. I—"

"I wanted Tom to post a letter for me. It was money for a doctor to visit an elderly retainer on the Wyndham estate."

It took a moment to absorb her meaning. When it did, he could only gape at her. A letter? To a doctor? A letter so important she had to crawl out of her bedroom in the middle of the night? "Could you not simply wait until the morning? I would have happily franked it for you."

She shoved out of her seat, pacing before in him an agitated swirl of muslin skirts. "But it is not for you to frank!"

"Of course it is!" he said, losing his grip on his temper. "I am your guardian!" He stopped himself, running his hand through his hair as he tried to comprehend the most confusing woman he had ever met. "Where is the letter? I will send it posthaste."

"I already sent it. Tom took it the next morning."

He glared at her. Lord only knew how she got it to Tom while bedridden. "Amanda, you would try the patience of a saint."

She shook her head, her hands clenched into fists. "No, my lord, I try your patience."

"I never claimed—"

But she was not listening to him, too intent on her own thoughts. "I know what you think of me. How you despise my common ways, but the woman is . . ." She stopped herself, taking a deep, shaky breath as she fought for control. He watched her close her eyes to concentrate her effort, and for the first time he realized her descent out her window was not a lark or even a secret assignation, as he'd feared. It was something much, much more important to her.

"The woman is . . ." he prompted.

She turned to him, her eyes glittering with unshed tears. "Mary Ames was a mother to me. She cared for me when it would have been a good deal easier for her to just throw me away. Now she is ill, so I wanted to send a doctor to her."

He did not miss her odd phrasing. How could a servant throw away the young miss of the manor? But his attention was too focused on her thoughts about him to ask about another odd reference to her childhood.

He stood slowly and moved out from behind his desk, wanting to touch her, to soothe her sudden agitation. But all he could do was throw more questions at her. "Why would I not understand that?"

She rounded on him, her eyes flashing brilliantly in the afternoon sunshine. "I see the way you watch me when I speak with the servants. You do not approve. You want me to treat them the way Lady Sophia does, as if they existed solely to meet my whims. It is just one more proof to you that I shall never be a lady!"

He shook his head, trying to get her to perceive the truth. "I do not despise you for that, Amanda. I envy you! Can you not see? Since the moment you arrived in London, you have turned this whole household upside down. You have given my mother the vapors; you have me tearing my hair out in fear or shock or amazement, and you have completely unsettled the entire staff. And yet . . ." He took a deep breath. "And yet they adore you. Even my mother adores you. They will do anything for you. My mother is planning your wedding to nothing short of a duke. I watch you, and I am amazed. I do not understand how you do it, but you have completely captivated the entire household."

She stared at him, her eyes impossibly large in her face, her expression tragic, as though her whole life rested on the next moment.

"And you, Stephen, do you adore me, too?"

"I . . ." What could he say? Rather than sort through the sudden surge of conflicting emotions assaulting his thoughts, he concentrated on the one thing he was sure of. "I worry about you. I am your guardian, and yet I cannot keep you safe even in my own home."

It did not take a genius to see his words were the wrong choice. Where before she looked vulnerable, open, even hopeful, now she looked away, her face as closed as the library door, her eyes equally blank.

"Amanda—" he began.

"I am not a lady, my lord, and I do not think any number of lists will change that. Perhaps I should have realized it earlier, but I failed to, and now we are stuck with it." She lifted her chin. "Will you banish me back to York?"

He sighed, feeling completely at a loss, dumbfounded by how thoroughly he had botched this interview. "No, Amanda, you are not to be banished. But I will take a brief trip to Wyndham Manor tomorrow. You are welcome to join me." He glanced up, suddenly hoping beyond hope she would choose to accompany him. "You could visit Mrs. Ames and make sure she is properly cared for."

"You are going to Wyndham Manor?" Her voice was a tremulous whisper, and he watched in alarm as her face drained of all color.

"Yes," he said carefully. "I intended to leave two days ago, but your, um, escapade delayed me. I plan to depart in the morning."

"But . . . but why? Surely I can explain anything you need to know."

"It is past time I saw the estate, Amanda. Especially since . . ." He grimaced as he spoke. "Since you will no doubt be marrying soon and

258

the property will be part of your dowry."

"But surely it is not necessary. Not now, I mean, in the middle of the Season. Why not leave it for later?"

Stephen slowly walked back behind his desk, using the movement to buy time. She was clearly hiding something, searching for any excuse to keep him from York. But why? What secrets could be there that she did not want him to find?

He slowly looked up at her, his eyes narrowing as a seemingly inconsequential thought crossed his mind.

"Today is Sunday."

She blinked. "Yes."

"Today is Sunday, and yet you did not go to church."

She swallowed, her throat muscles constricting as she lifted her chin. "I was still resting from my ordeal."

"You are in perfect health." He patently ignored the ugly bruise on her temple for all that the sight still made his gut clench in horror. "You said it was nothing."

"Yes, but—"

"In fact, for the past two months you have never gone to church."

She straightened her body, as if defying him to challenge her, but he could not miss the panic in her eyes. "There is nothing odd about that. Many society ladies decline Sunday services. Especially since I love to dance until dawn the night before."

"Yes, but many society ladies have not had a religious conversion." He watched her closely, seeing not her upright carriage and defiant stance, but the way she twisted her fingers in her skirt and the darting shift of her eyes as she thought through her responses.

"I never said I had a conversion."

She was right. She had never actually said those words. He frantically scanned his memory, struggling to remember what exactly she had said that second night in his house. But instead of recalling that conversation, his mind ran to other conversations, other inconsistencies. He began with his strange discussion with Mr. Oltheten about Amanda and Gillian, touched on the night of her first ball when he found her clasping a maid's cap in her hands. Then his thoughts flashed through her unexpected compassion for the servants and unfortunates, her knowledge of medicines, and her willingness to maid herself, tend her own fires, and do all manner of things without thought— as though no one had ever waited on her before.

Then he lifted his gaze, finally focusing on her brilliantly rich auburn hair. What had Mr. Oltheten said? *Bitter, sickly little thing all encased in white. Looked like a shriveled-up mummy.* Looking at Amanda now, he saw something he had never noticed before. Even if she were wrapped in white and desperately ill, her hair would stand out. It was her crowning glory, a perfect complement for her flashing green eyes.

She would never look like a mummy. She was

too colorful a person, too bright a soul ever to fit that description.

"Tell me about your sister Gillian."

He heard her gasp, and the sound sent shock waves reverberating through his soul.

"Why?" she demanded, her voice almost shrill. "Why do you want to know about that worthless bitch?"

He raised his eyebrows, desperately fighting to gain a hold on his thoughts. "Strong words for your sister."

"Half sister. And if you want strong words, here are some more. She is a lying, scheming woman. You would despise her on sight, and you . . ." She took a steadying breath. "You would not even know why."

He could read the pain in her eyes, saw it lance through her expression as she fought a losing battle for control. She had never been like this, even in the midst of their most heated battles. Anguish seemed to beat at her before his very eyes. Yet she stood there, her chin raised in rebellion, as if she dared him and the universe to break beneath her exterior to the misery underneath.

She is Gillian.

The thought whispered through his consciousness with the force of a sledgehammer. He felt his jaw go slack as he stumbled to his desk. *Good God—*

He cut off his thought as ruthlessly as a surgeon cutting off a man's arm. It could not be true. It was not true.

He raised his tortured gaze to the woman before him, her face pale as she watched him, her eyes pulled wide with concern.

She is—

No! It was impossible.

It took all of his will to suppress his own mind, but somehow he pushed his own thoughts away. Then, for the first time in his life, Stephen looked straight at Amanda and gave her the cut direct.

He turned around.

He heard her gasp, knowing he had just hurt her, but he was ruthless. He turned his back on her, just as he turned his back on the answers in his mind. He closed his eyes as he closed out his thoughts, shutting away everything he wondered, everything he thought, because suddenly he did not want to know.

And more important, he did not want to probe the anguish tormenting the woman he loved.

He closed his mind to it all, blocking everything from his thoughts and his memory. "You may go now, Amanda," he said, his voice cold and implacable.

Then he reached for a bottle of brandy, trying to drown out the sound of her footsteps as she fled his hardened heart.

Chapter Thirteen

A lady is always in control.

He knew.

Gillian flew up the stairs, her blood pounding out that single refrain.

He knows!

He knew the truth about her birth. He knew she was a bastard, a liar, and a fraud. He knew, and he despised her for it.

She had to leave. She had to escape this house, run from the hatred and disgust in his eyes. Run and never come back.

Gillian had her cap and her few meager possessions packed in a valise and was opening her bedroom window when the truth struck her.

She had nowhere to go.

She had thought to run to Tom and beg his

help to get her out of London. But Tom was gone to Shropshire, and all her money had been sent to the doctor. She thought about Geoffrey. Perhaps she could run to him, but he would want an explanation she could not afford to give him.

Gillian stepped back from the window and collapsed on her bed.

There was nowhere for her to go.

She pulled her knees up to her chin and closed her eyes. She needed to think. She had to be calm and rational and sort through her options.

First the facts. Stephen knew the truth. She could not stop a soft whimper at the thought. When he had turned his back on her, she felt as though he had cut out her heart. He had been angry with her before, but now he disdained her. Now he could not even look at her.

The tears ran freely down her cheeks, splashing across her knees.

He despised her.

Gillian grabbed a pillow and pressed her face into it. It felt cool against her skin—soft and somehow comforting. She curled around it and let the sobs come.

There were no more thoughts of her future, no more plans or facts or options. She could not get past the truth, could not see beyond the knowledge that he despised her and, moreover, that he had every right to.

She was a liar, the scheming bitch Amanda

always accused her of being. The pain she felt now was no more than her due.

All too soon she would hear the countess's outraged shouts, the horrified gasps of the servants. Even Greely's aplomb would not be proof against the news of her perfidy.

Then they would all storm her door, screaming at her to quit the premises, spitting their hatred at her. She would be tossed penniless onto the street, her marriage to Geoffrey impossible, Tom's help beyond reach, and the servants' friendship hopelessly destroyed.

Yet it would not matter. Nothing could matter more than the sight of Stephen turning his broad back on her.

Gillian fell into a fresh bout of silent tears, her body shaking against the pillow, her soul buried in misery.

What would she do?

She did not know how long she lay there, sobs racking her body. Eventually her eyes dried, and slowly she began to sense other things. She felt her muscles protest her contorted position on the bed, she smelled the heartening scent of fresh-baked bread, and heard the birds chirp merrily in the tree outside her window.

She did not hear the angry mutters of betrayed friendships.

Gillian lifted her aching head, then slowly uncurled her clenched body until she could sit up. Her dress was hopelessly crumpled, her face felt as if it were scrubbed raw, but nowhere did she hear the heavy tread of people come to throw her out onto the street.

What was happening? Why was she still here?

She stared at her closed door and willed it to open. And to her benumbed mind, it appeared to do just that. The latch turned and the heavy wood fell backward to reveal the shocked gaze of the countess.

"Sweet heaven, there you are. I could not credit it when Hawkings said you were not prepared for the Quinleys' rout, but here you are, and looking quite a fright, I might add."

Gillian could not think of a thing to say. She had expected angry accusations, hurt remonstrances, anything but this scolding for not being prepared for some ball!

"But—"

"Have you and Stephen fought again?" The countess sighed as she swept into Gillian's room. The woman looked stunning as always, this time in a silk ball gown of deepest sapphire. "Two months ago I would not have credited anyone could argue as much as I and my sweet Jonathan fought in our first year. But here you two are, at loggerheads again." She wrung out a cloth in the washbasin. "Has he banished you to Yorkshire again?"

Gillian blinked, then flinched as the countess pressed the wet cloth against her puffy eyelids. "I . . . I assume so."

"Well, do not assume. He has not said a word to me, so clearly he regrets his hasty actions."

Gillian pushed the soothing cloth away from

her eyes, coming to an abrupt decision. She could not live with the lies any longer. "I sincerely doubt it. In fact, my lady, I have—"

"Of course, he does."

"—something urgent to tell you."

"Why else would he run off to his club?"

Gillian paused. "Stephen has gone to his club?"

"Nearly two hours ago. Just between you and me, I think he feels guilty about how shabbily he treats you."

"Me?" Gillian squeaked.

"Oh, yes. He has not escorted us anywhere in nearly two weeks."

"But Lady Sophia—"

"It is bad enough that he treats me so, his own mother, but you . . . why, you are his ward, his responsibility."

Gillian took a deep breath. "Countess, please, I have something to confess. I am not—" Suddenly her face was buried under the suffocating press of the cold, wet cloth.

"Hush. We must get you looking right for tonight's ball. If Stephen wants to hide himself away in his club, then that is how men deal with the world. It is we ladies who must carry on. And right now, that means you are to look your best for tonight's rout."

"But—"

"Hawkings!" Gillian flinched at the countess's strident tone. "Come in here at once! We have much to do."

"But—"

"Shhh. Hawkings will know just what to do to set you in your best looks."

From beneath the wet compress, Gillian sighed. She could not see the door open and close, but she heard the rustle of silk as Hawkings removed Gillian's best ball gown from the wardrobe. It seemed despite everything, she was doomed to continue her farce. The countess would not allow her to speak, even if it were to announce her engagement to the crown prince himself. And she could not just blurt out the truth, especially not with Hawkings right in the room.

"Now listen to me, Amanda," continued the countess firmly. "Men think they know everything, and believe me, they certainly have their place. But do not make the mistake of thinking they run the world. It is simply a clever ruse we women allow them. It keeps them busy so they do not notice the important things."

"But—"

"Hush, girl. I am talking now."

Gillian sighed. "Yes, my lady."

"Stephen is a wonderful boy, and I adore him to distraction, but he always has been a bit stiff in his thinking. Whatever you have argued about will wash away soon enough. What is important now is that you are going to a ball tonight, you will be courted and feted and danced with until you drop with weariness. Then, in the end, you will make a brilliant match."

"But—" Gillian cut off her objection as Stephen's mother stripped away the now tepid cloth. "My lady," she began, "I simply must—"

"Amanda," the countess said as she loomed above Gillian in all her regal disdain. "*I* say you will attend the ball, and attend you will. *I* say you will make a brilliant match, and never doubt that you will. Do you understand, *Amanda? I* have said it."

Gillian nodded weakly. What else could she do?

For whatever perverse reason of his own, Stephen did not expose her fraud. Gillian did not understand it. She merely marked the time, watching as he remained absent from his own home, returning in the small hours of the morning only to leave each morning as soon as he was dressed.

She would lie in bed and hear his heavy tread as he passed by her door. Once, she heard him stop just outside, as if he wished to open the door and speak with her. She lay stiff in her bed, her breath caught in her chest, waiting for his decision. Then he passed on, and she was once again caged in her strange existence.

She went to parties, danced and laughed as usual, and pretended to a gaiety she did not feel. And every moment of each day, she waited to be exposed. She imagined every knock on her door to be Stephen, come to throw her from his life. She heard every whisper as the first rumblings of shock at her perfidy.

Yet all she could do was wait. Geoffrey remained away on estate business. Stephen did not leave for York. And the countess seemed obsessed with making Amanda a stellar success.

There was nothing to do but wait.

Stephen glared bleary-eyed across the dim, fetid air of the gaming hell. He searched for another victim, but unfortunately, no one appeared interested in being ruthlessly stripped of their money.

He growled something incoherent and reached for another glass of brandy.

Someone approached, so he looked up and grinned, gesturing with lazy movements at the chair across the table from him.

"Piquet, gentlemen?" he asked lazily.

The two dandies paled, shook their heads, then hastily retreated. Stephen took solace back in his glass. He had heard the rumors, saw the speculative glances. Mavenford was mad, they said. His humor was sadly out, due to an old war wound, and he was drinking and carousing himself in a futile effort to correct it, they whispered. Or better yet, two of his many mistresses were feuding over his illegitimate children, and he would rather bury himself in brandy than face them.

No one knew the truth. Not even Stephen.

All he remembered was that he was angry, more so than ever before in his life. And when he sobered up enough to almost remember who had made him so very furious, he crawled back into his bottle.

But all through his self-destructive drinking,

he knew the end approached. He could feel the tension coiling inside him like a spring wound tighter and tighter. He would soon snap, and God help the poor soul upon whom he finally unleashed his temper.

Especially if it was her.

But for now, he took another drink.

Geoffrey Rathburn, Lord Tallis, checked his pocket watch before mounting the front steps to the Earl of Mavenford's fashionable residence. He barely glanced at the house. He had seen it many times before, but even so, something within him registered the stately, aristocratic elegance of the building. It was the home of a family that had been rich and titled for generations.

It was hard not to envy it.

So he distracted himself by glancing at his pocket watch one last time. He had returned to town just this morning after completing the final accounting of his inheritance, if one could call it that. His father's debts were staggering, but with a good steward and some creative bookkeeping, he knew his situation was acceptable. It would take a determined effort for Stephen to discover Geoffrey's true financial status.

By that time, he and Amanda would be safely wed, her dowry giving his estates a much-needed boost.

Now all that remained was Stephen's official approval of the match. So immediately upon his return this morning, he sent around a message requesting an audience with the Earl of Mavenford and a later drive with Amanda. Hopefully all would go quickly, and by this evening Amanda could begin plans for their wedding.

His earlier intention to wait until after Sophia's engagement was discarded the moment he saw the ledgers. He could not wait any longer for his sister to bring Stephen up to scratch.

Geoffrey sauntered up the steps and pulled the bell cord, moving smoothly inside after the door slid ponderously open before him. "Good afternoon, Greely."

"Good afternoon, Lord Tallis," responded the stiff butler with an excruciatingly correct bow. "I am afraid Miss Wyndham is not here at present, but if you would be so kind as to wait in the front parlor, I am sure she shall be along directly."

Geoffrey frowned. Greely never confused appointments, especially those made in advance. "Actually I had an appointment with the earl."

The butler was well trained. He only blinked, pausing a fraction of a second before speaking. "Very well, my lord. I shall see if the earl is in."

Geoffrey nodded, watching the stately Greely closely. There was something decidedly odd about his behavior, something out of the ordinary, but quickly covered. But there was no time for questions as Greely stepped silently down the hall.

As Geoffrey waited, he let his eyes rove along the entranceway, missing nothing. In addition to the luster of well-tended furniture and the rich gleam of mahogany and oak, all brilliantly carved, he noted the pile of cards awaiting Amanda's return, the stack of nosegays and other flowers dotting every flat surface, and the number of invitations awaiting her attention. He expected as much, but it was nevertheless startlingly annoying to see how very popular Amanda had become.

It was good that he had secured her promise early.

As if on cue, Greely returned, gesturing to the open library door. "His lordship will see you now." Somewhere in the butler's formal tones, Geoffrey detected a hint of disapproval, and he instinctively bristled. His lineage was every bit as august as the earl's, if not quite as well feathered. How dare—

His thoughts were abruptly cut off as he entered the library. With a start of surprise, he detected the faint odor of brandy, saw the lurking shadows of a darkened room, and realized the butler's disapproval was not for him, but for the earl.

Geoffrey found Stephen immediately. The man looked immaculate as always, but his slumped posture, glittering eyes, and the disheveled mat of his hair told him the earl nursed more than his brandy. He looked like a man nursing a grudge.

This little interview would be a great deal more delicate than Geoffrey had originally anticipated.

Best get to it then. Geoffrey squared his shoulders as for battle. "Hello, Stephen," he said, gliding to a chair opposite the desk.

"Geoffrey." The earl's voice was low. Not slurred, just low. And cold.

Not an auspicious beginning. Geoffrey shifted uncomfortably in his seat. "Perhaps this should wait for another time," he offered.

"You have come about Amanda."

Geoffrey raised his eyes, wondering what had changed the usually urbane Earl of Mavenford into the cuttingly rude man before him. "Never one for subtlety, were you?" he drawled, relaxing into his chair even as his attention sharpened.

The silence stretched between them as they sized each other up. Geoffrey was the first to break, mindful of his upcoming appointment with Amanda. "Yes, Stephen, I wish to talk about her. She and I have an understanding."

"You want to marry her." The earl spoke as if Geoffrey wanted to do something loathsome with his innocent ward, and for the first time in many years, Geoffrey felt a shiver of self-doubt slide down his spine.

Not trusting his voice, Geoffrey decided to remain silent, his gaze locked with Mavenford's. Stephen obviously had his own agenda and timing. Geoffrey would gain nothing by trying to push it.

Suddenly Stephen pulled out a pristine piece of linen paper from his desk. On its face, Geoffrey saw a list, the handwriting marching down the page like tiny soldiers.

"I have some questions."

Geoffrey nodded. He expected something of this sort.

"If you answer them appropriately, then you will be allowed to . . . to further your understanding with my ward."

Geoffrey nodded again, his confidence returning as he found himself in more familiar territory. He knew his lineage was more than acceptable, his education stellar, and his financial standing, if perhaps his weakest point, would no doubt be overcome by his good breeding.

He was ready.

"First, how do you feel about ladies brawling?"

"I beg your pardon?" He could not have been more shocked if the countess had chosen to appear before them in her nightclothes.

"How do you feel about ladies brawling?" Stephen repeated in stentorian tones.

"Of course I do not approve of it," he snapped, wondering if the earl had taken leave of his senses.

"Would you teach a lady to brawl if she asked you?"

"Of course not!"

"What if she insisted it would protect her from cutthroats and thieves?"

"I would tell her she was wrong."

The earl's face twisted into a derisive smile.

"And if she went out barefoot just to prove you wrong?"

Geoffrey's thoughts whirled as he tried to make sense of this bizarre situation. His gaze went first to the bottle of brandy by Stephen's right elbow. It was nearly full, an untouched glass sitting directly beside it. If Mavenford was foxed, it was from a different source.

"Next question. How do you feel about said cutthroats as your personal servants?"

Geoffrey slowly uncurled from his chair. "Clearly, Stephen, you are not in the mood to discuss—"

"Sit down!"

Geoffrey stood, barely able to keep his temper in check. "I do not appreciate being the butt of some ridiculous joke or wager, Stephen—"

"Wagering! That is question number seventeen. We will get to it in due time."

"I doubt it."

Stephen looked up, his eyes coldly intimidating. "We will if you wish to marry my ward."

Geoffrey waited a moment, weighing his options. He had none. As Amanda's guardian, Stephen had the right to demand trial by fire, if he wanted. And given Mavenford's strange mood, Geoffrey half expected Greely to be heating some coals at this very moment.

"Next question," continued Stephen. "Are your locks proof against burglars?"

"I am sure Lord Tallis's locks are adequate to their purpose."

Geoffrey spun around as Amanda's low tones

cut through the still air. She stood in the doorway of the library, the sun splashing on her white gown, highlighting the tiny embroidered rosebuds on the dress until they looked like bright spots of blood.

"You did not knock."

Geoffrey did not think it possible, but Stephen's voice grew colder, and Geoffrey was stunned by the dark fury seething beneath his words.

"The door was open, my lord, as you no doubt intended."

"Last question for now, Tallis." Geoffrey glanced back at the earl, but saw the question was really intended for Amanda. "How do you feel about bastards?"

Geoffrey heard Amanda's horrified gasp and was not surprised to see her face drain to the color of parchment. Instinctively he shifted his weight, intending to go to her assistance, but she waved him away, quickly regaining her composure, if not her color.

"I see now why you were waiting, my lord," she said, stepping carefully into the room. "It appears you merely looked for the most humiliating moment to expose me."

Stephen pushed out of his chair, his eyes glittering with a black anger. "I was not waiting for anything, *Amanda*." He practically sneered her name. "And if you want to talk about humiliation, perhaps we should discuss my mother, who is upstairs right now planning your come-out ball, or the nosegays and cards from dukes out in the vestibule. Or maybe you would like to discuss this latest bill from the milliner for your court gown?" He waved a piece of paper in the air, but Amanda did not even look at it.

She was too busy being shoved aside by another person elbowing his way into the room from the side parlor.

"Do not feel ashamed, my lord," said the man who apparently had been waiting in hiding to spring upon Amanda. "Many are the souls who have been seduced by this lowborn witch."

Geoffrey heard Amanda gasp as everyone watched a rail-thin cleric swagger into the room. Geoffrey disliked the man on sight, starting with his fashionable haircut and ending with his austere ministerial clothing. But what most set his teeth on edge was the man's condescending smile and the lascivious gleam in his eyes as he took in every detail of Amanda's body.

"Reverend Hallowsby," Amanda said, her voice filled with contempt. "Come to create more sinners to punish?"

"Good afternoon, Gillian," the cleric returned, his attitude becoming even more derisive. "I have come to tell you of your mother's death. Four weeks ago."

Amanda swayed suddenly, and Geoffrey sprang forward, gently guiding her into a seat while the loathsome cleric continued mercilessly.

"Yes, I am afraid she died in sin, *Gillian*, neither repenting her base alliance with the late baron nor revealing your treachery." He stepped forward, using his superior height to look down his pointy nose at the pale girl beneath him. "How you managed to seduce the good Mrs. Hobbs to your cause, I shall never understand, but at least the doctor was able to give me your address."

Amanda—or was it Gillian?—glanced up, her eyes bright green emeralds in her wan face. "The doctor—"

"Arrived laughably late, as the patient was already buried. Beside your gravestone, I might add, tossed there on unhallowed ground. It makes me regret that I refused to bury you, Gillian, for the thought of the true Amanda lying in that place insults the soul of all good Christians."

Geoffrey reeled, fighting to absorb the information. Gillian had buried Amanda and put her own name on the gravestone?

"But at least the doctor could give me your address," continued the man, his words as relentless as they were cruel. "I, of course, suspected the heinous truth right away. I came straight to London to inform my lord of the unholy witch he bore in his midst." He turned to nod at Stephen, who looked to be carved in stone, his knuckles white, his emotions buried too deep to read.

"I feel it incumbent upon me to mention," the cleric continued, "that it was your sinful behavior, Gillian, that placed the final strain on your mother's failing health."

Beneath his fingertips, Geoffrey felt Amanda

tremble, as if her body physically could not bear the news and tried to shake it off. For his part, Geoffrey felt at sea, his mind reeling from the sudden knowledge of Amanda's—no, Gillian's—true heritage. He, of course, knew of Amanda's half sister. But could this be the girl? A by-blow passing herself off as legitimate?

Good lord, could it be true?

He looked down at the girl, trembling but stoic in the midst of her ruin, and knew it must be so. Still, he could not stop feeling some admiration for what she had done. It was bold and courageous, and a real joke on the haut ton.

He found himself liking her all the more.

Too bad he would not be able to marry her. Although in desperate need of an heiress, he knew what was due his family name.

Geoffrey sighed. *Too bad.*

Unless . . .

Geoffrey eyed Stephen. Mavenford was a man born to a wealth prudently, even brilliantly managed. He could not begin to understand to what depths desperation could drive a man or woman. Stephen stood there, behind his desk, the picture of betrayed trust, his compassion buried beneath generations of aristocratic duty and moral fortitude. But all that refinement had its weakness. The threat of a juicy scandal would cover a multitude of sins.

Geoffrey knew he could convince Mavenford.

The overweening cleric, however, was a different story. He would need to be eliminated somehow. The man was still droning on and on, detailing a whole catalog of Gillian's sins. It would be a pleasure to silence the bastard.

But before Geoffrey could think of a suitable method, Stephen managed it for him. The earl was curt and to the point, effectively shocking the cleric with his coldly delivered threat.

"Get out."

The reverend sputtered to a stop midword. "I beg your pardon, my lord?"

"I said get out of my house. In fact, get out of England."

"But—"

"If I ever—*ever*—hear one word of these accusations, I will hunt you down and kill you. I am a very rich and powerful man, Hallowsby. Do not test me on this, for I will do it."

The man stared at his would-be benefactor and sputtered, "But . . . but . . . but she is a bastard."

Beneath his fingertips, Geoffrey felt Gillian stiffen, but it could not compare to the earl's reaction. Without so much as a blink, he leaned down and retrieved something from his lower desk drawer. Lifting it up, he calmly loaded and cocked a pistol, then aimed it straight at the cleric's head.

"Was that your excuse for punishing her? Do you think her birth gives you the right?"

"It *does* give me the right!" exploded the man with holy zeal. "Every good Christian has the right to be repulsed by this witch, to be horrified and to exact God's vengeance!"

Bang! The gun discharged, blowing a melon-sized hole in the wood barely inches from the cleric's head.

"I said, get out."

Hallowsby literally shook in his boots. It took only a split-second's thought before the reverend grabbed his hat and ran for the door.

"Greely!" Mavenford barked. "Have two armed footmen follow him. Be sure some press gang finds him. He must leave England by tomorrow night."

The butler's pale but impassive face appeared just beside the smoking paneling. "Yes, my lord," he said, and then he quietly withdrew, closing the door silently behind him, only to appear at rigid attention in front of the gaping hole in the wall.

Geoffrey took a deep breath. It was time for him to enter the fray with his own agenda. "My goodness, Stephen," he drawled. "I did not know you possessed such a flair for the dramatic."

But Stephen was not attending. Instead the earl turned his fathomless eyes on Gillian, his gaze holding the look of a man in hell.

"I am sorry about your mother," he said, his voice hoarse with suppressed emotion.

Gillian did not respond, too lost in her own misery.

"Hallowsby will not bother you anymore. He will not bother anyone." Then he paused, as if searching for something to say. "I will supply you with whatever you need: money, transportation, whatever you wish to start a new life."

"What you will supply, Stephen," cut in Geoffrey coolly, "is her dowry and a promise to keep her true identity a secret."

Stephen's reaction was all Geoffrey could wish. The man literally gaped at him. "What?"

"As I tried to explain earlier, *Amanda* and I have an understanding. I intend to stick to that understanding, provided, of course, a suitable incentive on your part and your promise not to reveal"—he glanced at the gaping hole in the wall—"this entire wretched incident."

Stephen glared at him, and Geoffrey raised a mocking eyebrow, his expression designed to show the earl he was quite comfortable with the situation. Provided, of course, he received his stipulations.

For a long minute, there was not a sound except for the ponderous ticking of the clock. Even Gillian appeared to stop breathing.

Abruptly Stephen relaxed. He settled down in his chair with a wary look. Then suddenly Gillian turned to look at him, her eyes wide with confusion.

"Why, Geoffrey? Why would you still want to marry me?"

He looked down, pleased to see she had stopped shaking. "Because," he said softly, "ours was always a business arrangement. Your true heritage changes nothing. In fact, it doubles your dowry." He glanced at Stephen to make sure the man understood his price. Then he looked back at Gillian, casually caressing her beautiful cheek. "I still believe we will deal well together. I am sure you will work extra hard now to always appear a lady."

She swallowed. "Y-yes, of course."

"We can be married tomorrow morning by special license. No one need know the truth." He felt his smile grow as he looked back at Stephen. "Neither my mother nor yours need ever know."

"But," interjected Gillian, "what if the truth does come out?"

Geoffrey sobered, knowing he must tell her the truth. "Then I will be forced to annul our arrangement. I will not want to," he said softly, "but I have certain obligations to my family. I will, of course, see that you are well provided for."

She nodded. "I understand."

"But I would not worry," he added as gently as possible. "I doubt the cleric will talk after Stephen's little display." The smells of gunpowder and burning wood were still heavy in the room.

"No, I doubt he will," she agreed. Her eyes focused not on him, but on Stephen as she spoke, her voice growing more determined with each word. "Indeed, I can see you are most generous, my lord." She turned to face Geoffrey directly. "I accept your proposal, Lord Tallis. Now, if you will excuse me, I have a good deal of packing to do while you gentlemen arrange the details."

She nodded to both him and Stephen, then quit the room. Watching her regal retreat, Geoffrey smiled, knowing she would make him an excellent countess.

Yes, he decided with a satisfied smile, this was indeed a good bargain for all around. And with that thought, he turned toward Mavenford, prepared to negotiate in the full knowledge that he had the upper hand.

Chapter Fourteen

A lady is never in haste.

Her mother was dead. For the last month her mother had been dead and buried, and she had not known, had not been with the dear lady when it happened, had not even been nearby. Gillian had been in London wearing rich clothes and going to parties.

And now her mother was dead.

She swallowed, catching a harsh sob in her throat, and she bit her lip to keep back the tears. Still, the grief threatened to overwhelm her, surrounding her in a hazy cloud of pain that washed the world in gray.

"Amanda?"

Gillian blinked at her future husband, sitting across from her in his traveling coach. They were going to his family seat in the Cotswolds, where they would be married in the morning by special license.

In less than twelve hours she would be Lady Tallis.

"Do you want to delay the wedding?"

Gillian shook her head. She had set upon her masquerade as a way to save her mother. By all rights, with her mother gone, she need not marry. Her own requirements were few, and she had the whole world to choose from.

Except that her mother's one wish was for her daughter's happiness. Although Gillian could not quite predict whether her marriage to Geoffrey would bring her joy, she was certain it would bring a measure of security. And for Gillian, security was as close to happiness as she was likely to find.

It did not matter that it was Amanda's security and Amanda's marriage, she told herself. Whatever remained of Gillian had died with her mother. She was Amanda Faith Wyndham now, and soon she would be Lady Tallis. She would have fine clothes, food, and a place in society— at least as long as her true lineage remained secret.

That was enough. She did not need to be herself.

"There is no need to delay, Geoffrey. Mother would have wanted this for me."

He nodded, his expression pensive, his eyes amazingly astute. "Do you love him so very much?" he asked softly.

She did not ask to whom he referred. Stephen had never left her thoughts since he had turned his back on her nearly a week ago. And Geoffrey, with his dark gray eyes that missed nothing, would be sure to understand that she grieved as much for losing Stephen as she did over losing her mother.

Did she still love him? After everything that happened?

"No," she lied. Then her gaze slid away from Geoffrey to watch the evening glow fade into night. "And even if I did, he despises me now. The upright Earl of Mavenford could not countenance marriage to a by-blow, much less a liar and a fraud." She tried to keep the bitterness from her voice, but it crept in despite her efforts.

Then she felt Geoffrey's hand on hers. "We will proceed slowly, Amanda. Accustom ourselves to one another. In time I am sure we can come to some arrangement."

"Thank you," she whispered, grateful for his understanding. It would be a relief, after all that happened, to take a moment to rest before facing the obligations of marriage.

"It will all work out for the best, Amanda."

She turned to him, her question spilling from her lips even while she wondered why it was so important to her. "Could you not call me Gillian? Just when we are alone?"

His answer was softly spoken, but clear in the evening gloom. "I do not think it wise, Amanda. Someone might overhear. And besides, you must learn to accept your new identity. You are Amanda Wyndham now. All traces of . . . of the other person must be erased from your heart and soul."

"I understand." And she did. But she could not help feeling that in becoming Amanda, the best of Gillian had disappeared. If Gillian were gone, who would remember Mary Ames? Who would put flowers on a poor maid's grave? What would she say to her children about their grandmother? She could not speak of the sweet woman who sang nonsense rhymes by the fire to distract her daughter from an empty stomach. She could not tell them about a woman who lived with such simple wisdom.

Amanda did not know about these things, but Gillian did. And Gillian did not want to forget.

Stephen could not forget. He threw his empty bottle away in disgust while his head spun and his sight grew fuzzy.

She was gone.

Her small trunk had been loaded into the Tallis coach two hours ago, and then she'd followed. Her sweetly curving body and her tragic, pale face disappeared into the vehicle's dark interior with barely a backward glance. Then she and Tallis drove away.

She was gone.

The lying bitch. But his thoughts held no heat, no anger, only the aching emptiness of memories that haunted him despite the brandy. Would he ever forget the way her eyes had widened with too much innocence when she tried to fool him? Or the saucy sway of her hips when she laughed? Or the erotic press of her lips that brought such fire to his soul?

He groaned and reached for another bottle.

"Well, this is a sight to warm a mother's heart."

Stephen looked up, squinting past the brilliance of a single candle held close to his face.

"Mother," he said, his voice only slightly slurred. "Get that away from my eyes."

"You are foxed."

"Not nearly enough."

She peered at him, bringing the candle even closer; then abruptly she set it down, her disgust palpable in the fetid air. "Really, Stephen, I thought you were the sensible child."

Stephen shrugged his shoulders, stoically resigning himself to his mother's company. "I am sorry to disappoint you."

She sighed. "Well, you might at least offer me a glass."

He blinked at his mother in surprise. He could not remember the last time she had requested brandy. But at her impatient gesture, he poured her a glass, desperately struggling to keep from sloshing it over the side.

"What is this?" she asked, her voice cutting painfully into his concentration. The amber liquid spilled over the side.

"What is what?"

Cup-shot as he was, his reactions were slow.

He could not prevent his mother from grabbing a sheaf of paper from his desktop.

" 'Rules for a Lady,' " she read aloud. "I never did see the need for such folderol, but then I never did much understand the two of you."

Even drunk as he was, Stephen was strong enough to pull the page out of her grasp. It was the list from Amanda's—no, Gillian's—room. She'd left it behind, just as she'd left the delicate necklace and ear bobs he had given her. All three were folded neatly in her mobcap, tucked away at the back of her wardrobe.

Greely had said one of the maids found them while cleaning the room. Now the items sat on his desk, his last reminder of her. His mother was brutal as she casually inspected each piece, silently poking at each item while Stephen ground his teeth in frustration.

They were his, damn it, and he had no wish for anyone, much less his mother, probing wounds that had not begun to heal.

"Mother—"

"Greely tells me Gillian's mother died. How very wretched for her. I tried to express my condolences earlier, but I am afraid she was not attending."

Stephen blinked, frowning as he tried to sort through his mother's last words. Had she said Gillian? Impossible. His mother did not know Gillian's true name.

"I recall when my mother died," the countess continued as she reached for her brandy. "You were too young to remember, but I was stricken with grief. There is a special bond between mother and daughter that nothing can erase. I did not eat or sleep for days. All I could think was that I was alone in the world. I had a loving husband and three beautiful children, but I still felt so terribly, terribly lost." She glanced significantly at Stephen. "It is not the time to make important life decisions. One invariably makes the wrong choice."

Stephen shook his head. "Amanda's mother died years ago."

The countess set her glass down with an irritated click. "Well, what is that to the point? I was speaking of Gillian's mother. And that odious minister. I am so glad you dealt with him." She glanced pointedly at the hole in the wall. "I suppose you felt the, um, drama was necessary?"

Stephen stared at her in openmouthed shock. "*Gillian*'s mother died."

The countess folded her hands primly in her lap. "Why, yes. Did I not just say so?"

He gaped at her, trying to wade through his brandy-induced confusion to the truth. "How long have you known she is Gillian?"

"Why almost from the start! Stephen, you cannot think a baseborn serving girl could pretend to be a lady without my seeing the truth? I am not in my dotage, you know."

"But . . . but—"

"Good Lord, just because men are blind does not mean women cannot see these things. Why, there was nothing of my sister in her features whatsoever. And if that hair did not come from my brother-in-law, then it must have been the maid's."

"But . . . but—"

"Please, Stephen, try to clarify your thoughts."

Stephen took a deep breath, reached for his brandy, then pushed it away untouched. "Do you mean to tell me, Mother, you have known from the very beginning and yet you still pushed a . . . a—"

"Your uncle's by-blow," she supplied helpfully.

Stephen glared at her. "You mean you still outfitted her? And sponsored her Season?"

"Why, of course! Just because she was born on the wrong side of the blanket does not mean she is not family."

"But—"

"Really, Stephen, you are becoming quite tedious. Do you remember little Rebecca? The friend of the family I brought out when you were still in leading strings?"

He nodded, his thoughts stumbling back to a quiet little mouse of a girl, three years older than his oldest brother.

"She was your father's by-blow," the countess commented blithely. "Conceived before he and I ever met. My goodness, if I can bring out your half sister, then I certainly can do the same for Gillian."

Stephen gripped the edge of the desk as if it were an anchor holding him to reality while the rest of the universe spun out of control.

"Goodness, Stephen, I had no idea you were so correct. Surely you realize half the ton consists of bastards and by-blows pretending to a nonexistent heritage?"

"Half?" He gasped.

"Well"—she shrugged—"perhaps not half. At least two now."

Stephen pressed his fingers against his temples, trying to hold back the headache already throbbing behind his eyes. "Do you mean to say you knew about Gillian and did not tell me?"

"Well, I assumed you were more clever."

He let his hands fall onto the desk as he regarded the woman he thought he knew. "Mother—"

"The question now is, do you love her?"

"What?" He nearly roared the word, but his mother did not so much as blink.

"Come now. You cannot pretend this"—she waved at the empty brandy bottles—"is simply because she lied to you. I lie to you all the time, and you never go to these extremes."

Stephen stared at his mother, then abruptly closed off those thoughts. He did not want to know what she meant. He could only focus on one thing at a time. "Gillian committed a fraud. On all of society!"

"Yes, yes, we established that. I want to know if you truly love her."

Stephen felt as if his world were narrowing in on him, cutting off his air. He pushed out of his chair and went to the window, shoving it open until he felt the night air caress his heated skin. "She pretended to be my cousin."

"And you pretended to believe her."

Stephen tensed, unable to deny the truth. He had known. Perhaps not as soon as his mother, but he had realized Gillian's identity more than a week ago.

"She is illegitimate," he said through stiff lips. "I am an earl."

"Does that truly matter?"

Stephen was silent, considering. Of all his worries and thoughts, the difference in their birthrights was the least important of all.

"No," he finally said. "It does not signify." All his heart cared for was her smile, the open-hearted way she embraced the world, and most of all, the way he felt when they were together. She brought out the laughter within him, and a joy he never thought he could possess.

"Do you love her?" his mother pressed again.

That answer, at least, was painfully clear. "Yes."

"Then why let her marry another man?"

"I . . ." Why was he letting her go? he wondered. "Because she does not love me."

From somewhere behind him, his mother released a disgusted sniff. "Men! Stupid to the bone."

Stephen whirled around. "She wanted to marry him! He proposed, and she accepted right there in front of me."

The countess crossed her arms, staring at him just as she had the time he turned the front parlor into a battleground for his toy soldiers. "I already explained, Stephen. Two minutes after hearing of your mother's death is not the time to make life decisions."

"But—"

"Gillian will marry another man in less than ten hours. If that is what you want, then I bid you good night. But if that is not what you want, then I have already ordered the carriage brought 'round. Do you wish to take it or your stallion?"

Stephen stared at his mother as his world finally, irrevocably fell into an obvious order. He was in love with Gillian. He had, in fact, been in love with her from the first moment she had called him the most generous man in the world and then ordered him to hire Tom. He could not let her marry Geoffrey. Though a decent man, Tallis was nevertheless not the one for Gillian.

Tallis would probably teach her to brawl.

Suddenly he felt his world brighten as it expanded enough to admit a willful, disobedient, and thoroughly delightful by-blow. "My stallion, Mother."

The countess sighed as her stubborn son strode from the room. "Men," she said as she drained the last of her brandy. "Stupid to the bone, but at least you can kick them."

"I now pronounce you man and wife. You may kiss the bride."

Gillian trembled slightly as Geoffrey lifted her veil. His lips descended, and she felt the warm pressure of his mouth against hers. Then his lips were gone, and she was married.

Married.

She gave a tremulous smile to her new husband. Did he look the slightest bit pale? No, it was merely the difference in his coloring. He was fairer than Stephen.

Taking her arm, Geoffrey turned her to the small audience of servants and family gathered as witnesses. Except for Lady Sophia and his mother, they were all strangers to her. But she smiled at them nonetheless. After all, they were her family now.

"Come, Amanda. Cook has been slaving in the kitchen since before dawn. We cannot disappoint her."

"Of course." She did not think she could swallow a single bite, but knew she must find a way. She was the lady of the manor now, and she needed to be gracious.

The lady of the manor.

Lady Tallis.

She moved mechanically, her poise deserting her as she forced herself into the dining room. Geoffrey had barely seated her when they heard a crash at the front door. Beside her, she saw Geoffrey's spine stiffen as his eyes darted toward the vestibule.

What could it be?

But before she could voice her question, Geoffrey interrupted her.

"Look at me."

"What?" She still frowned at the hallway, trying to gaze past the other people who also twisted around to see the front door.

"I said, look at me!"

Gillian shifted her gaze.

"Kiss me."

She obediently tilted her head, and with startling speed, Geoffrey took possession of her lips. He was masterful in his touch, strong and demanding, but her thoughts were scattered, her mind numb from the events of the last few hours. She opened her mouth beneath his insistent pressure, but there was no heat in her motion, no thought other than simple compliance.

Then he broke it off, his expression incredibly sad. Then, when he spoke, the emotion echoed in his soft words. "Oh, Gillian, what have we done?"

She looked into his eyes, frowning as she saw regret, tenderness, and, most of all, the flat acceptance of a man resigned to his fate. She saw it, but she could not understand it.

Then all thoughts fled as a familiar bellow cut through the air.

"Tallis!"

Gillian spun around, scanning the room for Stephen. She had not thought to see him for months. Years, if she could manage it. Yet here he was, bursting into her new life, ruining everything even before it began.

Suddenly she felt anger burn through her soul. She pushed out of her chair with more animation than she had felt in the last twenty-four hours. She rounded on the dirty and disheveled man who shoved his way into the room, insisting on meddling in her life. "Stephen!" she said in a hiss. "How dare you burst in like this?"

Beside her, Geoffrey was more resigned in his greeting. "Mavenford. Fancy meeting you here."

Stephen looked exhausted and dirty, but his eyes betrayed an inner desperation, and Gillian stepped forward instinctively, only to be brought up short by her new husband as he grabbed her arm and pulled her back.

She glanced at Geoffrey, feeling her face heat with shame. "I am sorry," she stammered. Then she looked down at the floor while Geoffrey's hard voice cut through the tense air.

"I trust you have a reason for bursting into my house like this."

Gillian raised her gaze, unable to keep from looking at Stephen's chiseled features. A dull flush colored his cheeks as he cleared his throat. "Tallis," he said, though his eyes were trained on her, their blue depths dark with some intense emotion she did not dare label. "I, uh, I would like to speak with—"

"My wife?" interrupted Geoffrey as he lifted up Gillian's hand. There, glinting in the early morning light, was the elaborate Tallis ruby-and-gold wedding ring.

Stephen stopped, his gaze suddenly riveted on their hands. "Wife?" he echoed in a hoarse whisper. "You have already married?"

"Yes," Geoffrey answered, his pose casual as

he pulled Gillian into the circle of his arm. "Amanda and I were pronounced man and wife not more than ten minutes ago."

It was as though the life went out of him. Stephen's shoulders stooped, and his breath seemed to catch on the barest shudder. The sight hurt something inside Gillian, and despite her best intentions, she stepped forward again, needing to comfort him.

"Amanda!" Geoffrey's sharp voice broke through her abstraction, and she froze. She felt as if she were torn in two, pulled between the man she loved and the man to whom she had promised herself.

"I . . ." Her voice faded. What could she say? Then she looked at Stephen and all thoughts drained away at the sight of his anguished features.

Time seemed suspended as the three stood frozen in what could have been an Arthurian tapestry of love and betrayal. Then abruptly Geoffrey sighed, and again Gillian recognized his resignation. "It appears I must go speak with the minister," he drawled.

Gillian blinked, not understanding, but apparently Stephen did. His eyes slowly widened as he looked first at her, then her husband. She followed his motions, trying to fathom the undercurrents between the two men. Some secret message passed between them, and suddenly Stephen smiled.

"Thank you, Geoffrey," he said, his voice low and hushed. "I am forever in your debt."

"Yes, you are," returned her husband in an almost cheerful tone. Then he turned to her. "My dear, would you be so kind as to show our guest to his room? The first to the right at the top of the stairs."

Gillian turned in confusion. "But—"

"I am afraid I must speak to the minister."

"Surely your housekeeper—"

"Please, Gillian. It will take only a moment."

"Gill . . . ?" Had Geoffrey spoken her true name? She frowned in frustration. She did not wish to cause a scene in the middle of her wedding celebration, but she had the distinct feeling she had lost control of the significant events of her life. Stephen had taken over, and once again everyone danced to his tune. It was all so very odd, and yet there was absolutely nothing she could do about it.

So she sighed, giving in with as much grace as possible. She would escort Stephen to his room. Whatever needed to be said between her and her former guardian was best done up there. In private.

"Please, my lord," she said to Stephen with icy politeness, "follow me."

With as much hauteur as she could muster, Gillian stepped past the ogling servants and her silent in-laws and preceded Stephen up the stairs. Then, with deliberately abrupt movements, she shoved open his bedroom door and pointed inside.

"Your room, my lord."

Stephen grinned, suddenly looking more self-assured as he stepped inside and shook his head in mock horror. "I am sorry, Gillian. I fear this will not do."

"What?"

"Just come inside and look. There is no window, no trellis."

With a muttered curse, she stepped inside, only to spin around as he quickly shut the door behind her.

"Open that door," she ordered. "This is not proper."

She did not think his grin could grow, but it did indeed spread a little wider, giving him a boyish look that set his eyes dancing. "Ah, yes, the proprieties."

"Stephen—"

"You look beautiful in white, Gillian. Sometimes I cannot sleep at night just thinking of you surrounded by white satin, your hair tumbling free." He reached out to touch her, but she jerked away.

"I am a married woman now," she snapped, her heart nonetheless beating unaccountably fast at his passionate words. "You cannot treat me like a silly child, and you certainly cannot say those things barely ten minutes after my vows."

He eased his hand away from her face, but his eyes still held a longing that somehow called to her despite her anger. How could he be so handsome? Even disheveled, clearly exhausted, and coated with half the dust in England, he still had the power to make her heart ache with a hunger that could never be fulfilled.

Stop this! she ordered herself. She was married now, and she would not betray Geoffrey no matter how much she wanted to fly into Stephen's arms.

"You are not married, Gillian," he said softly.

"Of course I am."

"No, Amanda is married." He took a step forward, clearly intent on touching her.

She backed up, her thoughts hopelessly confused. "Amanda is dead. I am Amanda now." She shook her head, knowing she was not making any sense, but powerless to sort through her thoughts in the face of his determined advance. "Stephen," she said, his name breaking on a sob. "Please stop."

The pain in her voice halted him as nothing else could. She saw him hesitate, his hand halfway to her face; then he drew backward, his eyes clouded with his own torment.

"I rode all through the night to get here, Gillian. And for every mile, every moment, I kept thinking of the things I would say to you."

"It is too late, Stephen." Gillian wrapped her arms across her bodice, trying to hold back the tears. How could it be so hard to see him? She thought she was at peace with her decision, and yet here he was making her hurt for him all over, making her want him again.

"I wanted to be eloquent for you," he continued, his voice infused with a burning intensity. "I wanted the words to be perfect, but now that I see you, nothing seems right."

"Stephen—"

"I have been such a fool. I love you, Gillian." He ran a hand through his hair as he struggled to express himself. "I do not know how I missed it. You have run me in circles since you first arrived. No one else could make me hire a pickpocket or wander around an ancient crypt looking at centuries-old skeletons. I have even finished my speech for the House of Lords." He looked up at her, his face bemused, his eyes filled with love. "I adore you. Please marry me."

"Oh, Stephen." Gillian bit her lip and turned around, unable to bear the sight of her strong and correct guardian looking so vulnerable, his heart in his eyes.

What could she say? She felt as if her soul were being rent, inch by inch. To finally hear the words she longed for, to have Stephen say he loved her, and yet to know it all came too late. Ten minutes too late.

She pressed her fingers against her mouth, but a sob broke through anyway. Then she felt his hands touch her shoulders, brushing aside her hair so he could caress her neck.

"Tell me you share my feelings, Gillian. Tell me I am not alone in this longing." He gently turned her around until they were face-to-face, his breath heating her skin, which was still wet from her tears. "Do you love me?"

She could not say it. It would betray everything she had just said to Geoffrey.

"Yes," she whispered, unable to stop herself. Her sight blurred as the tears spilled from her eyes. She had thought she was accustomed to pain, that the misery of unrequited love was the worst her world could bear. Now she knew she had been wrong.

How much worse it was to finally share her feelings, to learn her love was returned, and yet still have it be impossible.

"Shhh, my love. Do not cry." Stephen pulled her close, his heartbeat strong as he enveloped her in his arms. "This is a time for joy, not tears." He tightened his hold on her, dropping little kisses on the top of her head. "You love me," he whispered. Suddenly he lifted her high in the air, spinning her around. "You love me!"

"Stephen!" She gasped, shocked and confused by his gleeful display.

"I was not sure. Good Lord, but you are constantly provoking me. I could not know if it was out of hatred or if you were merely contentious."

"Contentious! Why, I will have you know you are the most overbearing, egoistical, arrogant—"

"Yes, yes!" he said, finally setting her down on her feet. "And I love you, too, my beautiful, wonderful Gillian."

She felt her face softening into a gentle smile, her pain melting away as the words finally slipped easily from her lips.

"I love you, too, Stephen."

"Then will you marry me?"

She shook her head, her gaze drifting to the closed door and the people, her new family and her husband, waiting for her downstairs. "I am already married."

"No, you are not. I wish to marry Gillian Ames, not Amanda Wyndham."

"But we are the same—"

"You have never been the same. Gillian . . ."

She pressed her hands against her temples, trying to understand this bizarre turn of events. Had Stephen gone insane? Was she asleep and this another one of her twisted fantasies? "None of this makes any sense!"

He brought her fists away from her face, gently kissing each knuckle until her hands unclenched and her mind relaxed enough for her to hear him. "Geoffrey is already annulling your marriage, probably on the grounds of mistaken identity."

She took a deep breath. "You mean fraud."

Stephen shrugged. "It hardly matters. What is important is that I can marry you. I can marry Gillian Ames."

"But . . ." She shook her head. "What will people say? What will your mother say? You will be marrying a bastard."

He flashed her a carefree grin. "I do not care. And as for Mother, she has known from the very first. I want to marry you, Gillian, and if the tabbies do not like it, then the Earl and Countess of Mavenford will not grace their functions. Believe me, wealth and a title cover a multitude of sins."

Gillian bit her lip, hardly believing it was possible. Could all her dreams be coming true? "I . . . I am not a lady."

"Well, of course you are." He laughed, suddenly lifting her high above him again. "I forgot to tell you the most important rule of being a lady."

"What?" she said as he slowly set her down.

"Rule number eighteen: A lady must always follow her heart."

Gillian felt the last of her fears slip away. With an impish grin, she let her body sway indelicately against Stephen. Her fingers entwined in his hair, and he lowered his head to hers. "In that case, my lord, I have been a lady only when in your arms."

He grinned, his lips tantalizingly close as he drew her tighter against the whole length of his powerful body. "Then I hope you intend to be a lady for the rest of our lives."

She sighed, lifting her lips for his kiss. "Most definitely, my lord. Most definitely."

Epilogue

A lady always follows her heart.

Geoffrey smiled as he read the *Times* announcement of the wedding of the Earl of Mavenford to Miss Gillian Ames, the daughter of a dear friend of the dowager countess. All rumors of an aborted elopement with himself were miraculously absent, thanks, no doubt, to pressure from Stephen. As for speculation on Gillian's true lineage, he had not heard a single whisper.

All in all, things had worked out for the best, he supposed. He had escaped apparently unscathed from a marriage he had belatedly realized was all wrong. Gillian and Stephen seemed almost sickeningly happy. And, most important, with the disappearance of Amanda Wyndham, his sister became the newest diamond and was now courted by scores of eligible suitors willing to soothe her broken heart. That it was, in fact, only wounded pride made no difference to anyone but himself.

Sophia would be fine.

The only continuing problem was his family's precarious financial position. Geoffrey let his gaze wander around the slightly shabby breakfast room of their London home. What he needed was another heiress, but the list of possibilities remained dismal at best. They were none of them nearly as enticing as Gillian, nor could he easily contemplate a future with any of them. If only . . .

His thoughts were cut off as his butler entered and discreetly cleared his throat.

"Yes, Santon?"

"Mr. Jeremy Oltheten to see you, sir."

"Really?" he drawled, his curiosity piqued. What could possibly send his usually placid solicitor from his offices at this time of the morning? "Show him in."

The young man wasted no time in bustling in, fairly bursting with excitement. "My lord, I have wonderful news. I have found a sizable investor in your mining enterprise."

Geoffrey felt his attention sharpen with anticipation. "How sizable?"

Jeremy named a figure that made Geoffrey's heart stop. An investment of that caliber gave him considerably more breathing room. Enough, perhaps, that he could postpone his search for a wife until next Season at the earliest.

"Who is this mysterious benefactor?"

The young man colored and looked suddenly ill at ease. "I am afraid I cannot give you his name, but I can tell you he is one of my most august clients and quite trustworthy. He intends to leave all management of the company to you."

Geoffrey's eyes narrowed, suddenly suspicious. Someone who invested that amount of money without any control? "I do not believe it."

"Oh, no, my lord, it is quite true. The gentleman in question has recently become married and wishes to devote most of his time to his new wife."

Geoffrey stared at his solicitor, a slow smile spreading across his face. There was only one recently married man who was also one of Oltheten's "most august clients."

"Excellent," Geoffrey exclaimed, suddenly pushing away from the breakfast table. He had the most uncharacteristic urge to dance a jig. "Come with me to the library and let us see how we can best spend Mavenford's money."

"But . . ." The young man suddenly faltered. "I mean, I did not say—"

"Of course you did not, Oltheten," he said as he clapped the man on the back. "Now all that remains is to convince my mother that I have no need to become leg-shackled. At least, not this year. Two if we work hard, Oltheten." Then he winked at his startled solicitor. "And believe me, I intend to work very, very hard indeed."

Savage
Devotion Cassie
Edwards

Sailing the deep, clear waters of the Puget Sound, beautiful
red-haired Janice Edwards is bound for a new beginning.
Leaving behind the wealth and luxury she's known in San
Francisco, she hopes to find a simpler, sweeter life in the
towering forests of Tacoma . . . and a man who will love her for
who she is, not what she has. But when the steamer *Hope* is
wrecked by a sudden storm, Janice is rescued by a man like
none she's even known. Tall, with muscular limbs and a
powerful chest revealed by his buckskin clothing, he is a
Skokomish Indian—from all she's heard, a savage to be feared.
Yet in his gray eyes she sees tender caring, in his strong arms
she discovers untold passion, and in his wild heart she will
find . . . savage devotion.

___4735-7 $5.99 US/$6.99 CAN

Always

Lynsay Sands

Bastard daughter to the king, Rosamunde is raised in a convent and wholly prepared to take the veil . . . until good King Henry shows up with a reluctant husband in tow for her. Suddenly, she finds herself promising to love, honor, and obey Aric . . . always. But Rosamunde's education has not covered a wedding night, and the stables are a poor example for an untried girl. Will Aric bite her neck like the animals do their mates? The virile warrior seems capable of such animal passion, but his eyes promise something sweeter. And Rosamunde soon learns that while she may have trouble with obeying him, it will not be hard to love her new husband forever.

___4736-5 $5.50 US/$6.50 CAN

Five Gold Rings

Constance O'Banyon, Stobie Piel, Lynsay Sands, Flora Speer

In the Year of Our Lord, 1135, Menton Castle is the same as any other: It has nobles and minstrels, knights and servants. Yet from the great hall to the scullery there are signs that the house is in an uproar. This Yuletide season is to be one of passion and merriment. The master of the keep has returned. With him come several travelers, some weary with laughter, some tired of tears. But in all of their stories—whether lords a'leapin' or maids a'milkin'—there is one gift that their true loves give to them. And in the winter moonlight, each of the castle's inhabitants will soon see the magic of the season and the joy that can come from five gold rings.

___4612-1 $5.50 US/$6.50 CAN

Dorchester Publishing Co., Inc.
P.O. Box 6640
Wayne, PA 19087-8640

Please add $1.75 for shipping and handling for the first book and $.50 for each book thereafter. NY, NYC, and PA residents, please add appropriate sales tax. No cash, stamps, or C.O.D.s. All orders shipped within 6 weeks via postal service book rate. Canadian orders require $2.00 extra postage and must be paid in U.S. dollars through a U.S. banking facility.

Name_____
Address_____
City_____State_____Zip_____
I have enclosed $_____ in payment for the checked book(s).
Payment <u>must</u> accompany all orders. ❑ Please send a free catalog.
     CHECK OUT OUR WEBSITE! www.dorchesterpub.com

Cinnamon and Roses
Heidi Betts

A hardworking seamstress, Rebecca has no business being attracted to a man like wealthy, arrogant Caleb Adams. Born fatherless in a brothel, Rebecca knows what males are made of. And Caleb is clearly as faithless as they come, scandalizing their Kansas cowtown with the fancy city women he casually uses and casts aside. Though he tempts innocent Rebecca beyond reason, she can't afford to love a man like Caleb, for the price might be another fatherless babe. What the devil is wrong with him, Caleb muses, that he's drawn to a calico-clad dressmaker when sirens in silk are his for the asking? Still, Rebecca unaccountably stirs him. Caleb vows no woman can be trusted with his heart. But he must sample sweet Rebecca.

Lair of the Wolf

Also includes the second installment of *Lair of the Wolf*, a serialized romance set in medieval Wales. Be sure to look for future chapters of this exciting story featured in Leisure books and written by the industry's top authors.

___4668-7 $4.99 US/$5.99 CAN

Dorchester Publishing Co., Inc.
P.O. Box 6640
Wayne, PA 19087-8640

Please add $1.75 for shipping and handling for the first book and $.50 for each book thereafter. NY, NYC, and PA residents, please add appropriate sales tax. No cash, stamps, or C.O.D.s. All orders shipped within 6 weeks via postal service book rate. Canadian orders require $2.00 extra postage and must be paid in U.S. dollars through a U.S. banking facility.

Name_____
Address_____
City_____State_____Zip_____
I have enclosed $_____ in payment for the checked book(s).
Payment <u>must</u> accompany all orders. ❑ Please send a free catalog.
CHECK OUT OUR WEBSITE! www.dorchesterpub.com

A Promise of Roses

Heidi Betts

Spunky Megan Adams will do almost anything to save her struggling stagecoach line—even confront the bandits constantly ambushing the stage for the payrolls it delivers. But what Megan *wouldn't* do is fall headlong for the heart-breakingly handsome outlaw who robs the coach, kidnaps her from his ornery amigos, and drags her half across Kansas—to turn *her* in as an accomplice to the holdup!

Bounty hunter Lucas McCain stops at nothing to get his man. Hired to investigate the pilfered payrolls, he is sure Megan herself is masterminding the heists. And he'll be damned if he'll let this gun-toting spitfire keep him from completing his mission—even if he has to hogtie her to his horse, promise her roses . . . and hijack her heart!

___4738-1 $4.99 US/$5.99 CAN

Dorchester Publishing Co., Inc.
P.O. Box 6640
Wayne, PA 19087-8640

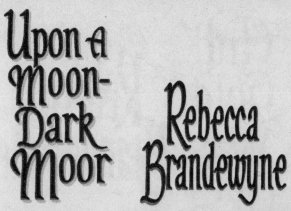

Upon A Moon-Dark Moor
Rebecca Brandewyne

From the day Draco sweeps into Highclyffe Hall, Maggie knows
he is her soulmate; the two are kindred spirits, both as mysterious
and untamable as the wild moors of the rocky Cornish coast.
Inexplicably drawn to this son of a Gypsy girl and an English
ne'er-do-well, Maggie surrenders herself to his embrace. Hand
in hand, they explore the unfathomable depths of their passion.
But as the seeds of their desire grow into an irrefutable love, its
consequences threaten to destroy their union. Only together can
Maggie and Draco overcome the whispered scandals that haunt
them and carve a future for their love.

___52336-1 $5.50 US/$6.50 CAN

Dorchester Publishing Co., Inc.
P.O. Box 6640
Wayne, PA 19087-8640

And Gold Was Ours

Rebecca Brandewyne

In Spain the young Aurora's future is foretold—a long arduous journey, a dark, wild jungle, and a fierce, protective man. Now in the New World, on a plantation haunted by a tale of lost love and hidden gold, the dark-haired beauty wonders if the swordsman and warrior who haunts her dreams truly lived and if he can rescue her from the enemies who seek to destroy her. Together, will they be able to overcome the past and conquer the present to find the greatest treasure on this earth, a treasure that is even more precious than gold. . . .

___52314-0 $5.99 US/$6.99 CAN

Dorchester Publishing Co., Inc.
P.O. Box 6640
Wayne, PA 19087-8640

Please add $1.75 for shipping and handling for the first book and $.50 for each book thereafter. NY, NYC, and PA residents, please add appropriate sales tax. No cash, stamps, or C.O.D.s. All orders shipped within 6 weeks via postal service book rate. Canadian orders require $2.00 extra postage and must be paid in U.S. dollars through a U.S. banking facility.

Name_____
Address_____
City_____State_____Zip_____
I have enclosed $_____ in payment for the checked book(s).
Payment <u>must</u> accompany all orders. ❏ Please send a free catalog.
      CHECK OUT OUR WEBSITE! www.dorchesterpub.com

Fairest of Them All
Josette Browning

A true stoic and a gentleman, Daniel Canty has worked furiously to achieve the high esteem of the English nobility. Therefore, it is more his reputation than the promise of wealth that compels him to accept the ninth earl of Hawkenge's challenge to turn an orphan wild child into a lady. But the girl who's been raised by animals in the African interior is hardly an orphan—and his wildly beautiful charge is hardly a child. Truly, Talitha is a woman—and the most compelling Daniel has ever seen. But the mute firebrand also poses the greatest threat he has ever faced. In the girl's soft kiss is the jeopardy which Daniel has fought all his life to avoid: the danger of losing his heart.

___4513-3 $5.50 US/$6.50 CAN